The House in Amalfi

Praise for Elizabeth Adler's novels:

'The women in Elizabeth Adler's novels are courageous and creative . . . her books entertain and delight.'

Cosmopolitan

'The popular Adler gets the dynamics of a new relationship pitch-perfect . . . But it's the detailed, realistic description of the trip to France that makes her latest great vicarious vacation reading.'

Publishers Weekly (The Last Time I Saw Paris)

'Sensuously creamy suspense . . . a literal cliffhanger.'

Kirkus Reviews (All or Nothing)

'Like Tuscany's beauty, this book is helped with delicious words and literary creativity. It's thoroughly engrossing.'

North Wales Chronicle (Summer in Tuscany)

'A heartwarming, romantic adventure . . . a great one for Francophiles, features real places, restaurants and hotels in France.'

Hello! (The Last Time I Saw Paris)

About the author

Born in Yorkshire, Elizabeth Adler is married with one
daughter and lives in California.

ELIZABETH ADLER

The House in Amalfi

HODDER

Copyright © 2005 by Elizabeth Adler

First published in Great Britain in 2005 by Hodder and Stoughton
A division of Hodder Headline

The right of Elizabeth Adler to be identified as the Author
of the Work has been asserted by her in accordance
with the Copyright, Designs and Patents Act 1988.

A Hodder paperback

1

A CIP catalogue record for this title
is available from the British Library

ISBN 0 340 89660 4

Printed and bound by Mackays of Chatham Ltd, Chatham, Kent

Hodder Headline's policy is to use papers that are natural, renewable
and recyclable products and made from wood grown in sustainable
forests. The logging and manufacturing processes are expected to
conform to the environmental regulations of the country of origin.

Hodder and Stoughton Ltd
A division of Hodder Headline
338 Euston Road
London NW1 3BH

For my lovely Red and dearest Jerry—

who do not appear in this book!

Life is granted to no man on a permanent basis. It is a privilege, and we must use our time wisely. It is up to each of us to make of it what we can.

—MIFUNE

ONE

Lamour Harrington

FOR TWO YEARS I HAVE LIVED ALONE, NOT ALLOW-
ing even a dog or a cat to intrude on my solitude. My friend
Jammy Mortimer, who I've known since we were little kids,
says I'm getting creepy. "All this loneliness is not good for
you," she says in her usual forthright manner. "You'll end up
a fat, eccentric recluse, refusing to open the door even to me."

Of course that's not true—my door's always open to
Jammy. But as far as the weight is concerned, I have to admit
I've gotten even skinnier over the past few months. I have a
busy life—by day, that is—and eating is a habit I seem to be
forgetting. I work as a landscape architect, bringing beauty to
other people's homes, creating outdoor "rooms" for them,
some small and fragrant, others rambling and wild, but always
enhanced by the drift of water, the ripple of a pebbled
stream, a simple fountain. I love transforming barren lots
with living things: grasses, shrubs, flowers, trees. But most of
all I love the trees. Sometimes I ask myself what would life be
without them?

Now I think about it, it would be like my own life, barren
and empty since I lost Alex, my husband, in a car crash two
years ago. It was the second time in my life that I'd lost a man
I loved to a tragic accident. The first was when my father died
in a mysterious boating mishap when I was just seventeen.

It's my belief that you can never recover from the agony of

being rent apart from your loved one within the space of just a few seconds and then having to face the sheer terror of going on without him. My husband was my love, my best friend, my companion. "You just have to pick yourself up and get on with living," friends advised me, after a few months. And I tried. I went back to work all right, but somehow I've never learned to "play" again.

Sitting here now, twenty floors up in my urban Chicago aerie overlooking the blustery windblown gray lake, a cooling mug of coffee clutched, half-forgotten, in my hand, I'm thinking about happiness and trying to remember what it felt like. My dwarf ficus trees out on the small terrace tremble in the chill breeze, reminding me of the pampered lemon trees on Italy's Amalfi coast, sequestered for winter in their cozy greenhouses, emerging again in the spring with a burst of blossoms so fragrant it takes your breath away.

And quite suddenly, because I haven't consciously thought of this in ages, I'm thinking of my father, Jonathon Harrington, who'd named me Lamour after his beautiful but flighty New Orleans great-grandmother, and about the time he took me with him to live in Rome while he wrote his novel.

It was sure to be a success, he told me—how could it not be when he was writing it in a city filled with history, culture, and sex? He didn't actually say the word *sex;* after all, I was only seven years old. I believe he used the word *sensuality* instead, though I wasn't sure what *sensuality* meant, either. And later, to my surprise, because to me he was just my father, his novel did become a huge success, which he said went a long way to blotting out the pain of the whole writing experience.

Again, I didn't know what he meant, since he seemed to spend most of his time happily in the bar in the piazza near our apartment. Not for us one of those beautiful Renaissance palazzos whose chiseled facades decorate Rome's better streets and whose parquet and paneled, gilded, and mirrored interiors have sheltered wealthy Romans for centuries. Ours was just the top floor of an ancient peeling stucco building with reluctant plumbing and possibly dangerous electricals in what was still the workmen's quarter of Rome known as Trastevere. And for a seven-year-old let loose on its cobbled alleys and squares, it was Paradise.

When we first stepped off the Alitalia flight into the hot sunshine of a Roman summer my father, Jonathon Boyland Harrington from Atlanta, Georgia, told me from now on to call him Jon-Boy instead of Daddy, reasoning it would make me feel more grown-up and him, I guess, more of the "southern writer" and less of the single parent. This was the role he'd been playing since I was three, when he'd picked me up and we'd left my mother because, he told me, of her "drinking and carousing." Again, I wasn't sure what *carousing* meant, but young though I was, I knew all about Mom's drinking.

"I'll never drink and carouse, Jon-Boy," I reassured him that day at Rome's airport, and he gave me that crooked grin and the lift of a black eyebrow that made him more than just handsome and said, "You betcha won't, girl; Italian women don't behave that way." Which I guessed also meant that from now on I should consider myself Italian—at least for the duration of our stay in that country.

We lived at the center of a maze of narrow, winding, secretive streets, more like alleys really, with tall, thin buildings crowding each side. The old gray stone showed where centuries of different-colored stucco had peeled off, and there was always laundry hanging overhead—snowy-clean undershirts and colorful tablecloths and the whitest of sheets. Up on the roofs you could catch a glimpse of scrawny little trees and shrubs sprouting among the TV aerials. The alleys smelled of cats and fresh-ground coffee, of laundry and heat vibrating off stone.

My new neighborhood was far from glamorous, just "homey" in a foreign sort of way. It was certainly light-years from the grassy-lawned suburban street I had called home for most of my short life, and where the aromas were mostly of buttered popcorn or freshly mowed grass. These Roman smells were new and exciting.

My alley was called vicolo del Cardinale, though I can't believe any real red-robed cardinal ever lived anywhere near there. Perhaps he just took a walkabout once and the name stuck. I was usually out on my *vicolo* early, waving to my new friends visible at the windows of their tiny kitchens or already on their way back from the market—in which case I knew I'd overslept.

These local women knew, via the grapevine, that I had no mother, and because I was usually on my own they watched out for me. They always asked where I was going and shook their heads disapprovingly when I told them I did not attend the *scuola elementare* and that Jon-Boy was teaching me himself. But they still liked him. How could they not? He was Mr. Charm personified, and he always had time for a chat with them.

In their black dresses and flat-back granny shoes and with their kind, lined faces they were all grandmas to me. I ate homemade pasta in their kitchens, admired pictures of their grown-up sons and their "real" grandchildren, and promised to always be good so that one day I would marry someone like that and give Jon-Boy a grandson of his own. "That would straighten him out," they said, nodding, satisfied at having solved our family problems so simply. How I wish they had.

Still, out in the early-morning alley, with my face hastily

splashed with water, a cursory brush of the teeth, and my long dark hair in a thick, clumsy braid swinging between my shoulder blades, I felt the heady rush of freedom for the first time as I followed the sharp sweet smell of freshly ground coffee and sugary buns until the tall, shadowed alley burst onto the piazza in a shock of sunlight and activity.

The news vendor had already set up his stand and a van was delivering copies of the morning papers and sport magazines that seemed, along with Italian crossword puzzles, to make up most of his stock. Almost immediately behind him, separated by a scattering of small tables with metal chairs that scraped the uneven paving stones with a terrible screech every time someone took a seat, was the Bar Marchetti, already with a few male customers propping up the counter. One foot on the brass rail, they leafed through the early news while knocking back an espresso piled high with sugar.

Across the way in her small wooden hut, Adriana, the flower seller, waved to me from behind a bank of multicolored blossoms, and I made a fast detour from my predetermined route to the bar just to receive her quick kiss. She tucked a pink carnation into my braid and asked anxiously when I would start school like a normal child. I quickly reassured her that Jon-Boy would be giving me a math lesson later that day. This was of course untrue, because Jon-Boy had about as much knowledge of math as any seven-year-old and about as much money sense as your average flea. But that's another story.

Off I sped again, pausing only to peer through the tall wooden doors of the flat-fronted little church topped with a classic pediment and a small verdigrised cross. The plain exterior led into an intriguing ornate gold and frescoed dimness lit by flickering candles. I did not go in because I was heading to the bar for my coffee and *cornetto,* the staple breakfast of every Italian, of whom, after just a couple of months, I now counted myself as one.

"*Buon giorno, Angelo.*" I stood with both feet on the brass rail, elbows propped on the bar. Switching my braid over my shoulder I chewed on the end, smiling my gap-toothed seven-year-old smile at him.

Angelo was in his thirties, a big man, broad shouldered, strong necked and shaggy haired, with a wide face inset with glossy dark brown eyes and long straight lashes, like a cow's. He had a perpetual overnight growth of dark beard from which his teeth gleamed large and shiny white.

I had a kind of flirtation going on with Angelo, my very first. In fact I had not known how to flirt until I came to Rome and sat alongside Jon-Boy in the cafés, watching elegant pretty women walk a little slower as they passed, smiling from the corners of their eyes at him, turning their heads and giving him a long slow look that said whatever was said between a man and a woman. I practiced this new knowledge on Angelo and like most Italians with children, he humored me and allowed me to twist him around my little finger— something I doubt I could do with a man today.

"*Ciao, bella,*" he said, accepting my money and handing me a *scontrino*, a receipt, which I then gave back to him in exchange for my breakfast. This was the way it worked in Italy. Angelo knew my "order" and was already at the hissing, sputtering machine fixing my cappuccino, a drink invented by the Capuchin monks long before espresso machines were thought of, and to whom I shall be eternally grateful.

Angelo piled my cup high with froth, flung a lavish dusting of powdered chocolate on top and shoved it across the counter at me. He picked out the crispest *cornetto*, wrapped it in a small square of wax paper and handed it to me. Next to Italian ice cream and real Italian pizza, this was my favorite thing on earth. I loved the way the crisp layered pastry crunched when I bit into it, powdering my T-shirt with crumbs, and then the soft sweetness as my teeth and taste buds encountered the center. I took a deep slug of the cappuccino, wiped the chocolate dust and crumbs from my mouth with the back of my hand, and beamed up at my hero. "Great," I said, forgetting all about speaking Italian I was so lost in my pleasure.

"Great!" he replied in return, and I laughed because coming from him it sounded funny. *"Ecco,* so what you do today?" he said in the kind of simple Italian I had just mastered. (Conjugating verbs was a mystery never to be solved.)

"I'm going to the market in Campo de' Fiori to buy salad for tonight's supper." I patted the money folded in my jeans pocket, filled with the importance of my task. "I'll buy salad and cheese and prosciutto. And bread, of course."

"But shouldn't you be in school?" Angelo asked the question I knew was going to haunt my childhood days in Rome. I shrugged it off as nonchalantly as I could, though I admit I was starting to get worried. What if the police came looking for me? Arrested me right here on the piazza with everybody looking on? What if they hauled me off to face the principal at the school in front of all the other kids? The humiliation of that thought left my mouth hanging open—not a pretty sight when it was still half-full of *cornetto*—but Angelo merely smiled and patted my bony shoulder. "Hey, be happy while you can, *piccolina,"* he said. "Remember, life is short." And he slid a second *cornetto* across the counter with a wink that said it was free, then went to attend to his other customers, piling in now for their morning espresso fix.

Caffeine was already thundering through my veins, giving a fast lift to my skip as I headed past Pizzeria Vesuvio, my favorite pizza joint, threading my way through a maze of familiar alleys and dodging the speeding Roman traffic that stopped for no one.

I stood for a moment on the corner of the Campo de' Fiori, taking in the crowded square. Awninged stalls were piled high with vegetables and fruits whose scents tickled my nostrils and whose rainbow of colors dazzled my eyes. Wasps buzzed over the peaches and a rattle of female chatter hovered in the air. Smart Roman ladies, long legged in short skirts and heels, perfectly made up, perfectly coiffed, picked over tiny yellow-flowered zucchini and moist dove gray mushrooms as expertly as the local black-clad grandmothers, giving the same intense scrutiny to each piece because nothing less than perfect was good enough.

The displays of flowers near the central fountain put Adriana's to shame. Towering orange gladioli, buckets full of coral roses and banks of greenish-white lilies whose smell captured you at twenty paces, and always the tiny baskets of dense purple violets. I bought one of these to put in my room; then I purchased a single tall white lily. I would present it to my father at the dinner table that night, when my salad and ham and cheese were artistically arranged on plates next to a glass of his favorite local white Frascati wine. It would be a sample of my love, because no girl ever loved her father more than I did.

Dragged back to a cold Chicago evening by a sudden blast of wind that sent the ficus leaves scattering across the terrace, I recalled how I had felt that Roman morning, with the sun hot on my back and my pigtail bouncing. How Angelo's bright white smile had sent my heart racing and the way the sugary taste of the *cornetto* had shocked my taste buds and how Adriana's concerned kiss had made me feel so wanted. I could smell again the lilies in the Campo de' Fiori, and I smiled, suddenly realizing that what I was remembering was that elusive emotion called happiness.

I didn't know it on that sunny morning in Rome, but I had yet to experience *true* happiness. The "real thing" would not come until the following year, when Jon-Boy took me to live in the house in Amalfi. The place where, ten years later, he would die so mysteriously.

TWO

THE QUIET OF MY APARTMENT WAS SHATTERED BY
the insistent buzz of the intercom from the downstairs foyer,
jolting me from my dreams and sending cold coffee flying
from the mug. "Damn," I said, mopping the pale chenille
chair arm with a Kleenex. "Oh, damn it, who can that be?"

I ran to pick up the house phone in the kitchen and said
hello, rather testily. Jammy's sigh was like the wind gusting
outside.

"Earth to Planet Zero," she said in the high little-girl voice
she has never managed to lose, which only adds to her charm
and is probably the reason that, like Jackie Kennedy, she'd
kept it.

I signed too, knowing why she was here and what she
would tell me—again. Jammy was never a quitter. "Okay,
come on up," I said resignedly.

"I'm not coming up. You are coming down. I'm taking
you out for drinks and dinner. And no, I don't care what you
have on—just throw a coat over the sweats; we're only going
to the local Italian."

"But it's only five thirty," I objected, with a quick glance at
the kitchen clock. "I can't drink yet."

"Did you never hear the old saying it must be six o'clock
somewhere in the world? Now, put on some lipstick, throw
on a coat, and get yourself down here, pronto. Otherwise I'll

talk the ear off Serge and you know how he hates that. It'll be you he gets mad at and it'll cost you an even bigger tip at Christmas to soothe him, so hurry up, girl."

This time there was a laugh in my sigh. Serge was the concierge. An old-guard Russian, he'd lived in this country for forty years and still spoke as little English as possible. *Difficult* would have been an easy word to describe him, but he'd been at the building far longer than I, and he was here to stay. We just had to make the best of him.

I quickly changed from the sweats (Jammy knows me only too well) into jeans and a black turtleneck, shoved my feet into boots, and glossed my pale lips. I stared in the mirror. I did not look great. Tall and so skinny the jeans bagged on me, shadowed eyes, hollow cheeks, billowing curly black hair in dire need of a cut. Dracula in a turtleneck. I dragged my long hair into an elastic band with a dismissive shrug. What did I care? No one would notice me anyhow.

"You look like hell," Jammy said when I emerged from the elevator.

"Thanks." I flung a bunny-lined jeans jacket over my shoulders. "A compliment is always nice."

We waved good-bye to an indifferent Serge, and Jammy held open the big glass door while I flounced through. "I didn't want to come anyway." I scowled. "It's cold and miserable out here, and besides I don't want a drink."

Jammy thrust out an arm and stopped me in my tracks. "Shit, Lamour Harrington, who else is gonna tell you the truth if not me?" Her big blue eyes glistened with tears— probably of anger by now.

"Okay, so you're right," I said, turning to hug her, "but what woman wants to hear it?"

"This woman—*you*—*needs* to hear it. And she also *needs* a drink."

Jammy slid her arm through mine and we strode down the street, hip-to-hip, heads down into the wind, hair whipping wildly. Jammy's legs were as long as my own. We were always the tallest in our class, even when I first lived next door to her, which was when Jon-Boy was still in the early days of the single-parent role and had moved us into respectable middle-class suburbia.

We lived in the smallest house on the old tree-lined block in Evanston, dotted with browning lawns and basketball hoops, and right next door to Selma and Frank Mortimer and their three kids. Jammy was my age and we became instant best friends.

Jammy's house had everything mine lacked: a mom always there fixing meat loaf or mac-and-cheese or peanut butter and jelly sandwiches, and there was always purple Kool-Aid that we got to fix ourselves. In summer, when the soft fruits were in season, Mrs. Mortimer brewed up great vats of jams and jellies, stirring and sifting as the sugary scent pervaded the entire street, making our mouths water. That's how Jammy got her name; she was always licking out the bowls and had a permanently jam-stained mouth, sometimes for days on end. So Jammy she became instead of her given name of Jamie.

My artistic father, of course, was not happy in suburbia. He'd only moved there because he thought it was the best place for me. And he was right, though unexpectedly, it also turned out to be good for *him*. The Mortimer house became mine, lifting the parenting burden from his shoulders, so he was able to meet his girlfriends and old college cronies with whom he could talk books and music and of course, about the novel he dreamed one day of writing. He taught English at the local college and when not there could usually be found in the coffeehouse or the local bar, scribbling in a notebook. To him the written word was exactly that. Written. By hand.

He said it came out better that way than on a word processor.

Meanwhile I had practically moved in with the Mortimers. "Sleepovers" would go on for days, sometimes even as long as a week, and gradually I became part of their happy family. So you see, Dad really did do the best thing for me then. And he also did the right thing later, shocking the Mortimers to their very souls, when he said he was taking a sabbatical for a year or two and going to Italy to write his novel. And that he was taking me with him.

Of course, I was nervous about going to live in a foreign country where I didn't know any other kids and where they didn't even speak my language, but I was also thrilled that my father loved me so much he couldn't bear to leave me behind.

A couple of years later, when we returned to Evanston, I picked up my friendship with Jammy exactly where we had left off. Then, when Jon-Boy returned alone to live in Italy, I became a permanent member of the Mortimer family. He came home a couple of times every year, but I was busy with school and I never visited him there. The last time I saw him was when he returned for my high school graduation.

Jammy is a sister to me, as well as a friend. We've suffered through each other's teenage dramas—Jammy's quite the drama queen—through first boyfriends and treacherous lovers. All the usual girl stuff. She'd helped me get over the awful desolation of Jon-Boy's death, out in a sailboat off the coast of Amalfi in a storm, and the fact that he'd just "disappeared" into the sea. I was seventeen years old, getting ready for college, and already living with the Mortimers as a sort of permanent boarder. Now I just stayed on.

There was a memorial service in Amalfi's beautiful ninth-century cathedral with its elaborate Moorish mosaic facade, but I refused at first to acknowledge Jon-Boy was dead, and I did not attend. Frank Mortimer went instead to represent me.

I had such happy memories of our time together at the little house Jon-Boy had bought there with, I suppose, some of the money earned from his novel that after he was gone for a long time I couldn't even bear to think about it. In all these years I'd never been able to bring myself to return to Amalfi and face my "ghosts."

There's absolutely nothing Jammy and I don't know about each other, and only Jammy knows the true extent of my second devastation, when my husband, Alex, was killed. She was there with me; she saw my naked soul tear apart; she stayed to pick up the pieces. She did not leave my side for weeks, telling her own husband he would just have to manage for a while because I needed her more. And good man that Matt is, he said, "Go ahead, baby; help her all you can."

And now she's here again, still trying to coax and bully me out of my funk and the rigid small life I've permitted myself, with its work guidelines and no play, because I've forgotten how to do that and anyway I just don't care anymore. And also, having lost two men I loved, I can't allow myself to be hurt again by falling for another. My life is on course. I have my work and that's it.

Jammy steered me down a couple of side streets out of the direct path of the wind coming off the lake to a small storefront trattoria optimistically called Tre Scalini. It was the name of a once-famous restaurant on Rome's Piazza Navona, the place Dad used to take me for their delicious *granita,* the espresso-flavored ice mixed with whipped cream.

"It's strange how food can trigger memories," I said, hoisting myself up on the bar stool next to Jammy and nodding meekly when she raised a questioning eyebrow. She went ahead and ordered two martinis with Ketel vodka and three Roquefort olives, shaken, James Bond fashion. "I remember the real Tre Scalini. . . ."

"In Rome, of course." Jammy propped an elbow on the bar. She shoved her blond bangs aside and gave me that sideways exasperated blue stare. "I swear you think you're Italian and that you never lived anywhere else but that old city. Except oh, where's the other place?"

"Amalfi." I turned huffily from her stare. "And I can tell you this trattoria has nothing on the real thing."

"Then if it's so great why don't you just go back there?" She put two elbows on the counter now and stared angrily into the mirror behind the bar.

I hoisted my martini to her reflection in a mock toast. "Here's to a long and happy friendship."

She turned to me, eyes blazing. "You know what, Lamour Harrington, you are turning out to be a miserable old bitch. I don't know what I ever saw in you. I've a good mind to walk out on you right now."

For a minute I was stunned into silence; then I said, "You wouldn't be the first. Remember Skeeter Malone? He left me at the senior prom for Melanie Damato."

"Melanie Tomato, we called her. She had tits out to here at age thirteen and we were all sick with jealousy."

"At least you caught up," I said, glancing enviously at her Victoria's Secreted bosom. "I was never so lucky."

I caught her eye in the mirror and we grinned. "Anyhow, Skeeter Malone was a shit to do that to you," she said, still loyal after all these years.

"Yeah, but he married those tits a few years later," I said, taking a gulp of my martini and coughing until my eyes brimmed.

"You should see them now," Jammy said, and then we were giggling again, silly as those two high school girls.

"Know how many years ago that was?" Jammy asked.

I shook my head. "Don't wanna count." I took a more

cautious sip of the martini this time, poking my fingers in it to catch an olive.

Jammy gave me a reproving shove. "Mom would have slapped your hand for that."

"And she would have been right. I seem to have lost my manners along with everything else."

"You haven't lost everything else, Lamour," Jammy said, suddenly serious. "Just your past. You—*we*—are only thirty-eight years old. There's a lot of future still ahead of us."

I contemplated my olives silently, then, "Trouble is, Jam, I like the past more." She was quiet, watching me as she sipped her drink. Then I said, "Before you called, I was trying to remember how 'happiness' felt. I was thinking about those days with Jon-Boy in Rome, remembering what it was like to be a little kid with all that freedom, in a new and exciting world where everyone was my friend. I could feel the sun hot on my back and smell the flower in my hair; I could see my first love, Angelo, and his big, white smile. I remembered the taste of my morning *cornetto* and the cappuccino foam on my lips and the scent of lilies in the Campo de' Fiori." I lifted my head and looked at her. "And you know what, Jammy? I remembered *that* was a moment of true happiness."

She rested her hand sympathetically on my arm. "But you felt that same happiness when you married Alex?" She seemed to be questioning me. "You were together for six years; you loved each other?"

I sifted through my thoughts about Alex, resurrecting him in my mind. Shorter than I, muscular, with deep dark eyes that were almost black in their intensity when he made love to me, the feel of his breath on my cheek when we'd slept together that first night, the way his body claimed my rhythm with his.

"Oh yes, I loved Alex all right," I said quietly, "but love and marriage are special responsibilities. The child I was in Rome was free."

Our eyes met in the mirror again, and I took another nervous gulp of the martini. I could tell Jammy was struggling not to say the obvious: that I was free now, so why couldn't I find that kind of happiness again?

"Let's eat," she said diplomatically instead, and we slid off our bar stools and headed for a table for two near the window.

A polished brass rail hung with red-checkered café curtains shut out part of the cold evening, though rain now misted the upper half of the window. Still, it was cozy in the little restaurant. A pizza oven glowed in the background and the aroma of ragù sauce and spicy sausage tempted. I ordered a bottle of Chianti, the kind in the straw flask that we used to drink illicitly at college and later we'd use the bottles as candleholders and that I don't remember ever seeing in Rome, since Jon-Boy bought only the local white Frascati.

I ordered lasagna and Jammy the spaghetti with ragù sauce. We tasted each other's food, mmming with pleasure. We were on our second glass of wine when Jammy dropped the bombshell.

"Matt and I are thinking of taking a trip to Italy this year," she said oh so casually. "We were hoping you would like to come with us."

I put down my fork and stared hard at her. "Did you just invent this, right now, this minute?"

"Of course not." She stuck her chin in the air, looking defiantly at me.

Twirling my glass in my fingers, I watched her squirm. "Liar, liar, pants on fire," I said, grinning, and then we were laughing again.

"Oh Jesus, Lam, it's just so good to hear you laugh again, I don't know if I can stand it," she said. Her long blond bangs fell over her eyes again and, as was her habit, she shoved them impatiently to one side. "Oh, so what if I did lie. I had good reason. What if Matt and I *were* to take a trip to Italy, would you say yes?"

She looked so solemn and earnest, the way she had when she was a little girl, it jolted me again to my own memories of being that little girl in Italy and the happiness I had remembered only hours ago. I thought of Jon-Boy and the small golden house in Amalfi with its wonderful green gardens tumbling down the cliff to the turquoise sea.

"Maybe I'd go," I said, suddenly tempted, "if I could guarantee I'd find that kind of happiness again."

Elated, Jammy grabbed my hand across the table. "You've gotta take chances in this world, kid. No guarantees."

I thought for a second, then I took it on the chin. "No guarantees," I agreed, "I promise I'll think about it." But as she linked her pinkie with mine in a wish for the trip to become true, I knew what I was wishing for. To have Jon-Boy and Alex back again.

THREE

Jammy

WHEN JAMMY GOT BACK FROM DINNER WITH LA-mour, her husband, Matt, was sitting on the flowered chintz sofa with Bramble, their ancient black Labrador, sprawled next to him. Matt's eyes were closed, and he was listening to the Stones playing loudly on his Bang & Olufsen.

"Remember we danced to this the night we met?" Jammy said. She patted Bramble, then sank into the cushions on Matt's other side, snuggling her head into his shoulder. He slid an arm around her neck and pulled her closer, dropping a kiss on her windblown hair.

"Didn't know you remembered," he said, but she heard the grin in his voice.

"There's a lot you don't know that I remember," she said with a tone of such dark foreboding that he laughed.

"And what exactly does that mean, dear Jammy?"

"Well, I remember we didn't have a honeymoon."

He pushed her away. "Are you gonna hold that against me forever? I was a poor business school student. You knew it when you married me. And you were a poor nineteen-year-old art student." He scowled suspiciously. "So what's the point of this little scenario, Jammy? You've got something up your sleeve; I can tell." She smiled too brightly at him and he groaned.

"I have no secrets from you," she said.

"For god's sake, tell me the worst."

"We're going on a trip to Italy this year. You and me. And Lamour."

"Lamour's coming on our honeymoon?"

"This is not our honeymoon. It's our 'getting Lamour over the bereavement' trip."

Matt closed his eyes and leaned his head against the flowered cushion. Jammy watched him anxiously. She could tell he was mulling over what she'd said and that he wasn't happy.

"You and I both know there's only one way to get Lamour over the bereaving 'hump,'" Matt said at last. "You have to tell her the truth about what happened with Alex."

Jammy had been afraid he would say that. "But how can I?" she asked, her voice strangled with desperation. "It'll kill her for sure."

"Or cure her," Matt said.

Jammy sat up and looked at him. She stared into his honest gaze until she could bear it no more and she turned her head away. "I don't want to be the executioner," she muttered, clutching his hand.

He held it to his lips. "Jammy, my love, did you ever think that you might in fact be the *liberator*? Tell her; then let's see if she wants to go on this trip to Italy."

She suddenly spotted a loophole in his reasoning. "You mean if I tell Lamour and she says yes, the Italian trip is on?"

Matt's laugh was muffled in her tumbling blond hair as he said, "I thought I was winning this round."

But Jammy was still thinking about Lamour and her heart was full of dread because now she had committed to telling Lamour about Alex. "I almost wish you had," she whispered. "Oh, how I wish you had."

FOUR

Jammy

SERGE, THE CONCIERGE, WAS HIS USUAL SURLY SELF, keeping Jammy waiting, her foot tapping, as he took his time about dialing Lamour's apartment on the house phone, but this time Jammy didn't even spare him a conciliatory smile. Fuck you, Serge, she fumed silently. I have more important things on my mind than keeping you happy.

"Ms. Harrington says to go right on up, Mrs. Haigh," he said, full of self-importance as usual. Jammy gave him a brief nod of thanks as she hurried into the elegant mirrored elevator and pressed the button for the twentieth floor.

The elevator opened directly into Lamour's private foyer, something both she and Jammy had considered incredibly grand in the early days of Lamour's marriage to Alex Monroe, coming as they both had from modest suburbia and progressing only as far as an equally modest rental apartment. Lamour said Lake Shore Drive had taken her at least a year to get used to, but get used to it she had, along with many other luxuries, because she had married a man of substance. Well, *a rich man,* anyway, Jammy quickly amended that thought, because in her view Alex Monroe had no "substance" whatsoever.

"Hi," she called, heading into the long living room with its thirty-foot spread of floor-to-ceiling windows and the view over the lake, calm this evening with a rosy sunset pinking the gray.

Lamour's sleek apartment with its minimalist decor never failed to make Jammy rethink her own sprawling ranch-style home. "Why is it when I come here I always feel insecure about my own place?" she grumbled as they hugged. "Why do I immediately want to lose all the tchotchkes and change the flowered chintz to black leather?"

A spark lit Lamour's amber eyes as she grinned. "As long as it's *Italian* leather."

"Back to Italy again, huh?" Jammy flung herself onto Lamour's own tan leather sofa, Italian of course, groaning at its unresponsiveness to her rear end. "Does it have to be so hard?"

"That's what makes it look good." Lamour knelt on the black rug in front of the oval glass coffee table centered with a bunch of perfect anemones in a perfect round glass vase. She poured martinis from a plain silver shaker into iced glasses, then added three olives to each.

"This is getting to be a habit," Jammy said, accepting the drink, but she sat up and took notice when Lamour suddenly said, "I'm just getting up my courage to tell you something."

"That you're not coming to Italy," Jammy finished the sentence for her. "I knew it! I just *knew* that's what you'd say. And that's why I have something I need to say to you." Shoving back her bangs, she looked nervously at Lamour from under her lashes. "Well, actually I have something to tell you. Something I think you should know."

Lamour looked surprised. Then her face dropped, "Oh no, don't tell me the college kid's in trouble?"

Jammy and Matt had married when she was only nineteen and they'd had a child by the time she was twenty. Now Jammy's daughter had just started college. She had never lived away from home before and the sudden freedom was going to her head.

"I almost wish it was about her." Jammy avoided Lamour's eyes and took a quick gulp of the martini.

"Jeez, then this must *really* be serious."

"Oh, it is, Lam. And for the life of me I don't know how to start."

Lamour uncurled herself from the floor and went to sit next to her best friend. "It's okay, sweetie," she said, patting her hand soothingly. "You can tell me *anything;* you know that."

"Trouble is," Jammy said, "this is something I should have told you years ago, only I wanted to believe it wasn't true. It's about Alex."

Lamour looked puzzled. "What could there possibly be to say about Alex that I don't already know?"

Jammy seemed to inhale all the air in the apartment before she finally caught enough breath to say it. "Alex was unfaithful, Lamour. He was having an affair."

There was a stunned silence. Then Lamour snatched her hand away. "Are you *crazy? Why* are you saying this? Oh, *I* know, it's to try and jolt me out of my grief, isn't it? You think you can shock me out of it by telling me my dead husband was a two-timing bastard, right?"

"Right on both counts. He *was* a two-timing bastard, and I *did* want to jolt you out of it and back into *your* life again."

Lamour was looking at her with such cold contempt, Jammy's innards shriveled with foreboding.

"How terrible of you, Jammy," Lamour said. "How *terrible* to demean my husband's memory; he was a good man, a wonderful husband. . . ."

"He cheated on you, Lam. He was leaving you for another woman."

"You are *contemptible,* Jammy Mortimer."

Lamour's voice was thin with the kind of inner rage

Jammy had never heard in any person before, but she was committed and went remorselessly on.

"The night Alex died in the car crash, he was on his way to meet the other woman. Her number came up on Alex's cell phone, as did Matt's—but not yours. The police called her first. When she showed up at the scene, Matt was already there. He said she was distraught, crying for Alex. She said he was her fiancé, that they were going to get married that fall. Matt swore she wore a diamond as big as the Rock of Gibraltar on her left hand. He had to tell her that there was already a wife—*you*—waiting at home. At first she refused to believe him, but when she heard Matt tell the police about you, she knew it was true. But after all, Alex was dead and there was no point in getting into a fight with you. She did the only decent thing: she left, and she never contacted you. Though she did keep that ring," Jammy added thoughtfully, "and judging from Alex's behavior she probably deserved it."

Lamour struggled to her feet. She stared blankly out the windows for a long moment. Then she swung round and with one wild sweep of her arm cleared the coffee table of the glasses and the martini shaker and the anemones. Silent with rage, she stomped the glasses into shards, grinding the olives into the black rug, kicking the silver shaker so hard it hit the window with a clang.

Her dark curly hair had escaped from its ribbon and flew wildly around her head as she turned on Jammy. "Please leave," she said in a low hard voice unrecognizable as her own. "Leave here, Jammy Mortimer, and never come back. You are not my friend."

FIVE

Jammy

JAMMY WAS CRYING SO HARD BY THE TIME SHE GOT home, she could hardly see to drive. The car was a Lincoln Aviator SUV that Matt had said was too big for her because she was used to the smaller Volvo she'd had for years. Now she swung too close into the garage, groaning as she heard the left wing mirror scrape the wall.

"Shit, oh shit," she moaned, "that's all I need. . . ."

Still sobbing angrily, she slid from the car, hearing Bramble's happy yap of greeting. Whenever she went out the dog would listen for the car and then come and wait by the door of the laundry room to be the first to greet her. He was older now and deaf and he didn't always hear the car anymore, but tonight he was right there, as though he knew she was upset, and his anxious licks made her smile through her tears.

Matt was right behind him, holding open the door to the kitchen. He looked warily at her teary face. "I gather the Alex talk was not a great success."

Jammy stood by the door, unable to move. "She didn't want to believe me. She said I was a terrible woman to say such things about her perfect husband. She told me, 'Please leave!' She didn't even say, '*Get out!*' She was in this weird kind of control of herself, Matt, except when she swiped the martini glasses from the table and stomped the olives into that perfect black rug. God, there's not even a cat hair in that place. There's no *life* there, Matt. And I love her and now I've blown our friendship, all because of that bastard Alex. Matt, oh, Matt, what am I to *do*?"

"Come here, honey." He took her hand and led her gently inside. Bramble trotted anxiously next to them. In the kitchen, secure in her own world, Jammy sighed as Matt put his arms around her.

"Wait, Jam, that's all you can do," he said gently. "Wait until the truth sinks in. Wait and see what Lamour does then."

SIX

Lamour

THE SOUND OF THE DOOR SLAMMING BEHIND JAMMY
reverberated through the apartment. Then there was silence.
A hard, ugly kind of silence. There was nothing alive in this
apartment except me and only the dull thud of my heart to
remind me of that.

My darling Alex had *not* been a traitor. I told myself that
over and over, as fat crystal balls of tears rolled down my
cheeks and into the pillow. Alex loved me; I knew it. There
had never been a wrong word between us. Besides, I would
have known if there had been another woman. Or would I?

Oh, *damn* Jammy; *damn her.* How could she put these ideas
in my mind? Alex was the perfect husband. We'd had the perfect life. Hadn't we?

Doubt slid like a traitor into my golden memories. I recalled with sudden terrible clarity Alex's frequent absences
"on business," his calls saying he'd be home late again, the
cell-phone ring answered with a terse "yes" or "no," and
how he would suddenly have to return late to the office for
some papers he'd forgotten. My thudding heart missed a beat
as I recognized there was a pattern to Alex's behavior. The
pattern of a man involved in a secret love affair.

I got up and walked into my smart living room. I stood,
staring bleakly at the familiar view from my bank of windows.
I remembered how thrilled we had been with that view, one

of the best in Chicago, Alex had told me proudly when he'd first shown me the place. Alex had bought it without me even seeing it, which upset me at first—but "I knew you'd love it anyway," he'd said. "How could you not? It's a class act, baby, and just right for you."

He was right of course, as he always seemed to be. Or perhaps it was that I just never questioned him. I was immersed in my work, my own separate life. Landscaping was my life; real estate development was Alex's. I allowed him to make the decisions and went along with them. He rarely asked about my work and he never volunteered much information about his, except to say how busy he was with a big deal pending.

Alex always seemed to have "big deals" pending, which was why when he died it had come as a shock to find out that we were not rich after all. There was simply no money. His only asset was this apartment, which was in his name and on which there was a substantial first mortgage as well as a second. I knew Alex was a wheeler-dealer, and I had to assume that business had not been going well before he was killed. We'd always had a good lifestyle, though, good restaurants, good clothes. At least Alex had good clothes; I was never much of a shopper, and after all, when I worked, which was most of the time, I wore jeans and work boots with a T-shirt or a sweater.

I had a couple of pieces of decent jewelry: my engagement ring, a nice three-carat emerald-cut diamond chosen by Alex, nothing too huge because Alex said my hands were small and slender and anything bigger would have looked "flashy" on me; a pair of diamond studs that I wore every day and was so used to I hardly noticed anymore; and the gold Cartier tank watch he'd given me for a birthday. I had a string of those diamonds you buy "by the yard" at Tiffany's. For a supposedly "rich" woman that was not much, I realized now.

In fact, Alex had not bought me any gift, not even flowers,

let alone jewelry, in a long time. For more than a year that I could recall, maybe even longer.

I sank back into despair. Alex couldn't have been planning to marry someone else. I *refused* to believe it. I remembered when we had met, how he'd sought me out across a room filled with middle-aged socialites to whom I'd just given a lecture on the art of landscape gardening. Alex hadn't attended the lecture; he'd been at a financial conference in the same hotel and had caught the last few minutes of my speech from the open door as he was passing.

"You were great," he'd said, fixing me with those dark eyes. "I'm Alex Monroe. And I know who you are. And won't you please have a drink with me."

He'd led me to the bar and bought me champagne and it had simply taken off from there. With never a hitch, until he died. *And until now.*

I stretched my weary body along the length of the Italian leather sofa, moaning softly. Jammy had been right: it *was* too hard. All for looks and nothing for comfort. Was that really the way I thought? Really the way my home was? Had Alex made me that way?

Confused, I sat up again. I sat for a long time on that smart, hard sofa, staring out the windows as night fell. Staring at the twinkling lights out along the lake, the little signals that life went on for some people. But not for me.

Self-pity overwhelmed my doubts and I began to cry again. I was truly a woman alone.

Despite the sofa's hardness, I must have fallen asleep, because I awoke with the dawn, stiff and swollen eyed, filled with doubt.

I got up, took a shower, dressed, and went to visit my local police precinct.

I had never read the police report of the accident; I hadn't been able to bear to see the details in print that made it all too real. Now I needed to know.

The kindly officer in charge summoned up the details on the computer and gave me a printout. The report said there were no other vehicles involved; Alex's car had simply aquaplaned on the wet road and hit a tree. He was already pronounced dead and in the ambulance on his way to the hospital when the police finally reached me. Matt's name and address were on the report, along with that of a woman listed under next of kin as "fiancée." My own name had been added later, with the word "wife" after it.

So now I knew that what Jammy had said was true. There was no mystery about Alex's death. The mystery had been his life. And I didn't want to know about that anymore.

There was a weight like a lump of ice in my chest. Jammy and Matt, my friends, had tried to protect me from knowing about my cheating husband. They knew I would grieve for him, but they'd expected me to recover—slowly, it's true—and that sooner or later I would pick up the threads of a normal life again. Instead, I had wasted two years grieving for a man who had been about to dump me for another woman.

Deceit is insidious; it crept around my heart, took over my mind, made me doubt my every moment spent with Alex.

I thought again about that elusive quality called happiness, about Jon-Boy and Rome. And about my long-neglected house in Amalfi. About finally facing my ghosts there.

I hurried back to the apartment. I was about to change my life completely. I called the real estate agent and told her to put the apartment on the market and that I wanted a fast sale. Then I called Jammy.

"When do we leave for Italy?" I said.

SEVEN

L'amour

SO HERE WE ARE IN ROME, JUST JAMMY AND ME. I almost felt like that little girl again, stepping off the plane and driving into the Eternal City, past the monuments and ancient buildings, the grand avenues and the jumble of twisting little streets thronged with traffic and people. It all reminded me again why I loved this place. In most cities you need to go to a museum to discover its history, but in Rome you *live* with it. It's on the streets where colossal crumbled statues lie where they have rested for centuries. It's in the *fontanelle,* the drinking fountains carved into stone walls flowing with water from aqueducts built by the ancient Romans. It's in the seven hills that make up the city and in the old churches, some splendidly ornate, decorated by a triumph of artists. And some deceptively simple, still used every day by the locals, and with sometimes an unexpected Michelangelo sculpture or a fresco by Raphael, a Torrite mosaic, or a Bernini fountain to make you gasp. It's in the grand piazzas, like the Piazza Navona, layered higher and higher through the centuries to prevent flooding, though even as late as the eighteenth century it was still being frozen and used for winter ice skating. You live daily with history in sight of the great dome of St. Peter's, as well as in the massive old plane trees that shade the streets and in the gossipy old cafés and the bars. There's something in the air in Rome that I swear adds a skip of excitement to your step, the way it used to when I was a kid, always expecting some new marvel, some new excitement just around the next corner.

Sadly, Matt could not make the trip with us—unforeseen business commitments, he'd said, though I suspect the truth was that he'd wanted Jammy to be the only one with me while I searched for my past. He'd been skeptical about my looking into Jon-Boy's death, too.

"Listen, hon," he'd said before we left, putting an arm around my shoulders and talking quietly. "It's been what, twenty years now? Face it, Lamour; Jon-Boy just made a mistake; he went out on a boat and got caught in a storm. I don't know; maybe he'd been drinking . . . a few too many glasses of grappa. . . ." He'd shrugged, knowing he hadn't convinced me, even though I knew Jon-Boy had been partial to a few too many glasses of grappa, though I'd never seen him drunk. And he *never* went out on boats.

But now Jammy and I are at the Hotel d'Inghilterra, originally an old palazzo but since 1850 an intimate, antique-filled hotel on the via Bocca di Leone, right in the heart of Rome's smartest shopping district.

"How convenient," was Jammy's appreciative comment as she sipped her first Roman espresso in the hotel restaurant, quaintly named the Lounge del Roman Garden.

Tired from the long flight, complete with all the usual air-travel delays, we went up to our pretty room, where we showered, then flung ourselves exhausted into bed. Soon I heard Jammy's quiet snores. She had always snored, I remembered from childhood. But I found myself unable to sleep. Excitement and apprehension filled my mind. Was I going to find Trastevere the way I remembered it? Or had the memories been enhanced by time, the way they so often are?

Too much time had passed to find my lovely "grandmothers" still in Trastevere. I wondered who lived in our old apartment now and whether if I knocked on their door and explained that I used to live there they might allow me to see it again. Just to breathe the same air that Jon-Boy and I had breathed together, smell that slightly musty air of a very old and rather decrepit building would bring back my memories.

Sleep was impossible. I could wait no longer. And besides, I needed to do this alone. I got up, dressed quickly, and with a last glance at the sleeping Jammy made my way downstairs into the suddenly quiet streets.

It was lunchtime and Rome had "closed down" for two or three hours. Only the sneakered, backpacking young still thronged the Piazza di Spagna, where I hailed a cab to take me to Trastevere.

My heart thumped from two jolts of espresso and nerves as each narrow traffic-clogged street brought me closer to my old home. When the cab finally dropped me off at the top of the vicolo del Cardinale, I gazed down its shadowy, empty length, unable for a moment even to move. A tall, slender man emerged from one of the apartments. Without looking my way, he strode off down the alley in the direction of the piazza. My heart skipped a beat. With his long dark hair and loping walk, it might have been Jon-Boy, out searching for me again, lost on my solitary ramblings.

After that I seemed to see the ghost of my father at every corner . . . a glimpse, a shadow. And I also saw the skinny little pigtailed girl I used to be, skipping down that alley where I now began my walk into the past.

I stared hopefully up at those old kitchen windows, but there were no more friendly "grandmothers" to wave at me. And the peeling stucco buildings that in my day had sheltered half-a-dozen or so apartments had been gentrified into smart homes with fancy wooden doors. Their polished brass handles gleamed, and the names of the apartment owners had electric buzzers next to them instead of the old bell pushes. No lines of laundry hung over the alley, and manicured tubs of flowers lined the fancy pergolas on the rooftop gardens, instead of rusty cans and old pots of wilting greenery.

I hardly recognized my old building. It was painted an immaculate rosy pink with dark green trim. I studied the names next to the six buzzers. There was no one I knew. I stepped back and peered up at the top floor with its tall shuttered windows and minuscule iron Juliet balcony. I used to hang over the edge of that balcony rail, looking out for Jon-Boy, waiting for him to come home for his dinner. Sometimes he did and I was happy, and sometimes he didn't and then I would sit on that balcony and eat my sandwich alone, waiting. Which now I recalled, surprised, was more often than not. I always seemed to be waiting for Jon-Boy.

I'd eaten many spaghetti dinners at my "grandmother's," hauled off my Juliet balcony by one or other of them, clucking angrily in Italian, too rapid for me to understand, though I knew it was about how bad Jon-Boy was to leave me alone. Again. And how many times had Jon-Boy finally come looking for me, smiling his easy smile, golden-brown eyes a-twinkle, agreeing with all their criticisms.

"Bene, bene," he'd say. "Sì la piccolina è mio tesoro, mia bambina. . . . Sì è una preciosa, chiaramente, signora, ed io l'adoro. . . . Va bene, and here I am to collect her."

He would charm them into reluctant smiles as I—the tesoro, the "treasure"—was handed back into my erring papa's loving care. And I would laugh because I knew he meant all those things and that he would always come back and that he would always guard me with his life.

Now, though, a tabby cat gazed calmly back down at me from my Juliet balcony, looking as if he owned the place. And of course, now he did. There was no trace of me or Jon-Boy left here.

I emerged onto the sunny piazza, relieved to find that at least the newsstand was still there, and the flower stall. The Pizzeria Vesuvio, with surely the best pizza in all of Rome, was still on the corner too, and most important of all, so was the Bar Marchetti, though now it was all glossed up with a shine of dark red paint and smart white *ombrellini* shading its outdoor tables.

I checked the newsstand but the vendor was a young man with disinterested eyes for an American tourist. A much younger woman had replaced the flower seller Adriana, and when I asked after her the woman merely shrugged her shoulders; she knew no one around here. For old times' sake I bought a pink carnation and tucked it into my hair, then walked apprehensively into the Bar Marchetti.

The men standing at the bar, some business suited, some in workmen's clothes, eyed me speculatively, the way Italian men always do, and I smiled and elbowed my way expertly through with a pleasant *"scusi, scusi, permesso."*

There was a young man behind the bar, not Angelo. He flicked me a brief glance as he wiped the portion of the tiled counter in front of me and said, *"Signora?"*

"Cappuccino, per piacere," I said, *"e un cornetto."*

He lifted a brow and threw me a skeptical look because no Italian would ever dream of drinking cappuccino after eleven A.M. and *cornetti* were eaten only at breakfast.

Glancing round, I saw that changes had been made. The cappuccino machine looked to be the latest large model and the bar had been expanded with tall stand-up tables. The menu chalked on a big board behind the bar now included a "pasta of the day" and salads, as well as soup and wonderful *panini* piled high with ham and salami, and mortadella and fontina and pecorino. The tables outside had always been half-empty because it cost more to sit while you ate. Now they were filled with tourists willing to pay more to rest their city-weary feet, and I smiled hearing that familiar screech of iron-legged chairs on paving stone.

A second man, younger than the first and with a waiter's white apron swathed around his middle, dashed back and forth bearing carafes of wine and enormous sandwiches. The young man behind the counter slid my cappuccino toward me. Eyes closed, I inhaled the familiar aroma of fresh coffee. Then I took a sip and was instantly transported back in time. I was that little girl again, balancing on the bar's brass rail with powdered chocolate and cappuccino foam on my nose, flirting with Angelo. . . .

"*Ciao, bella.*" Angelo's familiar voice sent my eyes flying open. "It *is* you, Lamour Harrington, isn't it?" His smile as he reached for my hand was so familiar, so warm, I beamed. "Welcome home, *cara*. What took you so long?" he said.

I clutched his hand in both mine, hardly able to believe it was true. Of course Angelo's hair was gray and his olive-skinned face was broader and crisscrossed with lines and maybe his teeth were not so big and white and shiny as I remembered, but his warm brown eyes with their long straight lashes were the same, and they welcomed me the way they always had.

Still breathless with shock, I said, "Angelo, the last time you saw me I was eight years old. How on earth did you recognize me?"

He lifted a shoulder in a shrug. "What other woman would wear a pink carnation in her hair and order cappuccino and a *cornetto* at lunchtime?" He grinned and handed me the familiar pastry in its square of wax paper. "Besides," he added, "you are as beautiful now as you were then, when you were just a lonely *piccolina,* haunting this piazza, looking after your father, and running wild in the streets of Trastevere."

"But I never felt lonely; you were my friends, the whole neighborhood. . . ." I didn't want to believe my memories were not as good as I remembered.

"*È allora,* the neighborhood has changed. Maybe it's for the better; at least that's what my sons tell me, but myself, I'm not so sure. The people who used to live here were like family to me; I miss them. Now I have tourists for customers. I make more money, but . . . ," he sighed and shrugged regretfully again, "I miss the old ways."

I dusted chocolate powder from my lips then licked my finger. "That's exactly what we were, Angelo. Just one big extended happy family."

He looked warningly at me. "*Cara,* please don't go searching for what no longer exists. Remember, we must keep up with the changes. And now, Lamour, tell me about you. Are you married? Children?"

He smiled hopefully at me but I glanced away. "I was married," I said. "He died." My tight lips told my unhappy story more than any words and Angelo's eyes narrowed with pity.

"Poor girl." He patted my hand gently. "I'm so sorry."

"It's okay." It was an awkward moment and I stared into my coffee cup, silent again.

Then Angelo said, "Did you know I married Adriana? You remember the flower seller? She will be pleased to hear about you again. These are our sons." He waved his arm at the two busy young men. "They are good fellows, and soon we hope to have grandchildren." He turned and looked deep into my eyes. "Perhaps it would have been easier, *carina,* if you'd had children. Life goes on through them."

I shook my head and the pink carnation fell, forgotten, to the floor. "Better I didn't."

Angelo's shrewd eyes took in my haunted expression and I knew he saw my unhappiness. "So, little one," he said, changing the subject, "your father the *dottore,* turned out to be a great man after all, though we all worried about the way he neglected you."

I had to smile at the way he used *dottore* to describe Jon-Boy. *Doctor* was a title Italians bestow on all men of letters.

"Neglect had its advantages," I said. "I was the free-est child in Rome. Free to go where I wanted, do what I wanted . . ."

"And always alone," Angelo said. He didn't add "just the way you are now," but I knew that's what he was thinking.

"I'm visiting Rome with a friend," I said defensively. "We just arrived. She was tired, but I'll bring her with me next time.

The bar was getting crowded and Angelo needed to get back to work. Life goes on, I thought, as I gathered up my bag, smoothed back my hair. *"Domani,* Angelo," I called, already edging through the crowd, though even then I knew I would not come back again.

"Wait. . . ."

I turned to look at him.

"You forgot your *cornetto.*"

I took it, smiling my thanks, already pushing through the customers crowding the doorway.

Back on the via del Corso, I hailed a taxi. I slumped in the seat and took a bite of the *cornetto,* tasting the familiar sugary pastry.

I had made a big mistake. Rome, *my* Rome, had changed. Jon-Boy was gone and so was my "family": the grandmothers, the neighbors . . . my friends.

I thought sadly that the old saying was true after all. You cannot "go home" again.

EIGHT

❧

Lamour

JAMMY INSISTED I GO SHOPPING WITH HER ON THE via Condotti, Rome's finest shopping street, conveniently situated almost outside our front door.

"You can count it under the heading of self-improvement," she said, eyeing my black T-shirt, black pants, and sensible flat shoes critically. In fact, looking at myself I realized I wasn't too far removed from the way my old Italian "grandmothers" used to look. Checking out the chic, sexy Roman women who all seemed to be wearing the very latest in designer clothes, I was torn again by doubt.

Since I'd found out about Alex, I had lost any feelings of self-worth as a woman. All I was, was what I did, and I was thankful that at least I did that well.

I stared despairingly into Gucci's windows. "There has to be more to me, the *real* me, than just some fancy new clothes."

"Of course there is," Jammy said, loyal as always.

But facing my somber reflection in that plate glass window I thought it was no wonder Alex had wanted to leave me for another woman. "Do you think she was sexy?" I asked.

Jammy had no need to ask who. "I guess so, but no more than you and me on a good day." She gave me an encouraging nudge. "So how about we give ourselves a 'good day'? See what trouble we can stir up amongst the Roman male population," she added with a mischievous grin that was meant to encourage me. Linking arms, we headed down the via Condotti.

That night I took Jammy to Da Fortunato, the *trattoria* on the via del Pantheon where Jon-Boy had taken me to celebrate my eighth birthday. Jon-Boy never seemed to have much money then, he also never really thought about things like clothes, so I didn't have many. I'd been forced to wear a pink sweater that had fit me on my seventh birthday with an old plaid skirt—my *only* skirt—and brand-new sneakers. I'd shot up like a sapling tree in spring, the sweater sleeves were halfway down my arms, and the skirt was daringly short. Only the new sneakers fit. And they were blindingly white.

It was winter and chilly, and we had taken a table indoors amid the good aromas of sauces and spices and a fabulous display of antipasti. But now it was a soft early-summer night and Jammy and I were at a terrace table looking out to the beautiful dome of the Pantheon, and I was a long way from that shabby little eight-year-old birthday girl. I was wearing a new silky dress in a coral color, sleeveless, with a deep V-neck that showed a fragment of a horribly expensive La Perla lace bra that Jammy and a persuasive saleswoman had informed me I simply had to have since it did wonders for my small breasts. "Besides," the saleswoman had said with that Roman-woman knowingness, "it is very seductive, no?" Her smile had clinched the deal. And seductive I hoped I now looked, with a peek of red lace at my breast and ruinously expensive high heeled red-suede mules on my long, narrow feet.

For once my dark curly hair was behaving itself, thanks to a pricey new cut, and it floated around my shoulders in a way I'd never experienced before. Remembering Adriana, I'd pinned a flower in it. I was beginning to feel a *little bit* Roman, but while looking good helped, inside I was still the wounded, insecure me.

Jammy looked delicious in blue that matched her eyes, and I noticed more than one man glance appreciatively her way.

"Jon-Boy turned me into a gourmet right here at Da Fortunato," I told her as the waiter opened the bottle of Frescobaldi Chianti I'd ordered. "I ate my first oyster here."

"And did you like it?" Jammy was starving as usual, already devouring the bread while scanning the menu. I don't know where she puts all that food; she's as slender now as she was at seventeen.

"Sort of, but I preferred the porcini risotto; I just loved that wild smoky mushroom flavor. I was a real sophisticated kid."

"To tell you the truth, I'll be glad to see you eat almost anything." Jammy looked me critically up and down. "Though I have to admit you do look pretty good tonight." She grinned and lifted her glass. "To you, sweetheart," she said, "and to your return to the living."

My spirits rose as we clinked glasses and I took a deep draught of the smooth, berry-tasting wine. Glancing up, I caught the eye of a man a couple of tables away. Older, experienced looking, broad shouldered, immaculately dressed. And handsome. He smiled and lifted his glass to me, bowing his head briefly.

I half-smiled back, then turned away, embarrassed. I'd forgotten that Italian talent for flirting. I told myself that of course it wasn't just me; Italians would flirt with almost anyone except their mothers.

"Did I just see what I saw?" Jammy grinned at me. "Did that guy really make a pass at you?"

I shrugged nonchalantly. "Of course he didn't; he just . . . smiled."

"Hmmm." Jammy did not believe me. She looked him over again. He was with a group of people and they were immersed in conversation. He'd already forgotten me.

"He looks pretty good," Jammy said, diving enthusiastically into a plate of fettuccine coated in butter and fresh Parmesan. "Oh God," she groaned, then took a deep, pleasurable breath, "this is the closest I'll ever get to Mom's mac-and-cheese." I laughed and told her she should be ashamed of herself, because this pasta had nothing at all to do with Kraft.

"And *this* is heaven," I added, tasting my porcini risotto and with it a basketful of memories, thanking God that at least some things had stayed the way I remembered.

We followed the pasta and risotto with grilled sea bream, the sweetest fish you've ever tasted, then a simple green salad and, after, even simpler ice cream, pistachio for me and chocolate, of course, for my all-American friend.

Dinner over, we sat lazily content, sipping grappa from tiny glasses. I leaned indolently back in my chair, wrinkling my nose as the liquor took my breath away. Crossing my legs, I gazed up at the night sky, heaving a sigh of something I thought might be happiness.

Take happiness where you can find it, I told myself. At this sweet restaurant with its view of the Pantheon and the moon shining down on it. In the soft night air, with the Romans milling past on their nightly *passeggiata,* children clasped in one hand, *gelato* in the other. In the violin music coming from somewhere close by, the lamplight, the flowers, the red wine, and the company of a good friend.

My eyes half-closed, I dangled a high-heeled red mule from the tips of my toes.

"Mi scusi, signora. . . ."

I looked up, straight into the eyes of the handsome man

who'd raised his glass in a toast to me. I stared blankly at him. Somewhere along the way I had lost that childhood capacity to flirt even when presented with an opportunity like this. I had no idea what to say to him.

He nodded politely to the interested Jammy and excused himself again for interrupting.

"Signora," he said, bending closer and speaking low so that only I could hear. "I couldn't help but notice how you swung your foot, the curve of your instep as you balanced the pretty red mule on your toes. It was one of the most charming things I have ever seen. I am by way of being a connoisseur of beauty and I must tell you, *bella signora,* that you have the most delicious foot in all of Rome."

"*Grazie, signore,* thank you," I managed to say as he smiled into my stunned eyes. Then he straightened up, bowed over my hand, said, *"Buona notte,"* and was gone.

Jammy stared suspiciously after him. "What did he say to you?"

I grinned modestly. "He said he thought I had beautiful feet."

"He said *what!*" Her face was pink with indignation. "What is he, some kind of *pervert*?"

"Uh-uh. He's a connoisseur of beauty. He liked my instep." I grinned at her, suddenly feeling good. I looked down at my long pale legs and my narrow feet with their coral-tipped nails in the expensive high-heeled red mules. I understood that all the Italian had wanted was to make me aware that I had innocently given him a moment of sensual pleasure. And in return, he'd made me feel feminine and sexy. Like a woman again, I thought, smiling.

The waiter came hurrying to our table. *"Signore,"* he said, "that was the great Italian couturier, the designer Giorgio

Vivari." He beamed at us, expecting us to know who he meant. And how could we not? It was a name that ranked up there with Valentino and Armani.

I was still smiling when Jammy and I left the restaurant. I would never see him again, but a well-known handsome man, a true connoisseur of beautiful women, had paid me a sexy compliment.

I was laughing as I took Jammy's arm. Italy was the place I needed to be after all.

NINE

L'amour

THE VERY NEXT DAY WE FLEW TO NAPLES. WE rented a car, a small Fiat, then headed out along the famous Amalfi Drive, the nerve-racking two-lane road that runs in a series of tight hairpin bends along the coast. We drove past hillsides dotted with sweet-looking creamy-colored cows, the *bufala* from whose milk the best mozzarella was made fresh each morning. We skimmed over gorges and ravines, past silvery groves of olives and leafy vineyards clinging to the rocky slopes on one side of the road while on the other tiny villages and hotels clung even more precariously to tumbling cliffs overlooking the rocks and the sea hundreds of feet below.

My heart in my mouth, I kept a stern eye on the road, trying to ignore Jammy's gasps of horror as a blast signaled yet another oncoming sixteen-wheeler.

She covered her eyes with her hands and moaned with terror. I grinned at her without taking my own eyes off the road.

"Oh, shut up," I said, "and keep a lookout for those round mirrors pinned to the rocks that tell us when something's coming."

"Something is always coming," she snapped. "And right now I'm wondering exactly why *I* did."

" 'Cause you're my friend." There was a happy lilt to my voice and she heard it.

"Well, okay, but can we please stop soon?" she begged.

"In five minutes we'll be there." I felt her accusing eyes on me.

"You mean you actually *know* where we're going?"

"Of course I do." I spotted the sign for the Hotel Santa Caterina, drove through a flowery orchard, and stopped in front of a low white building set like a jewel on a verdant hillside with a panoramic view of the coast.

Jammy gasped. I could tell she was pleased.

She said, "Oh!" when she stepped inside the charming flower-filled lobby.

The young man behind the desk greeted us with a smile. "We were expecting you," he said, and he proceeded to show us around the small, elegant hotel with its country-tiled floors and Belle Époque furnishings, its lovely gardens and extensive orchards. There was a swimming pool with a thatched-roofed café, and our pretty room had a view through the trees to the sea. I sighed happily. I had that comforting feeling of "coming home."

"I'm in love," Jammy said, standing in the middle of our large, sweet room, her arms outstretched, taking in the pretty decor, the big white bathroom with its huge tub, and the balcony with the perfect view. The scent of flowers drifted in on the breeze that felt soft as silk on the skin. "When do we eat?" she added more practically.

So, later, after a swim and a long soothing soak in the tub for each of us, we dressed in our new Roman best, sexy red mules and all, and went down to dinner.

But first there was a message from my Chicago real estate agent. She had an offer on my apartment close to the asking price. Would I accept it?

Yes, I would, and gladly, good riddance to the past, and we toasted our safe arrival with Prosecco, the Italian sparkling wine that doesn't even pretend to be champagne; it just is what it is: nice, fizzy, and fun. Then I ate the best potato gnocchi with fresh tomato sauce I'd ever tasted, while Jammy tucked into fettuccine again. A fish, a salad, cheeses. . . . We couldn't even make dessert.

Tired, well-fed, comforted, cosseted, I lay in bed, listening to Jammy's snores and the sound of the sea, thinking about my father. About that fateful night and the terrible storm, the capsized boat and the body that was never recovered.

For years after it happened I was terrorized by nightmares of Jon-Boy sinking beneath great black waves. In my dream his eyes were wide open, they stared beseechingly into mine, he held out his hands and I reached out to him. . . . But before I could catch him, he sank into the blackness.

I'd awake, sweating and trembling and praying never to have that dream again. I'd *willed* myself not to think about Jon-Boy's death, not to dream of it anymore. I never talked to anyone about it, except Jammy of course, and even then I didn't tell her about the dream. Somehow I managed to block the accident from my mind, allowing only the good memories to stay. But now I was here, at the place where it happened, and I began to question my father's death.

Jon-Boy was afraid of water. He'd always told me, "Keep your feet on terra firma, honey; it's the only solid thing in this life." He hated the sea. He was a bad swimmer. He had never sailed a boat in his entire life.

Then *why* had he been out alone in a sailboat, at night, with a storm brewing?

And why had I never asked myself these questions before? The reason was simple. I was afraid of the answer. But now I felt closer to him than I had in years. And tomorrow I was going to the house he'd bought in Amalfi, the house he'd left that night and to which he had never returned.

An image of Jon-Boy sharp as a photograph came into my mind: tall and thin, attractive, with a shock of dark hair falling over his brown eyes, a smile that charmed, and a long loping stride I'd always had trouble keeping up with. In my memory he was the young American writer in Rome—*il Dottore,* they called him, and it gave him a rakish kind of glamour—smiling tenderly at me. He was always tender with women, young or old. In fact, I never heard a harsh word from Jon-Boy, not ever. He was a friendly, open man, easy with his companions at the bar.

Behind my closed lids I saw him smile at me again, his hand raised in jaunty greeting. And I knew in that moment that though I could not bring him back, one of the reasons I was here was to find out exactly what had happened. How Jon-Boy Harrington had really died.

TEN

Lamour

THAT NIGHT, MY MIND MADE UP, I SLEPT AWAY those thousand nightmares. It was the best sleep I'd had in years. Early the next morning, I told Jammy I needed to be alone when I returned for the first time to the house in Amalfi.

I left her contentedly breakfasting on the shady terrace with the view through the trees to the sea. "Need we ever leave here?" she called after me as I closed the door. The magic had gotten to her, too.

Even after twenty years, I remembered every inch of the way, driving the narrow, twisting cliff-side road with the Pirata hill on one side and the lush green slope of the cliff and the sea glittering on the other.

I parked where Jon-Boy always used to, next to the wayside shrine, a small stone grotto with a plaster saint. His hands were outstretched in a benediction and I remembered this was Saint Andrew, whose bones lay in the crypt of the Duomo, the patron saint of Amalfi and the protector of sailors. A vase with fresh flowers had been placed in front of the shrine, and I wondered, surprised, who had bothered to put flowers in this forgotten little spot.

Up on the hill, the Castello Pirata stood proudly, as it had for centuries, its battlemented tower flying its strange flag with the bold skull-and-crossbones insignia of the Pirata family. Behind the saint's grotto, a sandy clearing led to the cliff and the *scalatinella,* the steps carved into the rock that zigzagged gently down through tangled green shrubs. Fifty feet below, the pale turquoise sea fluttered at the rocks, sending lazy flights of foam into the clear morning air.

As I walked slowly down the *scalatinella,* birds flew twittering from their nests and rabbits bobbed their white tails and disappeared into the tangled undergrowth. Then there it was. A small golden house gently folded into the green cliff side. I stood there, looking at part of my past. There was only the purr of the sea and the hum of crickets. I thought my house looked as lonely as I felt.

Jon-Boy had told me that it had been built in the 1920s to accommodate the mistress of the rich owner of the Castello Pirata. She was a pretty young opera singer from Naples, and the house was within easy reach of the Castello, if you were young and agile as the young lovers were, yet discreetly tucked away. Solid rock had been blasted to make room for the house, which in the end had turned out to be smaller than the mistress expected, but it was so beautiful she fell in love with it and forgot to grumble.

It was small and square, with four tall French doors facing the terrace on the ground floor and five square windows above. Its flat roof was topped with a little Moorish-style dome tiled in the blues and greens of the sea. Narrow fluted columns, twisted like candy, supported the three graceful arches fronting the shady patio and the veranda above. From this, broad shallow steps led to a series of terraced gardens and down to the small cove.

I could hear the soft trickle of a waterfall and remembered the fall spilled down the cliffside, guided by carefully placed boulders, meandering on through gardens, shaded, here and there, by a beautiful ancient cedar. Halfway down the slope was a fanciful marble belvedere, a domed pergola where I imagined the little opera singer used to sit watching the sunset and sipping wine, the way Jon-Boy so often had. Now it was smothered in trailing blue morning glory, bright as the sea.

But when I looked closer I saw that the ancient cedars were growing over the roof of the house and their branches had been twisted by years of winter winds into fantastical shapes. Wild creatures had made their homes in the undergrowth. The old wooden shutters were weathered to a silvery sheen and latched tight by bands of rusted iron, and over the upper windows tattered awnings flapped forlornly in the breeze.

I closed my eyes, summoning up a picture I had carried in my mind all these years. Jon-Boy and I were sitting on this very terrace. It was evening and as usual he had a glass of local Campania white wine while I had lemonade I'd made myself from lemons picked that morning from our very own trees. I'd run barefoot all summer and the soles of my feet were tough as leather, my dark hair was bleached copper by the sun, and there was a crust of salt on my skin from my latest swim. I could smell the salt on me, and the lemons, and the jasmine curling around the fluted white columns.

I was like a wild creature in those days, with no one to answer to, no one to tell me what I must do. When I was tired, I went to bed. When I awoke, I got up, eager for another day. I always headed straight to the white-tiled kitchen, where I'd butter a hard crust of yesterday's bread, or maybe it was even the day before's—Jon-Boy and I were not very good at shopping. I'd slather it with fig preserves that tasted of sugar spiced by the sun; then I'd put the espresso on to brew for whenever Jon-Boy woke up. Which might be noon or sometimes even later, depending on where he'd been the night before. And of course, who he'd been with, though I never really knew about that part of his life.

I never tried to wake him or peek into his room. Young and innocent though I was, somehow I knew not to go there. I just waited instead.

Sometimes a girl would be with him, young and pretty, some tourist he'd picked up in Amalfi the night before, and I'd be pink with jealousy, refusing even to talk to her. Jon-Boy would laugh and make some excuse for me and they'd drink the coffee I'd made and then go off together. I never asked where he was going and he never told me, and he never asked me to go with him. But I always knew he would come back for me.

I'd already be in my bathing suit. I remember it even now; it was bright red, very old, and way too small. It smelled of summer, that suit, and I never, ever, wanted a new one. I'd gallop down the million steps to the cove and head into the water, wading until it came up to my shoulders, cool and so clear I could see the dozens of little fish darting curiously around my toes. Then I'd hurl myself forward and head toward the horizon in the fast crawl I'd perfected in the Evanston school pool.

There was nothing to beat that feeling. It was total freedom, just me and the cool, crystalline blue sea, with the early sunlight sparking off it turning my spray to miniature rainbows. I could have swum on forever, all the way to Capri even.

I'd turn and float on my back, searching the lush, indented coastline. If you didn't know the house was there, you might never notice it, but I knew to look to the right of the *scalatinella*, to where the twisted cedars sheltered it. I'd catch a glimpse of its blue and green tiled dome, its green-striped awnings, and its golden walls, and I'd smile, secure again as I turned and swam lazily back to shore. To the fresh-squeezed orange juice that I knew, if Jon-Boy was there and he was alone, would be waiting for me.

ELEVEN

Lamour

I WAS JOLTED BACK FROM MY DREAM OF THE PAST by a new sound. From behind me came the shuffle of sandaled feet. I swung round, half-expecting to see Jon-Boy, but found myself looking instead at a Japanese man, so old he seemed ageless. A fragile gray beard drizzled to a point just below his chin and his wild gray eyebrows swept to points somewhere near his bald pate. He was thin and wiry, with skin the color of pale sandstone and a clear gaze that belied the wildness of his appearance. He looked like a faun carved in some ancient stone frieze or like a lean, benign Bacchus or a bit like the wild goats I remembered leaping sure-footedly, down a steep cliff on an island off the coast.

He was just such a natural part of the habitat, it seemed he might have grown out of it. Which in a way he had, for this was Mifune, the man who had created the very garden I was standing in, many years before I first saw and fell in love with it.

It was Mifune who had instilled in me my love of plants and trees, of boulders and running streams and fountains. Mifune who had taught me how the seasons worked with nature and Mifune who unknowingly had led me to my career as a landscape architect.

Next to Jon-Boy, Mifune was the most influential figure in my life. He'd been my only friend here. We had spent hours, days, weeks that led into months, and months that drifted into a year in each other's company. He had shaped my life with his practical words of wisdom, and even now I never took on a new project without first thinking what Mifune would have done with it.

Seeing him now, in this garden, *my* garden, after almost thirty years, shocked me into silence. He had seemed to me old then, and I'd thought he surely must be dead. For a long moment we stood and looked at each other. Then, "Mifune," I said, "of course you won't remember me, but I've never forgotten you."

"*Va bene, la piccola* Lamour Harrington." A wide toothless grin split his lined parchment face and his pale eyes sparked with pleasure. "Can it really be you?" he asked, in Italian. "After all these years, you have come home again?"

I wanted to run to him, to hug him, but I remembered his formal Japanese ways and instead I bowed deeply, giving him the respect he deserved. "But Mifune, you told me that you were going to return to Japan, that you would find your old life there, your old customs, your own people."

He, too, bowed his head with its few remaining wisps of hair. "I returned one time, signorina. But I realized that the world I had left behind as a young man no longer existed. All was changed and nothing was reality. So I came home again. To Amalfi."

Observant as always, he had noted my ringless left hand and called me *signorina*. "Like me, Mifune," I said, "but I'm only here on vacation. I've come to see my old house."

He laughed, a small, almost soundless chuckle, "This place possesses you when you are young. You can never be happy anywhere else. Haven't you found that out yet, *piccolina*?"

"Happiness is an art I lost years ago," I said. "I don't know how to find it again, Mifune. I don't even know what it is.

Recently I was thinking about when I was a child in Rome with Jon-Boy, and I remembered *that* feeling was what happiness was. And then he brought me to this house, this *paradiso*, and I found out there is a different, truer kind of happiness."

"Happiness is all in the spirit," Mifuni said, "and I can tell from your eyes that you have lost that. Part of it is losing Jon-Boy. What the rest is I will not ask. It is no longer important. You are here again, back where you belong."

"I need to find Jon-Boy again," I said. "I need to know what happened that night. I need to know how he died so I can banish my dreams, and my ghosts."

He nodded gravely. "I understand."

I thought quickly of my busy life in Chicago, about my business commitments and my few close friends. I thought of Alex and of his betrayal. I thought of Jon-Boy and Mifune. All my *good* memories were here, in Italy.

My apartment had been sold. I no longer had a home. I was alone in the world, and what, after all, did I have to go back to? My greatest pleasure was growing things, creating gardens from seemingly impossible spaces, like this one, where Mifune had allowed me to help him plant the sloping cliff side into a panorama of verdant green pleasure. Now it was a shambles of overgrown crumbling terraces that threatened to tumble into the turquoise sea. The dark green cedars sheltering the house bent under the burden of their untamed branches, and the sweet golden house I remembered as my real "home" looked neglected and desolate.

Like me, the house needed to get its spirit back, and I suddenly knew we would do it together. I would leave the past behind, make a fresh start. I'd become self-sufficient, grow olives on my hillside, grow lemons, tomatoes, cultivate my wild terraces. I'd buy one of those pretty cows and make my own mozzarella; I would keep chickens and eat real eggs, not store-bought ones. . . . I was dazzled by my unknown independent future.

"I guess I'm home again, Mifune," I said, smiling as that first pang of pure, true happiness danced through my veins again. "I'm back where I belong."

TWELVE

Lamour

I REMEMBER CLEARLY THE DAY I MET MIFUNE. JON-Boy and I had been in the little house for about a week and every morning we rose early and ran down to the sea for a swim. That is, I swam while Jon-Boy watched. "Don't go too far out, honey-bunch," he'd warn me. "I don't want to have to rescue you." Of course he knew I was a good swimmer, even then, far better than him, and in these safe waters I'd hardly need to be "rescued."

That morning, however, I'd knocked on his door to wake him and gotten no reply. I knocked again, but I didn't open it. I never did. I knew Jon-Boy would have answered if he was there. I ran down to the kitchen to see if he was already squeezing juice for me; then I checked the terrace and the garden.

Deciding he must have gotten up really early and gone to the market in Pirata without me, I threw on my red bathing suit and raced down the *scalatinella* to the cove.

Of course I also understood now that Jon-Boy had probably left me asleep the previous night and gone out on the town. I didn't blame him; a man with a seven-year-old kid couldn't be expected to stay home all the time. At least that's the way I thought then.

The boats were bobbing up and down at the jetty, and with a hand over my eyes I scanned the bright silvery sea. The sun was emerging from the clouds and it was a perfect morning. I waded out, then dived under.

After about half an hour, I emerged from my watery world and plodded, tired, back up the steps. I was looking forward to the cup of coffee I'd fix for Jon-Boy and me, and a slice of that lovely crusty bread, but when I pushed the front door it would not open. I pushed and pushed, but it was firmly stuck.

I tried the French doors. They were latched from the inside. I climbed up to the kitchen window. It too was latched. I contemplated scaling one of the columns to the upper terrace but had the sense to know I'd probably break my neck.

By now the sky had clouded over and the sun was hidden. I sat hunched on the terrace steps, shivering in my wet bathing suit, thinking longingly about that hot coffee.

"What are you doing here all alone, little girl?"

I hadn't heard anyone coming. I looked at the old man, a little scared. Even then, to me he seemed old and so thin, and wiry, with strange pale eyes and tangled eyebrows, I thought he was a ghost.

"Oh," I said, startled. "Are you a ghost?"

He laughed. "Not yet, *piccolina*. Are you?"

"No." I eyed him carefully. He was carrying a large watering can and a long-pronged rake. "Where do you live?" I asked, still a little afraid of the stranger, aware that Jon-Boy was not here to protect me.

"In my cottage, up at the Castello."

"Oh," I said again, impressed because I'd seen the Castello from a distance and it looked like a place a princess would live.

"I am a gardener, little girl. My name is Mifune."

"Mee-fu-nee . . . ," I repeated it, smiling. I liked the way it sounded. "My name is Lamour."

I was shivering by now and he said, "You should go indoors, Lamour, change your clothes, get warm."

"But the door won't open," I said. "All the doors are locked, and Jon-Boy isn't home."

Mifune didn't ask any questions about Jon-Boy or why a seven-year-old had been left alone. He simply said, "Then come with me, *piccolina*. We'll go to the kitchens at the Castello. The cook will find you some warm clothes to wear and give you a hot drink."

I went willingly, intrigued by my strange new friend skipping along beside him, chattering away, asking a million questions. Where did he come from? Why did he live here? What was Japan like? What kind of Japanese food did he eat?

He stopped in his tracks, grabbed my hand, and bent his face close to mine. "*Piccolina,* do you *ever* stop talking?" he said. "Stop now. Look around you. See what beauty there is. It is not always necessary to talk."

I stared back at him, dumbfounded. Where I came from every kid talked nonstop and usually over the top of other kids.

"*Look,*" Mifune said. And I looked.

I looked where he showed me he had planted new seedlings in the shade of the pine trees that he said by summer would be in full bloom. I looked at the rabbit burrows in the hedgerow and at the birds' nests and he told me the names of the flowers I saw, both the English version and the Latin that I repeated after him, intrigued that anything could have two names.

We walked through the pines, along the path to the back of the Castello Pirata, where the maids tut-tutted over the story of me being left all alone by my father, locked out of my house and wearing only a wet bathing suit. Garments were found to wrap me in—a too-large sweater, a pair of shorts—and hot chocolate was made specially for me.

Thrilled with my big adventure, I thanked them and said good-bye; then I followed Mifune back through the beautiful gardens that I now saw with wide new eyes.

When we got home, the front door was open and Jon-Boy was there, searching anxiously for me.

"Oh my God, there you are!" He hoisted me off my feet, hugging me to his chest. "You scared me, Lamour. I saw your bathing suit was gone and there was no sign of you in the sea. Jesus!" He crushed me to him again and I felt his heart pounding. He then suddenly noticed we were not alone.

"*Signore,*" Mifune said, bowing.

"*Signore.*" Jon-Boy also bowed.

"I am Mifune, the gardener at the Castello. Your daughter was alone. She could not get into the house. She was cold and wet."

Jon-Boy heard the reproof in Mifune's voice. "I apologize to Lamour, and to you, Mifune," he said politely. "It was un-avoidable but also inexcusable."

"Mifune took me to the Castello," I interrupted, still excited by my important adventure. "They gave me hot chocolate and these clothes."

"Then we must thank Mifune for helping you." The two men assessed each other. "I'm thanking you from the bottom of my heart," Jon-Boy added. "Lamour's my girl; she means everything to me."

Mifune nodded. "She is a fine *piccolina* even though she talks too much," he said, and Jon-Boy laughed. "I would be happy if you would take tea with me, at my cottage in the Castello's grounds, tomorrow, at four o'clock," he added, and Jon-Boy said we'd be delighted.

Mifune bowed and said good-bye, walking away with that

soundless loping walk. Jon-Boy said his invitation sounded like a royal command and we'd better go, so the following afternoon, dressed in my best, which wasn't much, a T-shirt and shorts, but at least was better than the old red bathing suit, and carrying a gift of some Amaretto cookies wrapped in pink tissue paper, I walked together with Jon-Boy through the pine trees to take tea at Mifune's house.

I'd never seen anything like it. It looked like a Japanese temple. Two columns supported a pedimented roof that rose to a peak, then swooped in a gentle curve to deep overhanging eaves. Three low steps led up to the porch, where a small brass gong awaited by the front door. The shoji-screened windows had, of necessity, been flanked by Italian wooden shutters against winter storms, but for the rest Mifune's home looked completely Japanese.

Feeling as though I were in storybook land, I struck the gong softly, announcing our arrival.

Mifune came to the door. "*Signore, signorina,* please enter," he said with that curious little bow.

I looked at the shiny bamboo floor, at the shoji screens dividing the single room, and at the tatami mats around the low table in its center. The only other piece of furniture was a long narrow table that Jon-Boy told me later was an antique elm-wood altar table. It held a small shrine where a candle was lit to honor the ancestors Mifune had never known.

The old man busied himself preparing tea, presenting the three thin porcelain bowls on a black enamel tray. He poured strong green tea from a pot with a bamboo handle and he and Jon-Boy talked while I stared around me, taking everything in.

I'd never seen a home like this, never met anyone like Mifune. And I was willing to bet he'd never met anyone like me, either. I looked at him and smiled. I knew we were going to be friends.

From that day on, Mifune kept watch over me. He always seemed to know where I was and when I was alone. He began to teach me about flowers and plants, about the earth they grew in, about the power of water in plant life and the need for sun and shade and wind. I began to learn about life from Mifune, and I never forgot what he taught.

THIRTEEN

Jammy

JAMMY SPRAWLED LANGUIDLY POOLSIDE AT THE Santa Caterina. A big straw hat covered her face and she gazed heavenward through the chinks in the raffia at the peaceful blue of the sky. Somewhere down below, waves broke gently on rocks, and a gull cried.

She heard Lamour's footsteps on the steps, quick, light, urgent. She would have known them anywhere.

"Jammy!"

The sun lounger next to her squeaked as Lamour plopped onto it. "Yeah?" Jammy said, acting casual and praying Lamour would too.

"Jammeeeee!"

Under the hat, Jammy grinned. "What?" she said. Then the hat was snatched off and Lamour's face was beaming into hers.

"Jammy Mortimer Haigh, stop pretending you can wait to know what happened."

Jammy sat up. "Okay, so I can tell it was good by the smile on your face," she said, adjusting the strap of her bathing suit.

"Jam, it's still *there*! My little golden house. Of course it's been abandoned since Jon-Boy . . . left. It's a bit run-down now. And the garden . . . well, let's just say it and the house need my TLC. But more than that, Jam, I met someone special."

Jammy listened quietly to Lamour's story about her old friend and mentor, about the sorry state of the gardens and the house. That is until Lamour said, "And now I've decided to stay on here. I'm going to fix up the house, and I'll work hard with Mifune to restore the gardens. I'm going to live there and be myself again. . . . I'll grow vegetables, keep chickens, a cow. . . ."

"Are you out of your mind!" Jammy jumped upright on the lounger. "For God's sake, Lamour, *a cow*! I know you're excited, but at least talk sense. You *can't* live here. Your life—your *real* life—is in Chicago . . . your work, your friends. You'll buy a new apartment; you'll finally get on with your life—God knows you've wasted enough time."

"I'm not coming back, Jammy." Lamour's eyes shone with the fervor of the newly converted. "I'm going to live in my house in Amalfi. I'm going to be self-sufficient—as far as I can, anyway. I mean I can't grow vines on my cliff side, but I do have a pasture on the hill across the road for my cow. . . ."

"And exactly how close have you ever been to a cow?"

"Well, of course I've seen them, you know, on farms, in the countryside. . . ."

"Driving by in a car. Right?"

"Well, right. But that doesn't mean I can't learn all about them, and after all, I only want *one*."

Jammy lay back on the chaise. She put the straw hat over her face again. "So you're going to milk the cow twice a day, right? At five in the morning, right? And again at about seven in the evening? Just when regular people might be thinking about going out to dinner somewhere nice, with a good bottle of wine to sustain them. Hey, maybe you could whip up a batch of mozzarella to sell at your little roadside stand the next morning, along with some fresh brown eggs—no doubt with double yolks—from your charming little chickens, who just can't wait to lay them for you in their neat little nests. And of course you'll make fresh lemonade from your

homegrown lemons to sell along with the eggs and the mozzarella, and of course you'll have knocked out a batch of
crusty rustic bread, still warm from the oven, to go with the
eggs and the cheese. What an idyllic life, Lamour; I can see
it now. . . . Away go the red-suede mules; good-bye, pretty
dress; good-bye, the possibility of a sex life, because you'll
soon be a grizzled, overworked old woman in a black dress
and granny shoes, wishing you were back in a peaceful Chicago apartment, tending other people's gardens for a living.
And a darn *good* living it is, Lamour. Which is one thing you
seem to have left out of your plan. Exactly *what* are you going to live on? After all, you're not *exactly* used to roughing
it." Jammy pushed back her straw hat and glared at Lamour.
"Sometimes you are such a silly bitch, Lamour, I don't know
how I put up with you."

Lamour's face fell, but then she grinned. "The Amalfi
house was Jon-Boy's; now, it's mine. It'll cost me nothing to
live there. Of course I know I'll have to work; I'm not that
stupid. But Jammy, I'll get a smaller apartment so I can go
back to Chicago to work on my commissions. I won't give it
up entirely, at least not until I'm sure I can make it out here."

Jammy slid the hat back over her face again. "What am I
going to do with you, Lamour Harrington? Whatever am I
going to do?"

"You could at least *look* at the house before passing judg-
ment," Lamour said, sounding hopeful. "I admit it needs a
touch of paint and I haven't even seen what the inside's like
yet, but Mifune is leaving the key under the lemon pot outside the door. We could look at it tomorrow. Will you come
with me, Jammy? *Please,* say you will."

Jammy's sigh almost gusted the straw hat right off her face.
"You know I will," she said resignedly, hearing Lamour's delighted laugh.

FOURTEEN

Lorenzo

WITH HIS UGLY WHITE DOG, AFFARE, IN THE SEAT next to him, Lorenzo Pirata flew the Bell helicopter low over the ink blue evening sea as though seeking that no-man's-land, the line where the darkening western sky meets the sultry water. To his left, ropes of glittering lights lit the resorts along the Amalfi coast, highlighting the charming inlets and coves and the terraces of the hotels. He spotted the red beacon atop the Castello Pirata and the hazy yellow lights of the tiny coastal town of Pirata itself. With a small sigh of relief, he brought the helicopter in lower.

Lorenzo's family had been living here for three centuries and he knew every inch of his land. He knew every man, woman, and child in Pirata. He looked after them like a father. He was coming home, and for him there was no better place to be.

The bird's-eye view of the pale terra-cotta Castello Pirata as he hovered before landing never failed to thrill him with its odd beauty. The central square stone tower with its battlements looked like Hamlet's castle in Denmark and was all that was left of the original Castello, built by an ancestor with good taste and a lot of money in the seventeenth century. The legend was that the ancestor had made his money by acts of piracy on the high seas, hence the name of Pirata, or "pirate," but apart from the skull and crossbones on the family flag and the fact that the family's business was shipping, that was now mostly forgotten.

Stuccoed wings and annexes had been added over the decades, as had the gardens. A grand terrace lined with tubs of lemon trees was fronted with a dozen massive sphinx heads, brought from Egypt in the early nineteen hundreds. Now they looked with disapproving expressions over the breathtaking panoramic view of the jagged Amalfi coastline.

A deep-blue swimming pool graced with delicate stone arches rippled in the breeze from the helicopter's rotors. The young woman swimming lazy lengths glanced up, then waved a hand in greeting, and Affare barked frantically. Lorenzo smiled, pleased. His twenty-one-year-old daughter, Aurora, was home unexpectedly for the weekend from her university in Grenoble.

He set the helicopter gently on its pad, then sat for a moment in the sudden silence, letting his ears adjust to the stillness. There was only the sound of Affare's panting, the hum of crickets, and the trickle of a fountain. The urban burden of his city life in Rome lifted from his shoulders and he was home again, in his own pocket of the world, in the place he loved.

He strode from the helipad with Affare bounding ahead through a little maze of thyme-lined paths and took the broad sweeping steps up to the house two at a time, shedding his jacket and loosening his tie as he went.

He was a big man of sixty-four years, always impeccably dressed, with a head of thick silvery hair brushed straight back, a hawkish nose and a firm chin, bristled now with a day's growth of beard. Lorenzo Pirata was the kind of a man who simply by his presence commanded attention and respect. With his easy charm, he had the ability to dominate any room he entered, and also any woman who fell in love with him. And there had been many.

But Lorenzo had been married only once, to his first love. When she died, he knew he could never replace her or their first rare true love. But his life had gone on. He was now father to two grown children, a man of the world, urbane yet earthy, happier cultivating his gardens or sailing his old fishing boat than at any grand party in Rome or New York.

Massimo, the houseman, who had been with the family since they were both boys, had heard the helicopter and was already holding open the Castello's heavy iron-strapped wooden door for Lorenzo. Lamplight spilled from the lofty Pompeian red hall as Massimo greeted him, holding out his arm for the cast-off jacket and tie as Lorenzo headed straight for the stairs to his room and a shower.

"*Scusi, signore*, but Mifune is here to speak to you," Massimo called after him.

Lorenzo paused on the steps. He swung round and saw Mifune standing discreetly by the door, his battered straw gardening hat clutched in both hands. The old man looked so frail, Lorenzo's heart went out to him. He wanted to say, "Mifune, there's no need for you to stand in my house. Please sit down here, on this comfortable chair." But he knew Mifune would never step over that boundary between master and servant, even though, to Lorenzo, he was more like a family member. The dog ran to greet his old friend, and Mifune bent to pat her.

"You are well, I hope, Mifune?" Lorenzo said, alarmed by the unexpected visit and the old man's frailty.

"I am well, signore, thank you." Mifune's reedlike voice could not carry far, and Lorenzo walked over to him, bending his head closer.

"The girl has returned, signore," Mifune said.

Lorenzo lifted his head. He closed his eyes and did not speak for a moment. He did not have to ask who Mifune meant. He said finally, "She waited a long time, Mifune."

"She is not happy, signore. She says she needs to leave her life behind. She has come back to find the happiness she knew here with her father." His faded eyes met Lorenzo's piercing blue ones. "And I believe, also to find out what happened to him."

Lorenzo paced the marble floor, hands behind his back, head lowered. "I shall not make her welcome, Mifune," he said finally.

The old man's thin shoulders seemed to droop with a new burden of sadness. His sparse grizzled beard sank into his chest and his wild eyebrows met in a frown. "Then I must, signore," he said quietly. "It is my duty." And with a bow, he turned away.

Lorenzo stood by the door, watching as the old man walked slowly down the wide stone steps and made his way back to the cottage in the grounds that had been his home since before Lorenzo was born.

They were both faced with a dilemma, and for once Lorenzo did not know what to do about it.

FIFTEEN

Lorenzo

LORENZO USUALLY ENJOYED HIS SHOWER, THE HARD
spray on his body, washing away the cares of the long work-
day. But not tonight. Mifune's news about Jon-Boy's daughter had come as a shock. After all these years Lorenzo had not
expected it, and he wished with all his heart she had stayed
home. Now he was put in the position of having to take a
hard line with her, and he didn't like it.

He lifted his face to the spray, letting it drum on his forehead as though it could erase the memories of the past. But it
could not, and he had no choice in what he had to do.

His suite of rooms was in the old tower, the original part
of the Castello. On the ground floor was his private sitting
room, where the walls were lined with shelves of books and
hung with fine paintings. They were not ones he'd inherited
but artworks he had chosen himself for the simple reason that
he had fallen in love with them. Each one gave him a great
amount of pleasure, and in many cases he'd sponsored the
young artists, encouraging their work and helping them get
gallery showings. He also had read every book on his
shelves—there were no leather-bound volumes here just for
show.

Three photographs in plain silver frames sat on his desk.
One was of Marella, his wife, taken on their wedding day. It
had been a small wedding with only a hundred guests, just

family and friends, because Marella was never a woman who craved grandeur. They had taken their vows in the Duomo di Sant'Andrea, the cathedral in Amalfi; then everyone had returned to the Castello for a feast served on the terrace, with its fabulous panoramic view of the coast.

Marella looked out from her wedding photo with solemn brown eyes. Her hair was pulled back under a billowing lace veil, anchored by a wreath of fresh flowers instead of the usual diamond tiara. She looked sweet and very young, and it was Lorenzo's favorite picture of her. Marella's death was the greatest tragedy of his life.

His son Nico's picture portrayed him exactly the way he was: brash, extrovert, a lovable charmer. What it didn't show was his inability to accept responsibility, both in business and in his personal life. Nico's refusal to work in the family businesses had hurt Lorenzo more than he cared to show. Instead he'd been harsh with his son, reminding him of his family responsibility. But Nico had gone his own way, dabbling in advertising and TV, and in fact, he was good at what he did. However, he was likely not to show up at work for weeks, going off on the spur of the moment on long vacations, which was not something his employers liked. In fact, if it were not that Nico was Lorenzo Pirata's son, he might not still have his job, no matter how good he was.

Nico's personal life was equally as erratic. He fell in and out of love rapidly and had a reputation for changing women as easily as he changed his clothes. Lorenzo did not approve of Nico's behavior and had told him so, but to no avail. All Lorenzo could do was hope Nico would grow out of it.

And then there was Aurora. She stared warily into the camera lens, like a deer caught in the headlights. Lorenzo's daughter's beauty was like that of a polished cameo, with her delicate bone structure, high cheekbones, big dark brown eyes, and full pouting mouth. Only Lorenzo knew that under that haughty beauty was an insecure young woman.

Aurora had always been a needy child. She had followed her mother everywhere, clinging to her, and when Marella died she'd been devastated and afraid. Aurora had held desperately on to Lorenzo, begging him never to leave her, and of course he'd promised he never would. He moved his little family to their palazzo in Rome so he could be close to them all week, but weekends they always returned to the Castello, the place he considered his true home.

Aurora had never lost that insecurity, nor her neediness. She acted brash and arrogant among her peers, and people thought she was selfish and spoiled, which indeed she was, but Lorenzo knew that inside she was still that frightened child, and felt he must do everything he could to protect her.

He toweled himself dry, put on casual pants and a linen shirt, and with Affare pattering at his side went downstairs to have dinner with his children.

They were waiting in the small sitting room that led onto the terrace. It was the place the family had always gathered, and in fact, the grand reception rooms were rarely used except for big parties or formal occasions.

Nico had a glass of whiskey in his hand and was staring out at the deep blue night sky while Aurora lounged in a chair flipping through the pages of a magazine. They looked up as Lorenzo came in.

"Papa!" Aurora exclaimed, getting up and running to him. "You are so late; where were you?"

Lorenzo gave her a great bear hug, making her laugh, and told her he'd been held up by a last-minute business problem.

"Oh, I hope it was resolved," she said, looking anxious, and he smiled at her concern.

"It was, sweetheart. Everything's okay." Aurora sighed,

relieved, and he went to greet Nico, who had not moved from his position by the open French doors. "Good to see you, son," Lorenzo said, clasping Nico to him, but Nico did not even put down his glass and merely patted his father's shoulder. There was a distinct coolness between them.

"We're running late," Nico said, glancing pointedly at his watch. "Dinner should have been an hour ago. I have a party to go to and I don't want to keep everyone waiting."

"A party? Where? Who with?" Aurora demanded, but Nico shrugged and said it was none of her business.

"I saw Mifune was here," he said to Lorenzo. "What's up? Is he sick?" There was genuine concern in his voice. He had known Mifune all his life, and the old man was his friend. Not so Aurora; she had always been a little afraid of Mifune's pale gaze and startling appearance and did not understand him the way Nico did.

Lorenzo went to the sideboard that acted as a bar and poured himself a Campari and soda over ice. He added a fresh basil leaf—a personal quirk of his—rubbing it with his fingers so the aroma opened up.

"Mifune told me that Jon-Boy's daughter is here from America," he said. "She has not been back since he was killed, and to tell you the truth, I wish she had not come back now."

Both his children knew the story of Jon-Boy's death and the body never being found. Now they were curious about his daughter.

"Her name is Lamour Harrington," Lorenzo said. "And since I have the unpleasant task of telling her she is not welcome, it would make things easier for me if you did not try to become friends with her. In fact I would prefer you not talk to her."

Nico stared at him, astounded. "Are you *serious*? What's she done, for god's sake?"

"She has done nothing. I simply don't want her opening up a past that is better kept under lock and key. Do you understand me, Nico? I don't want you to befriend her."

"I wonder why?" Nico said knowingly.

Aurora looked from one to the other, bewildered. "If Papa says we mustn't talk to her, he has his reasons," she said loyally.

Massimo appeared in the doorway. "Dinner is served, signore," he said, and Lorenzo nodded and led his children out on the terrace.

At the table, with the faithful Affare at his side, Lorenzo listened as his children chatted about their week. He wished Aurora had been the one to protest, but as always with her, whatever he said went. Sometimes he wished she would rebel, not depend so on him. He knew it all stemmed from her childhood, knew also there was nothing he could do about it.

"I want to go to the party with Nico," Aurora said.

Nico threw her a withering glance. "No chance."

"Why not? Papa, tell him I have to go, too."

"Tell her she's a spoiled brat," Nico retorted.

Lorenzo sighed. Children chose their own paths in life. His were no exception.

"I'll give you a game of backgammon after dinner," he offered Aurora, not wanting her to go to the kind of party he suspected Nico might end up at. And when she pouted, looking prettily at him, saying she really wanted to go, he said firmly she could not.

Much later, after Nico had left and Lorenzo had let Aurora beat him twice at backgammon, he and his dog went to the tower and climbed the spiral stairs that led to his bedroom. It was spare and masculine and not at all what you might have expected a rich man's room to be like. There was a bed with plain white linen sheets, a leather wing chair under the window, a simple Indian cotton dhurrie rug next to the bed, and a long table where he kept the books he was currently reading. The ceiling was beamed and the windows were tall and narrow.

When Lorenzo walked into his tower, he felt as though he was stepping back in time. His pirate ancestor had built it with the gold and silver that were the spoils of his trade, in the days when Amalfi was one of Italy's greatest trading ports. When Marella died, Lorenzo couldn't bear to stay in the room at the Castello they'd shared all their married life and instead he'd come here. The simple rustic atmosphere pleased him, and it held no sad memories. The tower became his retreat, a place of peace and quiet where, alone for once, he was able to rethink his life.

Eventually Nico and Aurora would inherit the Castello, but what worried Lorenzo now was that Nico was not worthy of it. He cared nothing for the Castello other than that it was a great party venue to bring his friends. He cared nothing for its history, nor for the people who had gone before him and who'd loved and embellished their home, each adding a part of him- or herself to its beauty. For Lorenzo, the Castello was an integral part of his family.

Lorenzo undressed and put on a robe. Affare was already curled up on her bed by the door, and he refilled her water bowl and put out a biscuit for her. Then he went to sit in his green leather wing chair, looking out through the tall windows at the half moon tipped with Venus, like a diamond brooch in the midnight blue sky. His thoughts turned to Mifune, whose trust he felt he had betrayed tonight. But he'd had no choice. He'd made a promise, and that was the way things had to be.

Sighing, he picked up a book and tried to read, but it was no good. His mind was on Lamour Harrington and the dilemma she had put him in, one to which he saw only one, unavoidable solution.

SIXTEEN

Lamour

THE NEXT MORNING I DROVE JAMMY TO SEE THE house. I parked at the little flower-bedecked shrine of Saint Andrew smiling happily because it seemed to me that his hand was outstretched in welcome. Jammy got out and stood looking up the hillside at the Castello and the bright blue flag flying over the battlements.

"Correct me if I'm wrong," she said, unbelieving, "but is that *really* a skull and crossbones? Who the hell lives there, the Marquis de Sade?"

"It's the heraldic symbol of the Pirata family. Pirata—pirate."

She gave me one of those you've-got-to-be-kidding glances, then looked at the empty green slope above us and the equally empty green cliff below. Not even a sailboat cut across the tranquil sea. Plus you couldn't see the house from the road, only the rocky steps. "You do know you're nuts, don't you?" she said, worried.

I slammed the car door, sending a scuffle of rabbits up the hill. "Jam, you're just too used to the urban mode," I said.

"And you are not," she retorted, but the rabbits were cute and she was smiling. "Is your cow going to live here then?" A discouraging sweep of her arm took in the empty hill.

I nodded. "Of course I'll have to build her a little barn so she can spend the cold nights out of the rain and wind."

"What rain and wind? I thought it was perpetual blue summer here."

"Into each life a little rain must fall," I said, thinking happily how a little winter rain would sprout new grass for my cow. "Of course I'll call her Daisy," I added. "In books, cows are always called Daisy."

"Shouldn't she have an Italian name? After all, she might not speak English." Jammy was getting into the spirit of things.

"I'll have to ask her," I said as we began to walk down the *scalatinella*. I heard Jammy grumbling softly, stepping gingerly behind me. "You don't mean to tell me this is the only access to the house?"

"Actually, yes, it is." I threw her a grin over my shoulder. Memory had shifted into gear and I was prancing down those steps like the child who'd climbed them a dozen times a day.

I jumped the final few, then waited on the little pathway at the side of the house. The old cedars filtered the sun, and tiny birds danced in the blue air and crickets sang for me.

Jammy came puffing down the last few steps. "All I can say is this better be good." She pushed the elastic back up her slipping ponytail and shoved the bangs out of her eyes. "Okay, so now—show me," she said in a voice that sounded like a challenge.

"Close your eyes and come with me." I took her by the hand and led her round the corner onto the patio. "Okay, now you can look."

Her blue eyes flew open. She clapped a hand to her forehead, turning slowly round, taking in my beautiful golden house and its blue mosaic dome, the twisted barley-sugar pillars, the shady tiled patio, the tumbling gardens, the waterfall, the ancient trees, and the marble belvedere entwined with morning glory the color of the sky. Below, the sea, glittering aquamarine and silver, merged with the horizon.

She closed her eyes again and just stood there.

"Jammy?" I said, worried she didn't like it.

"Shut up," she said. "I'm listening to the sound of peace."

"Then you *really* like it?" I said, relieved I wasn't going to have a battle over living here. But of course, I was wrong about that.

"I admit it's beautiful," Jammy said, "but it hasn't been lived in for decades. It's probably in terrible shape, and I'll bet anything the inside's a wreck. There's *no way* you can live here, Lam."

"We'll see," I said, confidently brandishing the heavy iron key Mifune had left under the lemon pot. I pushed the key into the lock and gave it a turn, but the lock was stiff and refused to budge. I tried again, aware of Jammy hovering nervously behind me. I knew she was hoping it wouldn't open and we would just call it a day, enjoy the rest of our holiday, then fly back to Chicago, where we would find me a new apartment and life would go on the way it always had.

I jiggled the key some more, praying for the lock to open. I wanted desperately to see my little house again. But the lock simply would not turn. Frustrated, I stamped my foot, wondering what to do next.

SEVENTEEN

Nico

CLAD ONLY IN RED BATHING SHORTS AND STILL WET from a swim, Nico Pirata sat in the cockpit of his sleek Riva, idly smoking a cigarette and watching his father painting the hull of a battered old wooden fishing boat. As always, the dog was with Lorenzo, sprawled, napping in the shade. No aristocratic hound for Nico's father—Affare was a mutt he'd found abandoned and brought home. As far as Nico knew, they had never been apart since.

To Nico's cynical eye, the boat looked like the toy ones he used to sail on the swimming pool as a child, the kind with a fearsome-looking bearded old salt at the plastic helm. Yet Nico's father was patting the peeling wooden planks with something that looked very like affection. In fact, Nico knew Lorenzo loved his old boat as much as Nico loved his gleaming silver Riva. Lorenzo said it was part of their history and that Pirata had been a fishing village for centuries and Nico should respect that. And right there was the difference between father and son: Nico had to have the latest, the glossiest. Lorenzo revered the old and their past.

Nico flung his cigarette over the side and lay back on the marine blue cushions. He was a beautiful young man, twenty-eight years old, lean and golden from the sun, with a mop of dark blond hair. He was also a terrible flirt. Women flocked around him, but he wasn't about to get caught in the marriage trap yet. At least, not unless the right eligible and beautiful girl came along.

It was early summer and there were several months of long lazy weekends like this one to look forward to, when, like everybody else that Nico knew, he would escape Rome's heat and retreat to the cool of the shore or to the mountains. Of course, he usually brought company with him, friends and a few beautiful girls to add spice to the mixture.

When he wasn't at the Castello, he worked as an art director at an ad agency in Rome. Of course his father wanted him to be in the family shipping and development businesses and also to help run the estates, but that simply wasn't Nico's style. He needed the excitement of big-city life and the flashy lifestyle his job gave him. And besides, he could always pay someone to run things.

Nico sat up and lit another cigarette, waving lazily to his father, who had finished painting and was heading for the elevator built into the cliff side where the rock had been blasted out, something quite common in this area. It would take him the hundred or so feet to the top and to the path back to the Castello. Nico thought that Lorenzo, wearing only paint-spattered shorts and carrying the paint can and brushes, with his dog bounding ahead, might have been one of his own employees instead of owner of all he surveyed. Yet, even in the old shorts, Lorenzo had an air of distinction. He carried his leonine silver head proudly, and his muscular body was tight and tanned. He looked fit and handsome, and dammit, he could still beat Nico in their weekly swim race across Pirata Bay. In fact, all his life Lorenzo had been better at most everything, and maybe that was what bugged Nico most about him. Nico's rivalry with his father had grown from those early beginnings, and that was one of the reasons he had opted out of working in his father's company.

The glass-fronted elevator slid smoothly up the cliff side with the dog and Lorenzo, still holding his paint can, in it. Nico thought the elevator was one of his father's best ideas. Prior to that, they'd had to walk down endless flights of wooden stairs, clamped to the cliff face with hoops of iron. Those stairs linked with the rocky ones leading to the abandoned little house, once known as the Mistress's House. Glancing up now at the house, Nico thought he caught a glimpse of someone through the greenery. It was probably Mifune, checking on his ruined garden again. Nico knew the old boy mourned that deserted garden. He turned his head away so he wouldn't have to look at those stairs. He didn't like heights. Never had.

He sat up abruptly and flung his cigarette into the sea. He hauled in the ropes, switched on the ignition, and idled the *Riva* from its mooring. Then with a roar he took off across the blue bay, heading for Pirata and the Caffè Bar Amalfitano. He'd always had the happy knack of being able to put bad thoughts behind him.

LORENZO STOPPED THE ELEVATOR HALFWAY UP THE cliff side and stepped out onto the platform where the old wooden stairs linked with those carved from rock. He hadn't been to the Mistress's House in years, but now because of Jon-Boy's daughter he needed to check on it.

Carrying his paint can and brushes, he took the stairs fast. The sun was hot on his back, and he felt the sweat spring onto his skin. Truth was, he enjoyed the stairs more than the elevator; he liked feeling his own strength.

Standing at the foot of the tangled green garden, he saw two women on the terrace. One was tall and dark, with her hair pulled severely back from her face in a tight knot, wearing large dark glasses. The other was a pretty blonde. She seemed apprehensive, as though she did not want to be where she was.

That lock had always been a problem, he thought, which was why in the past the door had always been left open. Until Jon-Boy's death, that is, after which the house had finally been locked up.

Telling the dog to wait, he strode through the gardens, up the steps onto the terrace. He stood for a moment, still unnoticed, watching them.

The dark one was obviously Lamour, Jon-Boy's daughter. She had the look of him, and besides, Lorenzo remembered her as a kid: a long-legged waif, skinny as a whippet, all big brown eyes and a floating cloud of dark hair. She hadn't changed much. They had met once before, though he doubted she would remember.

She was still struggling with the massive iron key he knew Mifune must have given her. She shoved it in the lock again and gave the door another push. It creaked loudly but still didn't open.

"Damn," he heard her say. "It's stuck, Jammy. It always used to stick."

"Oh, thank God," the blonde replied, sounding relieved. "It's a sure sign we're not meant to be here. Come on, Lamour, let's just go."

"I'm not going anywhere." Lamour jiggled the key in the lock some more, then gave the door another mighty shove.

"Are you aware that you are trespassing?" Lorenzo said coldly.

Startled, they shrieked and swung round, clutching at each other. Wide-eyed they stared him up and down, taking him in, old shorts, paint can, and all.

"Who are you?" Lamour demanded. "And why are you here?" she added a little haughtily, trying, Lorenzo knew, to look confident, because they were women alone and he'd scared them.

"More important, who are *you*?" he asked. Of course he knew exactly who she was, but he wanted to put her at a disadvantage. "There are severe penalties in Italy for breaking into houses that do not belong to you."

Lamour's face turned an indignant pink and her big dark eyes blazed at him. "We did not *'break in.'*" She dangled the old iron key on its string. "This is *my* house. It belonged to my father. I lived here when I was a child."

Lorenzo looked steadily at her. It was as though he were

looking at a memory. "I knew your father," he said at last. "You resemble him." He turned and walked back down the steps. "A warning." He threw the words over his shoulder. "It's better not to go exploring here after dark. It might not be safe."

And whistling for his dog, he was off, back through the garden to the stairs that he climbed as easily as any mountain goat.

NINETEEN

Lamour

JAMMY AND I STARED AFTER THE ARROGANT STRANGER striding through my garden as though he owned the place. "What do you think he meant?" I asked nervously.

"I think he meant keep your nose out of Jon-Boy's past and go back to Chicago."

"But why? Who is he? And anyhow, *why* did he think I was trespassing?"

"Well, of course he didn't know who you were until you told him," Jammy said.

"And then he warned me off." I didn't want to admit it, but I was unnerved by that warning. I shivered; could it have something to do with Jon-Boy's death?

"Hey, whatever," Jammy said with a grin, "he's surely a good-looking guy. Maybe you can hire him to paint the place; it looks as though it could use it."

But I didn't care what the man looked like; I was still thinking about what he'd said. I turned to look at the un-movable lock and sighed.

"Oh, the hell with it," I said, suddenly dispirited. "Let's just go get some lunch."

The village of Pirata was only a ten-minute walk away. It looked like a movie set, with tall pastel-colored houses sur-rounding the medieval piazza, flanked by stone arcades and centered with an ancient fountain. A series of slender arches framed the waterfront like a painting, and through them I could see the bluest of seas and the small harbor lined with traditional red and green wooden fishing boats. In the piazza was a greengrocer's with fruits and vegetables displayed in crates outside, and a general store that I remembered had hams and salamis hanging from the beams on giant hooks. They also sold dozens of different kinds of cheeses and home-made delicacies straight from the owner's kitchen: tomato sauces and pesto, the best meatballs, potato gnocchi, and ravi-oli so fine it was almost transparent. In fact, my mouth was watering just remembering the smell of the place.

They sold a multitude of other fascinating things too, like machetes and hammers and nails, patterned spaghetti bowls and olive-wood salad servers, tomato mashers and garlic presses, sewing needles and brooms and pestles-and-mortars, and all kinds of gadgets, as well as fresh-ground coffee.

On the other side of the square was the small pharmacy where I used to go for Band-Aids for my frequent scrapes and cuts and aspirin for Jon-Boy's headaches after too much grappa. Next to it was the barber's shop with a striped pole outside where Jon-Boy would occasionally get his hair cut.

Up on the green hillsides were little streets of white houses, their flamboyant gardens ablaze with color, and anchoring the tip of the inlet was a pretty tenth-century stone church. Be-low was the harbor, with its row of old fishermen's cottages, a beautiful place to linger at sunset over a drink.

I let out the breath I'd been holding. Pirata had escaped the tourist invasion, most likely because there was no space for a grand hotel. Plus the main road ran a few miles inland, diverting passing traffic from this little section of the coast. Miraculously, it remained the village I remembered from my childhood.

"Follow me," I said to Jammy, leading her unerringly

across the gorgeous little square and under the arches, turning left along the harbor to Jon-Boy's old haunt, the Caffè Bar Amalfitano. Like Angelo's place, it had been smartened up a bit, with a blue awning to shade its terrace tables and more comfortable chairs than the heavy wooden ones of old. But the tantalizing aroma of fresh pizza snaking from its tiled kitchen was the same, and from the bar came the familiar smell of the draft beer Jon-Boy used to enjoy. I noticed that the carafes of flowery local wine that miraculously appeared on the table as soon as you took a seat were the same, too, as were the frosted jugs of iced water and the stubby green glasses.

The proprietor was new, though. He was young and fresh faced, giving the pair of us the flirty eye as he greeted us. He announced that he was Aldo, plunked the carafe of wine on the table, then flourished his pencil over his pad and raised an eyebrow, waiting for our order.

"*Buona sera, signore,*" I said, giving him a smile as I ordered a pizza Margherita—large size—and a plate of *calamari fritti,* also large size.

Aldo hurried away, then came quickly back with a bowl of Parmesan cheese, a dish of olives, a plate of tiny orange-colored tomatoes—picked this morning, he told us—plus a bowl of garlic-and-lemon *aoili* for the calamari, and a hunk of rustic bread.

I poured wine into our green glasses and lifted mine in a toast. "To my house in Amalfi," I said to Jammy.

"Oh God, Lamour, you *cannot* be serious." Jammy's face was pinched with anxiety. "You *can't* live there. Besides, you don't know how much work the house needs." She looked at my smiling face and saw she was getting nowhere. "Anyhow, you have to at least forget about the cow," she added with a sigh.

"Daisy is already in my future," I said, tasting the wine. "And let's not forget the chickens."

She groaned. "You've *got* to come home, Lam," she pleaded. *"Please."* She took a sip of her wine. "This is quite good," she added, sounding surprised.

Then Aldo arrived bearing a basil-scented cartwheel-sized pizza and a huge platter of fresh calamari still sizzling from the frying pan. *"Buon appetito,"* he said, flashing us a smile.

As I bit into that first hot, aromatic slice of pizza a sense of well-being came over me. I *loved* this place. I *loved* this *caffè bar.* I *loved* the pretty harbor and the charming medieval piazza. I *loved* my hillside and my little golden house and the food and the wine. Of course the house would need work, but I looked forward to it, as I did to re-creating the garden with Mifune. And I looked forward, as I had not looked forward to anything in years, to being on my own and completely self-sufficient. I knew it was only when I had achieved that independence that I would find myself again as a woman. And a woman with no need of help from any treacherous man.

TWENTY

L'amour

WE MADE SHORT WORK OF THE *CALAMARI* AND I WAS already on my third slice of pizza when we heard the roar of a speedboat coming into the harbor. We turned to admire the sleek silver Riva as it slid alongside the stone jetty. We saw the young man piloting it, and we watched, interested, as he leaped nonchalantly ashore, tied the rope around the bollard, then pulled an old pink T-shirt over his head. Running his hands through his dark blond hair, he sauntered along the harbor toward us. Well, not exactly toward *us* but to the Amalfitano anyhow.

"My God," Jammy said, taking him in, bug-eyed, "this place is lousy with good-looking guys! Where do they all come from?"

I had no idea, but I had to admit he was a vision, gorgeous and golden. I also noticed the triangle of sweat on the front of his shirt and the sexy tangle of blond chest hair peeking above the V. He looked interestedly at us and I felt that old pull of attraction that I hadn't felt since I met Alex. But I forgot, I was not going to think about him.

The vision made a little bow to us. *"Buona sera, signore,"* he said, and I saw his eyes were alight with mischief and admiration as he looked at us. Of course I recognized at once that he was a practiced flirt. Still, I couldn't resist that smile and I smiled back. And so, I noticed, did Jammy.

"Buona sera, signore," we chimed, sounding embarrassingly like a chorus in a bad Broadway musical comedy.

The vision lingered by our table. "My name is Nico," he said. "Too bad you have already eaten, or I would have asked you to lunch with me. May I offer you more wine, though? Or perhaps a glass of *limoncello,* our local drink? Then you could tell me all about yourselves."

Jammy gave me a quick little sideways glance that said, *What are you waiting for, girl?* Then, sounding all charming and genteel and even *southern,* she said, "Well, that would be just delightful, *signore,* though of course, you'll need to tell us all about yourself, too."

The vision pulled up a chair, waving the proprietor over. *"Ciao, Aldo,"* Nico said, shaking his hand. It was obvious they knew each other well, and I guessed Nico must be a local. Jammy and I each primly accepted a glass of the *limoncello.* With it came a plate of tiny almond cookies. I didn't think I had room left for another morsel, but I nibbled on my cookie, looking through my lashes at our new "friend."

He raised his glass to us, suddenly serious. "To two beautiful women, whom I am most fortunate to find in my little village," he said.

I could have sworn he meant it, but even if he didn't, it was charming and so was he.

"And to our delightful new friend Nico," Jammy said, filling in the gap because I was trying not to choke on my *limoncello,* which had the bite of a shot of neat tequila. "I'm Jammy Mortimer," she said, "and this is Lamour Harrington. We are staying at the Santa Caterina."

I thought I saw a flash of surprise as he shook my hand. "Lamour, such a pretty name," he said, and, foolish woman that I am, I let my hand stay in his for a moment longer than I should have. I smiled right back into his eyes and found myself telling him the story of my namesake New Orleans great-grandmother. "Who was probably no better than she ought to be," I finished, taking another sip of the *limoncello,* startled by the way it seemed to fizz all the way from my mouth to my brain like rocket fuel.

"Then your great-grandmother was probably a very wise woman," he said, smiling. "And how did Jammy come by her name? Not another wicked great-grandmother?" And giggling, Jammy told him the story.

"Ah, but I must introduce myself properly," he said. "I am Nico Pirata."

"Oh!" Jammy said. "The skull and crossbones—the Marquis de Sade . . ."

Nico smiled, but his eyes were still on me. "Unfortunately, all I can lay claim to is a pirate ancestor."

I looked down at my glass, then up again at him through my lashes. Oh my God, I thought, I'm actually *flirting* with him. . . . Jammy's right; I am going crazy. I took another fortifying sip of the lemon rocket fuel and smiled some more.

"You really live in the Castello?" I asked.

"At weekends, and for a few weeks in the summer. Mostly I'm in Rome." He waved to Aldo for reinforcements. Aldo brought the bottle and put it on the table. Nico refilled our little glasses.

"It must be very beautiful, the Castello," I said, taking another cookie.

"It's beautiful, but I prefer Rome. But of course, Lamour, I know your name. You must be Jon-Boy's daughter?"

My eyes snapped open. I stared, astonished, at him. "Did you know him?" I asked eagerly. "Surely you're too young . . . ?"

He shrugged. "Everyone around here knows of the *dottore;* everybody liked him. Especially . . ." Somehow I *knew* he was going to say *"especially the women,"* but he stopped himself.

"I'm here to see my father's house," I said. "I lived there when I was a child. I haven't been back since he died."

Nico patted my hand. "Of course," he said gently. "It's normal that you should." And then he told us the story of how the house had been built in the 1920s for the pretty little opera singer from Naples who was the mistress of the then head of the Pirata family. *That* Signor Pirata had also had a wife and five children, though the poor wife had spent more time in Naples and Rome than at the Castello.

Jammy said, "If I owned the Castello I might never want to leave it." Then she took another sip of her *limoncello*.

I flashed her an astonished look; she hadn't even seen the Castello except for the battlements and the flag. I decided it must be the rocket fuel talking. I wanted to ask Nico about the storm and if he knew the story of how Jon-Boy had died, but this was neither the time nor the place. And besides, right now coming toward us at a rapid stride was a beautiful young woman with an angry scowl on her face. *Uh-huh,* I thought, *here comes the irate girlfriend.* . . .

She stopped at our table and stood, hands on her hips, glaring down at us and our half-empty bottle of *limoncello*. I felt like a guilty kid caught with a hand in the cookie jar. I had to admit she was gorgeous, though. Her long dark hair was braided and she was wearing a brief white halter top and impeccable white shorts that showed off her perfect tan.

She put a proprietorial hand on Nico's shoulder, and he tilted his head to smile up at her. "Allow me to introduce my sister, Aurora," he said. "Aurora, this is the Signora Mortimer and the Signora Harrington."

I felt rather than saw Jammy's piercing conspiratorial glance. I knew she meant: *Oh good, he's her brother, not her lover.*

I guessed they knew what she meant, too and I blushed. I could have killed her.

"Hi, Aurora, good to meet you," Jammy said, and I smiled and nodded hello, but the only response we got was a cold stare.

Aurora pouted, looking prettier than ever. "Nico, you know Papa said we were not to talk to *her*," she said, jerking her head in my direction.

My astonished eyes met Jammy's. What *was* Aurora talking about?

"That's never stopped me from talking to a woman before," Nico said, holding my gaze, ignoring his sister as she flounced angrily off.

"Forgive Aurora's rudeness," he said. "Sometimes she acts like a spoiled child."

Jammy and I stared, embarrassed, into our *limoncello* glasses and refused to have more. A few moments later, he pushed back his chair. "Jammy, Lamour," he said, "I'm so happy to have met you. You must let me show you around the Castello Pirata before you leave. I'll call you at the hotel to make an assignation." I stared at him. *Assignation* didn't exactly mean just "appointment."

He took Jammy's hand and bent over it in a little bow. Then he took mine and a little *frisson* passed between us. Of course he was younger, maybe by as much as ten years, but somehow, today, that didn't matter.

"I hope to see you soon, Lamour," he said softly. And then, with a casual wave, he headed back to his silver Riva, where we saw his sister was waiting for him.

TWENTY-ONE

Aurora

AURORA PIRATA DIDN'T KNOW WHY HER FATHER HAD forbidden them to speak to Lamour Harrington, but it didn't matter. Actually, *forbidden* was too strong a word: Lorenzo had said he would *prefer* them not to speak to her. Aurora was furious with her brother for so flagrantly disobeying their father's wishes. But more than that, they had looked as though they were having a good time, laughing and talking like old friends. She thought jealously that was just like Nico: he became instant best friends with everybody he met.

It was a happy knack Aurora did not possess. Despite her beauty, she was desperately insecure. Her mother had recognized her needs and indulged her, smothering her with love and kindness. But when her mother died when Aurora was only three years old she was cast into a well of despair so deep, her father had feared she might never recover. Psychiatrists and her father's steadfast love had gotten her through those long, tough, lonely years, but eventually she'd recovered, switching the full force of her love from Marella to Lorenzo.

This was no Electra complex; it was simply that Aurora's father was the rock on whom she depended. He understood her fears and her depression; he knew all her self-doubts, understood her shyness with strangers. Aurora had always been a child who needed extra attention, extra reassurance, and her father had made sure she got it. And so did Nico, when he thought about it, that is, because, like today, Nico was always going off at a tangent, easily distracted, easily amused.

Aurora preferred books and classical music; she loved her family and the Castello and her small group of friends in Rome and at the university where she was studying fine arts with the aim of one day becoming curator of a museum. When she was feeling good, she enjoyed giving small dinner parties for her friends, secure in their company. They discussed art and politics, and though she was shy, her intelligence shone through. When she was not feeling good, she stayed alone, often unable even to get out of bed, filled with a sense of doom and dark despair.

Beauty was the last thing on Aurora's itinerary. She accepted that she was pretty, but it didn't seem that important. She used little makeup, and though always well-dressed, she was not a clotheshorse. She had boyfriends, but she was no flirt, and she liked to go to movies and concerts, usually in a group. To an outsider, she might seem spoiled and petulant, and in fact she was. First her mother had spoiled her rotten and then her father. Only Nico stood up to her.

"How could you talk to those women when Papa said not to?" she said furiously as they sped across the bay in the Riva.

Her face was pink with anger, but Nico ignored her. He was still thinking about Lamour and Jammy. He'd liked their straightforward freshness, their willingness to laugh and enjoy the moment. Glancing out of the corner of his eye at his sister, he sighed.

"Aurora," he said, "just grow up, will you?"

Back at the Castello, Aurora ran immediately to tell her father what had happened.

Lorenzo was sitting in his study, reading over the plans for a new ship to be built in the French shipyards at Caen, but he stopped work to listen to his daughter.

"Don't worry about it," he said after she'd poured out the story of Nico's disobedience. "I'll speak with him."

Sighing, he watched her stride away and wished she had been the one to rebel and not Nico.

Still, he could see clearly now that he would have to do something about Lamour Harrington.

TWENTY-TWO

Lamour

BACK AT THE AMALFITANO, JAMMY SIGHED, "WHAT'S with the men around here? They all look like Greek—or should I say Roman?—gods, and they're all a bit crazy. Maybe you'll fit in here after all, Lamour."

I called Aldo for the bill, but he said not to worry; he had put it all on Signor Nico's tab. We had a bit of an argument in my stumbling Italian, because of course I couldn't allow that. In the end, I managed to pay for our lunch, but the rocket fuel remained on Nico's tab. Jammy and I walked back up the flight of stairs that led out of the inlet, between the hills, to the road.

"So? What d'you think?" Jammy asked.

It was like in our girlie old high school days: I knew exactly what she meant. "He's . . . interesting," I replied.

"What about the spoiled brat sister? *And* the controlling father who doesn't want them to speak to you?"

I lifted a shoulder in a shrug. "Who the hell knows what's going on?" I said. "I'll have to ask Mifune."

When we got back to the house Mifune was trimming the cedars overhanging the terrace with a fierce-looking machete. I remembered he had always used honed-steel machetes, and even now, with the waning strength of an old man, he moved with a smooth rhythmic certainty that was a joy to watch.

I'd told Jammy all about my mentor and now she was

about to meet him. He bowed solemnly as his pale eyes took her in.

"Welcome, Lamour's good friend," he said, and Jammy said, "Thank you."

"Come with me," he said, and he showed her his gardens, explaining in his reedy accented voice the concept of Japanese gardening. Jammy listened respectfully; then she thanked him.

"I've never met anyone like you before, Mifune," she said, not totally understanding what he was—who he was. "But I know you are a good man."

"Then we are equal, signora," he said, and with a bow he went back to his job.

Jammy looked at me, hands palms up. "At least someone is sane around here," she said with a grin.

TWENTY-THREE

 Lamour

LATER THAT EVENING, I LEFT JAMMY AT THE HOTEL with a headache, probably due to an overdose of rocket fuel at lunch, and returned alone to the house with a borrowed can of oil for the lock.

To my surprise I found Mifune sitting cross-legged on the flat slab of stone by the waterfall. He rose when he saw me, a tired smile on his face.

"Mifune, I didn't expect to see you here," I said.

"I come here in the cool of the evening to meditate," he said. "I like to clear my mind of the excesses of the day and leave myself at peace and open to new ideas. For me, it is a source of creativity, like a deep well that never dries up."

I had never thought of creativity in that way, but now it made sense. By cleansing your mind of the day's trials and tribulations, you were left with a clean slate on which new ideas could transcribe themselves.

"Then I shall try it, too," I said as we walked together up the steps to the house. "I have the feeling I'm going to need quite a lot of 'creativity' once I get started on my new self-sufficient life."

He didn't laugh at me as I'd expected; he simply nodded in agreement. "You had difficulty with the door today, *carina*," he said.

I stared at him, surprised. "But how did you know that?"

"The signore told me he met you here."

"The *signore*?"

"*Sì, il signor Pirata.*"

I stared at him, dumbfounded. Then the man I had thought was a painter was the owner of the Castello Pirata—and Mifune's employer. It was *his* grandfather who had brought Mifune to Amalfi as a boy, and now Mifune had been here more than seventy years.

Mifune told me how it had happened. The Grande Signore Pirata was on a visit to Japan. In Kyoto, he'd admired the elegant minimalism of the Japanese gardens. Mifune had been orphaned young and was apprenticed to a gardener there. The *gran signore* had recognized Mifune's unique talent as well as his spirituality. He admired the boy and arranged to bring him back to transform his own craggy Italian gardens into some form of Japanese sculpture. The boy had intended to return home, but then a year stretched into two and then three. He was so in love with his work the time just sped away. He was happy with his new "family" and he stayed on.

When I was a child, often Mifune would take my hand and lead me to the Castello, where he proudly showed off the landscape he'd created over a period of many years. It was a combination of the simple, almost architectural Japanese style and the natural Italian style of gardens that looked as though they might have grown wild. They were filled with fragrant herbs: rosemary and thyme, mint and oregano, lovage and lemon verbena, whose scent followed you as you brushed past. And there were *allées* of citrus, their carefully pruned trunks painted white and their dark green leaves clustered with bright fruits. There was the reedy lagoon where orange carp flickered through the green depths like slivers of molten lava from Vesuvius. And of course there were the tranquil Japanese oases that you came upon, quite by chance it seemed, at the turn of a gravel path, at the bottom of a flight of marble steps, or at the brow of the hill. Places with only a curve of pristine raked pebbles, yet each pebble was exactly the right size and chosen carefully for its color. The end result was a work of art—beautiful in its serenity. Shading this delicate simplicity might be a graceful three-hundred-year-old tree, transported all the way from Japan, or a piece of sculpture, a sleek fin of steel, bright in the sunlight, or a simple rustic bridge. And always there was the sound of water: the bubble of the stream, the trickle of a small cascade, the light gush of a fountain. Heaven existed in Mifune's gardens, and I was lucky enough to have found it.

I quickly brought my mind back to the present-day Signor Pirata. I remembered how arrogant he'd been *and* his odd warning.

"Mifune, I didn't realize the painter was the Signor Pirata from the Castello," I said. "I'm afraid I was a rude to him."

Mifune nodded and I guessed he had heard all about our little "confrontation."

"The signore enjoys to get away from his busy world; he enjoys spending time painting his old boat," Mifune said, gesturing toward the cove below.

I hadn't yet been down to the cove, but now I remembered the little jetty and that the Piratas had always kept a couple of boats there. I also remembered Nico Pirata's smart speedboat and guessed that's where it was moored now. Lucky Nico, I thought enviously, because I was a "water baby." I'd been a swimmer all my life and still had the broad shoulders and the smoothly muscled back and lean flanks that were the legacy of my Evanston high school swim-team days. Longing overcame me and I decided there and then that I would buy a small boat. I'd swim from it out in the bay; I'd sail it to Pirata to do my daily shopping; I would sunbathe naked on it. I couldn't believe how ideally my new life was shaping up. I only hoped I could work it all out. And I hoped I was strong enough.

Mifune gazed searchingly at me. I felt somehow lost in his pale gaze, as though he could see into my thoughts.

"When you unlock this door you unlock the past," he said quietly. "Remember there are other pasts here. Not only yours, also Jon-Boy's."

"But that is what I want," I said eagerly.

He bowed and I watched him walk slowly away, his knees bent like an old man's, back through the garden.

I was alone at my father's house.

TWENTY-FOUR

Lamour

THE DOOR SQUEAKED AS I PUSHED IT OPEN. THE slanting rays of the setting sun filtered in for the first time in twenty years and the musty smell of an unoccupied house hit my nostrils.

I was in a small terra-cotta-tiled hallway. Through an arch on my left was the *salone,* the living room. This was the largest room in the house, taking up most of the ground floor, with high ceilings and three French doors giving onto the patio. An arch to the right of the hall led to the white-tiled kitchen where I remembered eating some of the best meals of my life.

I walked into the living room and immediately had the welcoming feeling of coming home. Of course this was the only *real* home I'd ever had; the others had just been rented, and the Chicago apartment had been Alex's. But this house in Amalfi had belonged to Jon-Boy and me.

Then I saw his papers were still on the wooden table under the window and the blue couch had dents where people had sat, an empty glass, an open bottle of wine. . . . Shocked, I realized that the house had not been touched since the night Jon-Boy died.

Heart pounding, I climbed the stairs and walked down the narrow corridor to Jon-Boy's bedroom. I opened the door and, half-afraid, stood looking around. His books were on the shelves, his clothes still hung in the half-open armoire, and the

Cartier leather travel clock he'd bought to celebrate the night we left together for Rome was on the bedside table. Next to it was a photograph of me at my high school graduation.

I picked it up, remembering my graduation as though it were yesterday. Jon-Boy had told me he was going back to Italy to start his new novel and that he was leaving me with the Mortimers again. Of course I'd begged him to take me with him, but he'd said, "Lamour, we can't play at being irresponsible children any longer. You are growing up. You must go to college."

What he'd meant, of course, was that *I* couldn't go on playing at being an irresponsible child. But he, of course, could.

I said I didn't want to go to college, I wanted to go with him to our house in Amalfi, but he shook his head firmly and said, "Time for you to get on with your life, baby." He didn't say, "And it's time for me to get on with mine," but I knew that was what he'd meant. He wanted his life back, separate from mine.

I accepted it because those were the terms and conditions of life with my father. You took the lonely times along with the exciting ones, and besides, I thought he was serious about writing his new novel and I respected that he needed to be alone. Of course I was wrong. Jon-Boy never wrote it. I guess he was too busy just getting on with life instead.

He'd made me feel beautiful, though, on that graduation day, as well as loved.

I'd worn a dress for once, instead of jeans. It was cornflower blue, sleeveless, with a flippy little skirt. I'd felt different in it, kind of elegant and more grown-up. I had on my black graduation gown, cap tilted jauntily, tassel dangling over my right eye.

When my name was called by the principal there was the usual ramble of laughter. After all, Lamour was a pretty wild name for a seventeen-year-old girl—or at least the boys thought so. I'd walked proudly onto the podium to collect my diploma, head up, clutching my slipping cap. From the corner of my eye I'd caught sight of Jon-Boy, sitting with the Mortimer family, there in full force. There was a big smile on his face and he punched the air triumphantly.

My answering joyous smile practically wafted me off that podium, and then it was all over. Jon-Boy had put an arm around my shoulders. Looking at me, he said, "Honey, you are a beautiful girl and never let any of these young punks tell you otherwise." He'd grinned as he added, "And remember, your father is an expert on these matters."

TWENTY-FIVE

Lamour

AFTER ALL THE HIGH SCHOOL GRADUATION CERE-
monies and parties were over, Jon-Boy and I had dinner alone
together. I was sad because he was leaving the next day. I'd miss
the happy buzz he created when he descended on my simple
life, bringing with him the scent of exotic places: the market in
Campo de' Fiori; the fishermen's boats, the pines, the sea, the
hot sun of the Amalfi coast; the snuffly odor of Rome's ancient
ruins. The truth was I was still hoping and praying he would
say, "Forget college and come back with me."

I'd chosen a local Italian restaurant for our "celebration"
dinner. We sat opposite each other, silently eating pizza
Margherita that we both knew wasn't a patch of the Roman
ones but enjoying it anyway. Jon-Boy was drinking wine
and I was drinking Coke and we were talking, of course,
about Rome. I'd never seen the new apartment he'd rented
there, but I knew it was much grander than our old place in
Trastevere.

"Don't you miss it, though?" I asked.

"The old neighborhood?" He lifted a black eyebrow in a
question. "Sure I do, but one thing I've learned in my life,
honey-bunch, is that you always need to move on. Going back
is not in the cards; it never works." He saw I didn't want to
believe that and added, "Well, maybe that only applies to me."

He leaned his elbows on the table, watching, amused, as

I picked the tomatoes off the pizza Margherita, the way I'd always done. "Some things don't change, though," he said with a grin.

He looked up as two women approached our table, holding paper and pens, requesting his autograph. I watched shyly while they told him how wonderful his book was and that he was even more handsome than in his photographs. It had never really sunk in that my father was a famous writer, probably because I'd never shared that part of his life. He had written his novel after I'd left, and his success had swirled all around me without ever touching. I'd lived in Evanston with the Mortimers, and he'd lived in Rome and toured the world promoting his book. Anyhow, a few years had passed since then and now he was about to write his second one.

As the women fussed over him I watched, eager to share in the afterglow of his fame, seeing how easily he charmed them. He was so good-looking and so interested, making each woman feel she was the only person he cared about at that moment. It was a technique that had never failed him with women. He asked each woman her name, then called her by it; he signed their pieces of paper and added a little personal message about "meeting in Antonio's Restaurant"; he thanked them for enjoying his book, said he would never forget them, and sent them away aflutter with delight.

"Now they're in love with you as well as with your book," I said, a touch jealously, making him laugh.

"You're almost old enough to fall in love yourself," he said.

I didn't tell him I'd already fallen in and out of love a dozen times. Had he forgotten I was seventeen? "I guess so," I said instead. "Except there's no one here to fall in love with." This was true. I'd already gone through my list of possibles and now I'd run out of boys, and so had Jammy. We were heading off to college—me to Michigan State, she to the Rhode Island School of Design—unencumbered by boyfriends.

"Are *you* in love?" I asked, suddenly suspicious. I didn't want to be presented with a new Italian "mother" out of the blue.

"Aren't I always?" he said, catching my hand across the table, pulling a face when he found it greasy from the pizza. But I saw a wariness in his eyes and knew he was hiding something from me.

"No, seriously, Jon-Boy," I said as he wiped my hand clean with his napkin.

He looked solemnly back at me, something he rarely did; we always seemed to be laughing when we were together.

"Honey-bunch," he said, "you're getting to be a grown-up girl. You're moving into an adult world and with that comes responsibility. It's time to move on, *carina*. Your life will be new and exciting—college, deciding your future. . . ."

My heart sank. He wasn't going to ask me to go with him after all. "And yours will be your new novel and a new woman," I said, still hurting from being banished from his life.

"You'll come out to Amalfi for holidays," he promised. "The house is ours now. You can help me fix it up; it still looks the way it did when you were there."

"All those years ago," I said, remembering it clearly, as I always had.

He took a good long look at me. "You know you haven't changed one bit," he said. "Still the same big brown eyes, looking to find out my secrets. Still the same wild curly dark hair, still the same little girl you always were. *My* girl," he added, gripping my hand tightly.

I was so choked up I couldn't speak, but then the spaghetti Bolognese arrived and the moment passed. We finished our meal, chatting about school and college, my friends, Roman restaurants . . . anything and everything except that the next day he was leaving me.

We walked home together, arms around each other's waists—by then I was almost as tall as Jon-Boy. He came in to say good-bye to the Mortimers and thank them again for looking after me; then I walked him back down the path to his rental car. He put his hands on my shoulders, looking into my eyes.

"Never forget I'm your father and I love you," he said. And then he kissed me and was gone to a new life that did not include me.

I never saw him again.

TWENTY-SIX

I WIPED MY TEARS ON MY SLEEVE. JON-BOY HAD NOT been there for my college graduation. He had never even met my husband. I wondered what he would have said if he had. Would he have warned me against Alex? After all, who knew more about such things?

I put the photograph back on the table amid the years of dust.

Sniffing, I caught the room's faint masculine odor. I opened the armoire and inspected Jon-Boy's clothes: a smart suit, a soft cashmere jacket. Rome clothes, because mostly he just wore shorts or jeans here. But, surprisingly, hanging next to them was a beautiful red chiffon evening dress.

Of course there had always been women in Jon-Boy's life. Had this one lived here with him? Was he in love with her? Was she here with him the night he died? And where was she now?

I couldn't breathe. I ran to the window and threw it open, letting in the sweet evening air for the first time in all those years. After a few minutes I recovered and walked down the corridor to my own room.

I was afraid to look at it in case it wasn't as I remembered. But it was. A plain whitewashed room with faded blue-green shutters, a narrow lumpy bed with an ornate iron headboard, an old wooden cupboard and a battered old chair under the window. There was a table with a green-shaded lamp and the bed was made up with the bedspread neatly smoothed. My room had never looked this good when I occupied it; then it was a jumble of sheets and a trail of clothes and piles of books, with forgotten sandwiches hidden in the mess.

The big chair under the window was where I used to wait for Jon-Boy to come home, reading in the lamplight until my eyes bugged with fatigue. They hurt just remembering. And then there it was again: that old memory of waiting for Jon-Boy that I had refused to acknowledge. I felt the old pang of fear that he would not come back for me and now I remembered that this was what I had really felt. I had repressed the memory all these years. I'd always told myself he would come back for me. And finally, he had not.

Sighing, I went to my cupboard. Tossed on the floor was my old red swimsuit. I picked it up, seeing the holes in it. I'd worn it until it practically fell off me. Some of the happiest times of my life had been spent wearing that suit.

I went next door to the bathroom. There was still soap in the dish and shampoo. Towels had been flung over the shower rail to dry. It was as though Jon-Boy and the girlfriend who'd worn the red dress might walk in any minute.

I hurried downstairs to the kitchen. I loved this room, even though the white tiles needed a wash and the old propane stove was dirty and the dusty provisions of a bachelor household were still on the larder shelves.

I stood at the scrubbed pine table in the center of the room in the house that used to be the center of my world, and the sudden tears trickled down my cheeks.

"Oh, Jon-Boy," I moaned to the empty air, "whatever happened to you?"

"Lamour?" A voice brought me back to reality.

I looked up, startled. Nico Pirata was standing in the doorway. I glanced quickly away, not wanting him to see that I was crying.

"I was in the cove," he said. "I moored my boat at the jetty. Somehow I thought you might be here. I just came by to say hello."

"Go away," I said, turning my back on him.

"I'm sorry, Lamour," he said quietly. "I understand what you are feeling and I'm sorry."

I felt his hands on my shoulders; then he turned me to him. He put his arms around me. I smelled his salty sweat and felt the beating of his heart. It was comforting being held like that, and he was so beautiful, so vibrantly alive.

"I understand," he said, stroking my hair. "I understand, *carina*. Everything will be all right now. Trust me."

I'd forgotten how easy it was to sink into a man's arms, to become the vulnerable little woman again. *Too easy,* I warned myself. And besides, he was a Pirata and, because of his father, I didn't know if I could trust him.

I wiped away my tears with the back of my hand. Mustering as much dignity as I could with my swollen eyes and red nose, I said, "I'll be all right. It was just seeing everything here, just the way it was."

"The house has been closed since your father died. Nobody ever came here." He stepped back, watching me, arms folded across his chest. For a moment I was tempted to sink into his arms again and just cry on his shoulder.

"Well, thank you for coming by," I said, and he took the hint and walked to the door.

He stood silhouetted by the setting sun. "May I see you again, Lamour?" he asked.

"If your father lets you," I retorted. And this time I managed a grin. He waved as he left.

After a while I left, too. I didn't bother to lock the door. It had never been locked all the time I had lived there and I was not going to start now. I stood on the terrace, letting my little golden house wrap its charm about me. Then I drove slowly back to the hotel, to tell Jammy everything that had happened.

TWENTY-SEVEN

Lamour

A FEW DAYS PASSED WITHOUT ANY SIGHT OF NICO. Jammy had been here over a week. She was leaving the next day, but currently she was up a ladder painting the ceiling of the *salone* cream.

"I feel like Michelangelo," she called. "I've got the same crick in my neck."

"How d'you know he had a crick in his neck?" I said. "And anyhow, didn't he paint lying on his back on scaffolding or something?" I was busy painting the shutters a cool sea blue. We'd sponged the walls yellow, the color of dawn just as the sun comes up, and already the house was beginning to look like it was mine.

"So how did he keep the paint out of his eyes, lying on his back like that?"

I laughed and said, "Oh, Jam, are you about ready for a break?"

"I didn't want to be the first to admit it," she confessed. She clambered awkwardly down. "I'll never grumble again about the cost of having my house painted; they earn every penny."

Carrying a couple of bottles of Coke, we sat on the front steps, stretching our aching backs and breathing un-paint-fumed air. We'd been at it since early that morning and it was now four in the afternoon. I was ready to call it quits, but

Jammy was determined to finish her ceiling before she flew off to Chicago.

"I hate going home without you," she said.

"I'll be right here," I replied serenely, "at the other end of a phone."

"Lam, are you absolutely sure you want to do this?" she asked, giving it one last try. "Why not just think of it as a holiday house? We can all come out here in the summer; even the college kid will love it. I mean it, Lam; just think of the times we'd have together, eating pizza, swimming in the cove, fighting with the Pirate of Pirata. Also known," she added, "as the Painter of Pirata." She giggled, liking her new name for Lorenzo.

I laughed with her and suggested we have a farewell dinner at the Amalfitana that night.

She put an arm around my shoulders. Her face close to mine, she looked searchingly into my eyes. "Seriously, Lam, are you *sure*?"

I nodded, but I had a sudden sinking feeling in the pit of my stomach. It was all right when Jammy was here to keep me company: I had someone to laugh with over the upsets with the Piratas and all the work to be done. But when she was gone it would be another matter. I would be on my own in a foreign country. There would be no shoulder to cry on when things went wrong, no friend at my side to look out for me. I sternly reminded myself of my new vow of independence. So, where's your backbone, girl? I chided silently. Stiffen your lip like the Brits. You've chosen this road and now you must travel it. Alone.

We spotted Mifune, heading for his meditation stone, and Jammy ran to greet him. "Mifune, you've known Lamour since she was a child," she said. "I know you love her. Can I trust you to look after her when I'm gone?"

Mifune bowed. "Your trust is safe with me, Signora Haigh," he said, and Jammy bowed back and thanked him, satisfied that as long as he was here no harm would befall me.

Later, freshly showered, hair still damp, dressed casually in white cotton capris and T-shirts, we lounged gratefully in the Amalfitano's chairs, drinking white wine and nibbling on salad.

"I'm almost sorry to leave," Jammy sighed. "I'll miss all this."

"Come back anytime," I said, sounding hopeful, though of course I knew she had her own life to lead.

"I'll bring the college kid; she's gonna love it here."

We had run out of conversation, and for the first time I felt a gap between us. "Jam," I clutched her hand across the table, "I promise if it doesn't work out, if it's all too hard . . ."

Her face lit up. "Yes?" she said hopefully.

"Then like the little pig whose house blew down, I'll just try, try, try again," I said with a grin, and we were laughing again. Friends forever.

I saw Lorenzo Pirata before he saw me. He was with a group of people that included his daughter though not his son. Aldo and the waiters hurried to push three tables together to form a long one, slapping paper place mats with the map of Pirata and the Italian flag in front of them, slamming down silverware and a couple of glasses containing paper napkins. There were no frills at the Amalfitano. But this was a chic bunch, casual in a different way from Jammy and me. The women were elegant in thin white linen, sleek hair and gold bracelets and the men in fine polo shirts, shorts, and expensive loafers.

"We've got company," I said quietly.

Jammy glanced quickly over her shoulder. She turned back to me, brows raised. "It's his home turf." She shrugged. I saw

Aldo hurrying to take their orders while the waiters brought bottles of wine. I kept my gaze firmly away from them, concentrating on my wineglass, but I had the uncomfortable feeling that eyes were on me. I took another sip of wine, trying not to hear their conversation.

"Signora Harrington. Signora Haigh. *Buona sera.*"

Lorenzo Pirata was standing next to me. I lifted my eyes to him, aware of Jammy sitting breathlessly opposite, waiting for what was to happen.

"Good evening, Signor Pirata," I said coolly.

"I hope Aldo is treating you well," he said, smiling. "I can recommend the eggplant; it's his wife's specialty."

I hadn't even known Aldo had a wife, much less that she did the cooking. "Then I must be sure to try it," I said, matching his smile and thinking what a good-looking bastard my enemy was. Because one thing I knew for sure: he was my enemy.

"Then I'll wish you both a pleasant evening," he said, returning to his table.

I could feel Aurora Pirata's eyes burning into me, but I ignored it. The eggplant Lorenzo had recommended was meltingly good, draped in the wonderful local mozzarella and as calorific as anything I'd eaten in years, except of course the pizza and the calamari and the bread. . . . I sighed.

"Don't worry; you could use a few pounds," Jammy said, ordering another carafe of wine.

And of course I could. My lanky thinness was no match for the sleek women sitting with Lorenzo. "How could such a cute kid grow up to look like me?" I demanded, scooping up more eggplant and burning my mouth once again.

"Neglect." Looking up from her plate where she was busy demolishing a very large deep-fried fish, Jammy eyed me critically. "Actually, you look better than you've looked in years.

The haircut is great and you've got color in your cheeks. I swear you've even got a curve here and there."

I grinned. "It's all the pasta, and I'm hoping the 'here and there' are in the right places?"

"Yup. Small but perfect," she said, and we laughed together. Everything was going to be all right; I knew it.

A while later, we nodded our good nights to the Piratas and wended our way, arm in arm, back to the steps and the parking lot. We stopped to take a look at the village, lit by yellow globe lamps and the ruffles of fairy lights outside the Amalfitano.

"It's a picture postcard come to life" Jammy said, pointing out the illuminated belfry over the old church and the arches leading to the waterfront.

We were up early the next morning, slinging Jammy's bags into the car, heading for Naples Capodichino Airport. We checked Jammy in and went and hung out over coffee and *sfogliatelle*, the sugary pastries with a custard filling that were a Naples specialty. I talked about the house and said I was going to call in an architect and an engineer to make sure everything was structurally sound before I began my renovations, though I intended to start work immediately on the gardens.

"With Mifune's help," I added, "because nobody knows better than him what's under all those weeds and overgrown shrubbery."

And then Jammy and I were hugging each other and saying our good-byes. She walked quickly, as she always did, into the tunnel leading to the plane, pausing just once to look back and wave. She was smiling, but I caught the troubled look in her eyes. I had chosen a new life, and now I had to get on with it.

TWENTY-EIGHT

Lamour

AS FAR AS I COULD TELL, THE HOUSE NEEDED NO major work. The cliff was another matter. Mifune and I discovered erosion in areas where the shrubs and undergrowth had been cut back. I didn't think it was a problem, especially as I planned on replanting it later, but to make sure there was nothing major wrong with it and the house I called in an architect from Sorrento.

He came skittering down the steps on tiny feet, a short, round man with a tight mouth, a thin pencil mustache, and large black-rimmed glasses that gave him a look of importance. He wore a narrow black suit, a silver tie, and a Panama hat. Behind him came a couple of harassed-looking young assistants, carrying his briefcase and an umbrella, plus various surveying instruments.

Il architetto barked a *"Buon giorno"* at me and with a wave of a pale hand set his minions off to survey the land, to make sure, he told me, that it was not all about to cascade into the sea. Then, with the air of someone speaking to a mere assistant, he asked me importantly where *il signore* was.

"Il signore?" I looked puzzled and he looked impatient.

"Sì, il signore, the owner of the house. The one I am to consult with."

"But I am the owner."

He stiffened, turning to look fully at me for the first time. "Signora?"

"I am the Signora Harrington. It was I who arranged for you to come inspect my property, *Dottore.*" I threw in the title as well as a smile in the hopes of softening him up. After all, I didn't want to get on the wrong side of the local town council with a bad property report; nor did I want to spend a fortune putting to rights problems that might not even really exist. I was beginning to wish I hadn't bothered with this inspection.

Il architetto pulled himself to his full height of five-four and, mouth pursed, inspected me slowly from behind the blockade of his eyeglasses.

"*Perdona, signora,* but I had reason to believe I was to inspect the property for *il signor* Pirata."

I shook my head, and he looked most put out at having humble me for his client instead of hobnobbing with the *gran signore.* I said firmly, "Well now, *Dottore,* since we have established that I shall be paying your fee, perhaps we can get on with inspecting the house."

I led him briskly indoors and gave him a quick tour. "All I really need to know is that the building is in sound shape," I said. "Nothing has been touched since it was built in the nineteen twenties."

He stood in the hallway, peering into the pretty *salone* and then into the kitchen. His nose wrinkled in contempt.

"Is a very small, this house, signora," he said. "Is meant to be a guest cottage, no?"

"No," I said firmly. "This is my home, and I'm very anxious to make sure that everything is in order before I begin work on it."

"Hmmm. . . ." He thought for a minute, then went outside

and summoned his boys. He gave them what sounded like a long haranguing lecture. I wondered if he was telling them off for not informing him that he was not about to meet the *gran signore* and asking why he had been dragged all the way from Sorrento to meet a woman who intended to live in a place obviously meant for servants.

He turned to me finally. "My men will conduct the inspection of your property. We will submit a report in due course," he said.

My heart sank. "In due course" could mean any time between now and next year.

"And now, signora, I will bid you good day." And with a pointed glance at his watch, no doubt to let me know exactly how much of his valuable time I had wasted, he unfurled his umbrella and marched back up the *scalatinella*. I watched him go, plump and pale and sweating, looking, I thought, like Dirk Bogarde promenading the Lido in the movie *Death in Venice*.

Sighing, I went to the kitchen. I took a couple of almost cold Peroni beers from the ancient refrigerator that was scarcely big enough and certainly not strong enough to chill much more, then went out onto the terrace and called the "boys." I waved the bottles at them in case they didn't understand my stumbling Italian. They glanced at me, then quickly at the *scalatinella*. Their boss had disappeared and they smiled and accepted the beer, mopping their heads in relief.

They were young, olive skinned, and shadowy eyed, probably from overwork, I thought, but they perked up considerably with the beer.

"Is beautiful, your house," the spiky-haired one said, with a shy smile.

"*Grazie, signore*. I think so," I said modestly, but I was pleased.

I heard steps and swung round to see Nico bounding down the stairs. He was in bathing shorts and I guessed he was on his way to the boat.

"*Carina*," he called, giving me the big warm smile that always drew a responding one from me. "I just passed a strange man on the road. He looked as though he was dressed for a grand luncheon party, circa 1927. What's going on?"

I laughed; he had described *il architetto* perfectly. I explained who he was, offered Nico a beer, and said I had to get back to work.

"Why not come out on the boat with me instead?" He looked pleadingly at me. "It's such a beautiful day, we could have lunch in Capri."

I hadn't been to Capri since Jon-Boy's time. "But I have my 'boys' to look after." I gestured to the surveyors dragging equipment through the garden, measuring the cliffside. "And besides, I was going to paint my bedroom."

"Oh, come on, Lamour; there's always time for work. A beautiful day like this was not meant to be wasted."

I thought guiltily about the cans of apricot paint and the new rollers waiting for me upstairs. "Well, but what about them . . . ?" I said doubtfully.

"Don't worry; I'll take care of them."

I heard him call, "*Ciao, amici*," as he walked toward them, and somehow I knew he would charm them into doing whatever he wanted. I thought it must be nice to have that kind of special confidence, knowing that everyone would just love you and do your bidding. *Love:* the thought slipped into my mind. I decided not to think about love and instead ran upstairs to change into something suitable for a boat ride and lunch in Capri. In the end I wore white shorts and a green halter top and clipped my long hair firmly back. Just in case, I put a bikini into the straw bag I'd bought at Umberto's in Pirata, along with a straw hat, sunscreen, and lip gloss. I was ready in less than five minutes.

Nico was lounging on the patio. There was no sign of the boys. He grinned at me. "They went to the Amalfitano for lunch," he said. "I told them to put it on my tab."

I shook my head doubtfully. I knew all about those long lunches at the Amalfitano. "So when are they going to take care of my job?"

"They promised to come again tomorrow. I'll work it out with their boss. I know who he is; he's the kind of guy who'll be thrilled to get a call from the Pirata family."

I laughed; of course he'd called it right.

"So now you're free," he said, taking my hand and leading me to the elevator.

We stood close together in the little wooden box, looking out the glass door as it slowly descended. I avoided his gaze. "I haven't been to Capri since I was eight years old," I said, trying to fill the hot silence. I was going to say, "And that was thirty years ago," but decided against it, suddenly aware that there was a terrific difference between twenty-eight and thirty-eight.

"Here we are," Nico said as the elevator doors opened. He took my hand and we ran to the stone jetty and the waiting Riva.

He helped me in, then untied the rope and leaped in after me. The boat rocked under his weight, then the engine roared to life, and we slid silkily out of the small harbor. Then we were flying across the water with the wind in our hair and the cool sea spray anointing us, along the beautiful coast, past secret little villages reached only from the sea and small cliff-side hotels, and dark green caves and azure inlets.

It was so beautiful and so exhilarating, I laughed from the sheer pleasure of the moment. The wind snatched my laughter away, as well as the clip from my hair, so that it whirled around my head in a cloud.

"Like Medusa," Nico yelled, and I laughed some more. Happiness was, after all, in the moment.

TWENTY-NINE

AFTER ABOUT HALF AN HOUR THE ISLAND APPEARED on the horizon, its rugged limestone cliffs white against the deep blue sky and topped with a fluffy areola of greenery.

"Wonderful," I yelled to Nico.

"Wait," he yelled back, catching my hand and bringing it to his lips in a kiss.

I felt the blush stealing up my neck and turned away. No man had kissed me, not even my hand, in a long, long time. I treasured the moment, feeling that little bubble of happiness fizzing inside me.

"Look now, *carina*." Nico slowed the boat and I turned and looked into the famous *Grotta Azzurra,* the Blue Grotto.

The still water was a deep wine dark blue flecked with aquamarine. It hardly seemed possible that the sea could be this color.

Nico said, "The legend is that centuries ago a ship was passing by carrying a cargo of Tyrian purple dye. It was a special color that only the Roman emperors could use. The ship foundered and sank in the grotto, dying the waters this magnificent blue."

I trailed my fingers in the water, looking up at the cavern's iridescent walls, reflecting all the colors of the sea like a giant opal. Great natural beauty always gave me, a landscape architect, a sense of awe; it was something only God and time could achieve. Then Nico suddenly threw the boat into overdrive and we were off again.

He moored the Riva next to other similar sleek craft at the Marina Grande; then, with him holding my hand, we took the funicular along with other tourists up to the piazzetta, the bustling main square.

I'd forgotten how beautiful the little whitewashed town was, with its cobbled streets and miniature piazzas and the narrow flights of steps between the buildings. Arches tumbled with hot pink and purple bougainvillea, and winding lanes led to grand Moorish villas hidden behind high white walls fringed with oleander.

Nico held my hand and we wandered around, staring into shopwindows that offered a million temptations, like hand-made sandals, jewels, bikinis and couture dresses, bags and shawls and bed linens that made you dream of curling up in them.

I lingered in front of Alberto and Lina's jewelry store, tempted by a delicate coral bracelet.

"Why not get it, *carina*?" Nico said, as though expensive trinkets were something I bought every day on the spur of the moment.

I hesitated. The chunks of coral looked as though they had grown out of the gold. It was lovely in its simplicity.

"Maybe later," I said lightly, letting him lead me away from temptation. Besides, I had more important things to spend my money on these days.

Nico was still holding my hand, but it seemed so natural, and anyhow, I loved it. It made me feel I belonged.

We went to a pretty terraced restaurant off the Piazzetta called La Capannina, where he was greeted enthusiastically by the patron and shown a table ("Your usual table, Nico") on the veranda. Instead of sitting opposite, Nico came to sit next to me. He took my hand again and I looked questioningly at him. He laughed and put my hand to his lips. "Enjoy, *carina*," he whispered, looking tenderly at me.

We admired the other diners, chic in their Dolces and Versaces, as beautiful and colorful as a flock of chattering parakeets, and Nico ordered those fresh peach and champagne cocktails called Bellinis. We sipped them and without looking at a menu he told me exactly what we should eat. It was easy to be seduced into the delicate little woman role with Nico, allowing him to make the small decisions: where to go today, what to order, what to drink, what to buy. . . . I was a pampered female, purring into my Bellini, so when Nico started laughing, I asked him, puzzled, why.

"Because today you are a different woman," he said. "You've lost all that prickly get-out-of-my-hair attitude. I almost believe you are enjoying yourself."

He let go of my hand when our *insalata caprese* arrived. The tomato and mozzarella salad was interleaved with sprigs of fresh basil. The salad was invented on Capri and named for the island, and though I must have eaten it a thousand times, it had never tasted quite like this. First, the cheese was *burratta*, a creamier version of mozzarella. The tomatoes were grown in somebody's garden plot on the island and picked that morning and the basil was cut straight from the garden. Drizzled with local olive oil and lemon and spiked with black pepper, it was the freshest taste in the world. I need not have eaten another thing, especially as Nico and I were holding hands again, which I liked enormously, and now sipping a chilled light pink wine.

We smiled a lot at each other, talking about nothing in particular . . . the other diners, the color of the sky, and whether I should really buy the little bracelet I had admired at Alberto and Lina's. I found myself telling Nico about my life in

Chicago and about my work. He became very solemn when I told him about Alex's death, though I had the sense not to tell him Alex had been about to leave me for someone else.

"Poor Lamour," Nico said, caressing my hand gently. "It must have been so hard for you. You deserve a holiday like this."

Then the *linguine con lo scorfano* arrived, pretty as a picture, though the spiky scorpion fish were a bit intimidating looking.

I thought back to that cold, rainy winter night with Jammy at the *trattoria* in Chicago, drinking Chianti and dreaming about Italy. And now here I was with a charming, beautiful man whose eyes rarely left my face and whose only desire in life seemed to be to please me. I buzzed with happiness.

"Nico, *caro, there* you are!" A girl stood by our table, slender as a model in a low-slung miniskirt that showed off her gem-studded navel and her exquisitely brown thighs. She tossed her long blond hair, looking impatiently at us, as Nico got to his feet.

He put a hand on her shoulder. *"Cara,"* he said softly, "I didn't expect to see you here. I thought you were still in Rome."

"How could I stay there without you?" she demanded. Nico glanced at me, and with a murmured *"scusi"* he led her away.

I put down my fork. The gloss had suddenly gone off the day. The girl was not only gorgeous; she looked all of nineteen and was obviously more than just a friend. Feeling foolish, I poured more wine and sipped it, staring down at my plate.

The two of them were in the piazza. I saw him put his arms around her. They were so close their thighs touched. He took her face in both his hands and put his lips close to hers. For a moment he held her like that, and then he kissed her. A *long* kiss.

After a while, she stepped back and I saw that she was smiling. He said something and then she walked away, turning to wave to him. He waited until she was out of sight before returning to the table.

"I'm sorry, *cara*," he said easily, "but that was an old friend from Rome."

"Hardly an *old* friend," I said more sharply than I should have. "She's just a baby."

He looked at me, surprised; then he burst out laughing. "Come, Lamour, let's finish our delicious lunch," he said, pouring the last of the wine and signaling the waiter for another bottle.

But it was different now, and he knew it.

We walked back across the piazzetta no longer holding hands. From time to time I felt, rather than saw, him glance my way. He said nothing until we passed Alberto and Lina's jewelry store. "Wait," Nico said cajolingly. "What about your bracelet?"

I shook my head. "I don't want it after all," I said, sounding like the spoiled child I wished I was. I wanted to be that eight-year-old again, back with Jon-Boy, the child without a care in the world.

On the boat ride back to Pirata there were no happy calls back and forth this time, just the roar of the engine and the sound of the wind. I thought how foolish I was to have imagined even for a few moments that a young man like Nico could have been interested in me as a woman.

Back at the jetty, he tied up the boat, then helped me out. "Thank you for a wonderful day," I said politely, offering him my hand.

He looked at me for a long moment. "It was a pleasure, *carina*. And I mean that," he said.

I picked up my straw bag and walked quickly away. "Thanks

again," I called over my shoulder. "No need to see me home. I'll be okay." And then I remembered what I'd wanted to ask him.

I turned at the steps. "What do you know about Jon-Boy's death, Nico?" I asked.

He froze; then he turned and looked at me. "Nothing. I know nothing," he said. "You must ask my father about that."

I turned and walked away. I didn't believe him for a minute. And anyhow, why did he tell me to ask his father?

THIRTY

Lamour

I PLODDED UP THE STEPS TO THE HOUSE. I'D BROKEN my rule and allowed myself to be flattered by Nico's attention. Seeing him with the pretty young girl had brought me back to my senses, before it was too late. All I'd been for him was a local "flirtation."

I was too needy. Too vulnerable. And too damn old anyway!

On the terrace I stretched out full length on the old chaise lounge. I could feel the sting of sunburn on my shoulders and tasted sea salt on my lips, mementos of a pleasant day. I had no right to think Nico had behaved badly. Obviously he knew lots of girls, and of course they were in love with him. The fact that this one was beautiful and young was my problem.

I must have dropped off to sleep on the terrace, because the next thing I knew it was dark. I sat up and looked at my little house. There were no lights gleaming in its windows and no Jon-Boy there to welcome me. Loneliness swept over me in a huge wave. I huddled on the chair, arms clasped around my knees, head sunk, thinking of the happy times in the past. I'd been so confident I could re-create them, but now I wasn't so sure.

I wished Jammy was here sharing secrets, telling me in her high little-girl voice I couldn't possibly live here. For the first time I thought maybe she was right; then I told myself not to be so foolish. How could I allow a mild little flirtation gone wrong to make me change my mind? I must be crazy after all.

I picked up my straw bag, dusted myself off, and went into my house. Lying on the terra-cotta hall tiles was an envelope. Somebody must have pushed it under the door. I went into the *salone* and turned on the lamps to read it.

Signora Harrington was written in a large firm hand on the envelope. I tore it open and unfolded the single sheet of creamy handmade paper. It was from the Castello and written in English. *Dear Signora Harrington,* it began, *I would like to discuss your situation re the Mistress's House and would be pleased if you could join me for lunch next Friday at 1:00 P.M. here at the Castello. I understand from Mifune that you are a landscape architect, and I shall look forward to showing you around my gardens. Sincerely, Lorenzo Pirata.*

I thought the politeness and the offer to show me around his gardens were probably the sugarcoating on the bitter pill of what he really wanted to discuss. The house had belonged to the Pirata family before Jon-Boy bought it, and now I got the feeling Lorenzo wanted it back. And he also wanted me out of here and out of the Piratas' lives. Telling myself he'd soon find out he was dealing with the wrong woman, I quickly dashed off a note accepting his lunch invitation. I would give it to Mifune to deliver tomorrow. I would also ask him what he thought Lorenzo Pirata wanted to talk about, because I suspected Mifune knew everything that went on around here. Maybe he even knew what had happened to Jon-Boy.

I told myself I was being ridiculous; of course Mifune would not deceive me. I was just feeling sorry for myself.

I put a record on the long-unused record player, poured myself a glass of wine, and curled up on the sofa, letting the lush strings float rather squeakily around me.

What I *really* needed, I decided gloomily, was a dog.

THIRTY-ONE

Lamour

THE NEXT MORNING I WAS UP EARLY, SITTING OVER a cup of coffee, listening to the purr of the waves and waiting for Mifune. I knew he would come because he was obviously the letter carrier between me and Lorenzo Pirata. I'd put all thoughts of Nico behind me and resolved simply to get on with my life.

Today, for instance, I intended to paint my bedroom the color of ripe apricots. The narrow little bed of my childhood was too small, and I would order a new one to be delivered as soon as possible. I'd go to Amalfi and buy inexpensive but beautifully embroidered linens and thick new towels, and a soft rug for my bedroom. I'd buy new sandals, though now I regretted not getting the lovely handmade ones sold in Capri. And best of all, I would buy a boat. She'd be small, of course, and inexpensive, and she'd be my water taxi. I would call her *The Lady Lamour.* Remembering how lonely I'd felt last night, I thought, hell, I might even buy that dog.

I grinned; there was nothing like shopping to raise a woman's spirits. I saw Mifune coming toward me and I asked him to please take a seat and share some coffee with me.

He refused and I remembered too late he drank only Japanese green tea. He'd told me the Piratas imported it specially for him, with other Japanese condiments and delicacies that, when he'd first come to Italy, had helped make him feel at home. Now he ate Italian like everyone else, though I could see he ate very little and he confessed his diet was mostly the vegetables that he grew at the Castello.

Il architetto had sent a report on the erosion, as well as on the state of the septic tank, but I didn't even want to think about that. As for the erosion, Mifuni and I agreed all would be well when we had cleared the rest of the scrub. We would bring in new topsoil and replant with sturdy young trees and new shrubs whose roots would eventually knit the earth together again.

"Did you enjoy your day in Capri, Lamour?" he asked.

"It was pleasant," I said. "Capri was as beautiful as I remembered and the people as glossy and cosmopolitan as ever."

"Capri was the home of gods in ancient times, even before the Roman emperors," he said in his thin, quiet voice. "It has always been a mystical place submerged beneath a layer of hedonism. It has not changed."

Of course he was right. You felt Capri's secretive underlayers as you sailed around its limestone cliffs peering into the many caves, knowing that it had scarcely changed since those early Roman times and that the summer life floating over it was only a temporary thing. That come winter it would be left alone to dwell in the past again. Capri offered all visitors exactly what they were looking for. If they were clever enough, they would seek and find more than was on the surface; they would find antiquity and myths, stories of dryads and centaurs and nymphs, princes and pirates and Renaissance courtiers, mermaids and poets, writers and artists. At heart Capri would never change.

"And did you find what you were seeking in Nico?" Mifune asked.

There was no need to tell him what had happened; he sensed that I had been foolish. "Nico is a charming young man," I said warily. "He was a delightful companion—for an afternoon."

"Wisdom sometimes comes slowly, and with it pain," he replied. "Your father knew about such pain."

I stared at him, surprised. "You mean Jon-Boy fell in love and got hurt?" I asked.

"Your father had the same charm Nico has," he said. "He loved many women. And women loved him."

I waited for him to expand on that, but he did not. I gave him the envelope addressed to Lorenzo Pirata.

"I will take this to the Castello right away," he said. "I will come back later and we will walk through your garden again and discuss its future." He smiled for the first time that morning, a lovely toothless smile that lit up his milky eyes, animating his face until he almost looked the way I remembered when he was younger. "But now it is *you* who are the artist," he teased. "It is Lamour who will teach Mifune the new ways."

"No one will ever teach you anything," I said. "And I would be honored if you would have tea with me this afternoon. We can go through the garden then, and make our plans."

He bowed his acceptance and left, walking hesitantly, silent as a cat, back through the garden to the elevator, because he had finally admitted the steps were too much for him.

THIRTY-TWO

JAMMY HAD BEEN GONE A COUPLE OF WEEKS AND I missed her. I'd bought a laptop computer, but e-mail, though instant, isn't the same as real-life contact. Too restless to paint my room, I got in the car and drove into Pirata, to the Amalfitano. Aldo greeted me cheerfully, pulling out my chair and whisking crumbs off my usual table.

"Signora Lamour?" he said with a cheeky little grin at using my first name. "We know each other well enough now, signora," he added, "now that you live here."

"Indeed we do, Aldo," I said, ordering a cappuccino and the *sfogliatelle*. I'd gained five pounds since Jammy left, my clothes no longer hung on me, and I even had a few curves, no doubt due to the amount of pasta I was eating.

I sipped the cappuccino, as usual getting froth on my nose. I was thinking about what Mifune had said about Jon-Boy: that he was a lot like Nico. Jon-Boy was the same kind of charming, good-looking man who attracted women wherever he went. Of course I wasn't looking for my father in Nico; I'd simply been hankering after a bit of attention, a few compliments, a little kiss on the hand.

I waved good-bye to Aldo, then drove into Amalfi to shop. I was early enough to find a parking space, and I walked down the narrow hilly streets toward the waterfront. In a small dark store I found my sheets. They were a beautiful soft cotton with the hems embroidered in blue and green hydrangeas and I thought they would go well with my soon-to-be-apricot walls. I bought a pair of raspberry-colored thong sandals, then ate a pistachio ice cream from the *gelateria* on the harbor, its sludgy green color telling me it was the real thing and not made with artificial flavoring and bright fake color. Tucked away in a corner I found an old woman sitting on the steps selling eggs. Beautiful speckled-brown eggs, exactly the kind I would like my own chickens to lay.

"Signora," I said, "I will take a dozen of your beautiful eggs." She gave me a dazzling smile as she wrapped each egg individually in a twist of newspaper before placing it gently in my straw basket. I suddenly had a brainstorm. "Signora," I said, "I wish to buy the same kind of chickens that lay these beautiful eggs."

Her glance was shrewder this time. She told me she might just have some of those very same hens for sale and of course a rooster, because everyone knew that with chickens you needed a rooster. I hadn't known until she told me, but I agreed that of course I would need a rooster, too. Soon a deal was struck for four hens and a rooster at a price that seemed reasonable. It was arranged that I would pick up my chickens in the parking lot the next morning at seven sharp. We shook hands and she murmured a blessing and I took my eggs and drove back to Pirata, to Umberto's general store, to buy chicken wire and stakes for my new chicken run. I also ordered a small coop so they could have their very own house.

Coming out of Umberto's, I bumped into Aurora. Our eyes met; then she pushed past me into the store without so much as a *"ciao."* I sighed. I didn't need a fortune-teller to let me know I was among the enemy. I wondered what I had done to deserve her hatred. I had no claims on her father. Nor on her brother. Besides, "love," whether for father or brother or family or lover, could only go so far. This girl was the most insecure, unstable person I had ever met.

I drove quickly back home to spend the afternoon hammering stakes into the rocky ground behind the house for my chicken run. Winding the wire netting around the stakes was a bit more difficult than I'd thought. I kept getting it snagged, but I struggled through, pinching my finger in the pliers and scratching my elbow on the wire. Dripping blood, I decided my chicken run looked decidedly ragged. The netting looped unevenly and the stakes stuck out at odd angles. I sighed. It would have to do for now.

I took a long, luxurious shower. I stuck a Band-Aid on my raw elbow and got dressed. I went downstairs feeling pleased with the day's accomplishments.

Mifune arrived for tea wearing his Japanese straw gardening hat and bearing a bottle of sake in a beautiful wooden box, and a pair of wooden sake cups.

"Mifune, this is such a treat!" I exclaimed, making him welcome as a guest in my home for the first time. First, we walked the garden, deciding where to cut back the undergrowth and how to simplify things and how to bring stillness and serenity back again.

Later, I warmed the sake on the stove and he poured it into our wooden cups. We raised them to each other in a solemn toast.

"To our happy meeting again, Mifune," I said. "This is the best thing that's happened to me in years." I knew he could see I meant it.

"To you, Lamour," he said, "and to your future happiness. Wherever you might be."

I looked at him, surprised because there was no more "wherever" in my life. I was here to stay.

The sake loosened my tongue and I talked to him about my

life in Chicago and about what had happened to my marriage.

"It's that old problem love, Mifune," I said seriously. "It lets you down every time. Look what happened with Jon-Boy. I loved him so much and yet he left me, too. He came back here and got on with his life, and told me to get on with mine. Tell me, was that any way for a father to behave?"

I was voicing the feelings I had kept repressed all these years. My sense of abandonment when Jon-Boy had left me again and those long nights when I was just a little girl waiting for him to come home. "So you see, nothing much has changed," I said. "Here I am, all alone again. Perhaps that's just the way I'm meant to be, Mifune, a woman alone."

"Jon-Boy would want you to be happy, *cara,*" he said quietly. "You know he loved many women, but his little girl was the true love of his life."

"If only I could believe that," I said longingly, because it would have been so nice to believe I had been the center of his world.

"It is the truth." Mifune paused for a moment, like a man editing his thoughts. Then he said carefully, "Jon-Boy loved one woman very much, but as always with Jon-Boy, she was the wrong woman."

"Tell me about her," I said eagerly, thinking that at last I was on the track of something.

Again he thought for a long time before he spoke. I sipped my sake and listened to the sound of the sea, letting my old friend take his time, though by now I was burning with curiosity.

"He met her in Rome," Mifune said. "She was very beautiful. She had long black hair that hung straight and shiny as a blackbird's wing to her waist. She would wash it, then sit out here on the terrace, letting it dry in the sun. Your father would look at her as though he had never seen such beauty in his life. He was a man besotted with love, crazy for her. And she . . . well, she enjoyed him. You know Jon-Boy, handsome, a charmer, fun to be with . . . what was not to enjoy? But love? No, I don't think she ever loved him. And that was your father's big mistake. Women had always loved him; he couldn't believe that this one did not. She dangled him from the tips of her pretty red-nailed fingers and drove him crazy."

He finished his sake in a gulp, then got slowly to his feet. I rushed to help him. "And then what?" I asked urgently. "What happened to her, Mifune?"

"And then it was over," he said. "One day she was here; the next she was gone. I never saw her again."

"But didn't Jon-Boy?"

He shrugged his thin shoulders as we walked together to the elevator that would take him back up the cliff to the Castello. "I cannot say, Lamour. I was just the gardener. I knew nothing."

"At least tell me her name," I pleaded.

The elevator opened and Mifune got in. We bowed politely to each other. I looked pleadingly into his eyes. "You *must* tell me," I said. "I need to know."

But he shook his head; then the doors closed and he was wafted away from me, up to heaven, which was the way I had always thought of the Castello Pirata's gardens. Leaving me alone to spend a long restless night alone, wondering about the black-haired woman Jon-Boy had loved.

THIRTY-THREE

L'amour

I WAS UP BEFORE DAWN AND IN THE AMALFI PARKING lot promptly at seven the next morning, waiting for my chicken delivery. I paced around, sniffing the morning air like a pointer, enjoying its cool freshness before the noontime heat. At ten past seven I consulted my watch. It was late, but I thought perhaps they'd had trouble rounding up the chickens. By seven-fifteen I was pacing, wondering whether the signora with the great smile and astute bargaining power had misunderstood me. Or I her? Had she mentioned some other day? No, I was sure it was this morning. But what if she'd meant next week? What else might she have misunderstood? What if she showed up with five *dead* chickens, ready to be plucked and put in the oven? My thoughts were running wild, but just then a shabby dirt-spattered truck chugged into the lot and an old man with a lined brown face in bright blue overalls and a flat cap got out.

I heard a great clucking coming from the back of the truck and ran toward him "Signore, signore, it is I who bought the chickens," I called, smiling.

"*Sì, sì, signora.*" He shook my hand briefly. His was crusty and hard, a farmer's hand. "Where is your truck?" he asked. I waved a hand at my little Fiat and saw his brows raise to meet his cap.

"I thought we could put them in the backseat," I said,

though truthfully I hadn't even considered the problem of getting four hens and a rooster home. Muttering under his breath, he said *"Va bene, va bene"* and plucked a couple of chickens from the back. He tucked them, squawking loudly, under his arms and headed for my car.

I followed him, panicked. I'd expected they would come in a nice neat crate, and now I was going to have to share the ride home with, quite literally, a bunch of free-range chickens!

"Wait! Wait!" I called, running after him, but he already had the door open and the chickens inside. He slammed the door and they stared at me through the window, obviously as surprised as I was by this turn of events. As if in protest, they turned up their tail feathers and deposited neat little greenish piles on my car seat.

"No, no," I protested, waving my arms wildly, "take them out; take them *out,* signore. We must arrange something better." My Italian had fallen to pieces under the stress, and the old boy looked stonily at me from the corner of his eye.

Then, "Okay," he said, *"necessitan un plastico e della corda."* And he marched back to the pickup again, with me following, still protesting that I needed *una gabbia,* a cage.

He shrugged his shoulders and told me there was no cage. He grabbed another chicken from under the netting covering them and quickly tied her legs together with a piece of string and set her on the ground. He grabbed another and did the same to that. We watched them flapping wildly for a minute. He took a couple of plastic bags from the cab of the truck, muttered a couple more *"va bene, va benes,"* and was off again to my car.

I hurried after him. How was I going to drive with a bunch of flapping chickens crammed behind me? And how much damage were they going to do to the rental car? And how would I explain that to the Avis lady?

By now the old man had tied up the first two chickens. He spread the plastic bags over the backseat and the four birds sat there, glaring furiously at me, while he went back to get the rooster.

I heard the rooster's powerful squawk before he'd even gotten the bird out of the truck. He let out another high-pitched protest, flapping his strong wings violently, rising up into the air like a hawk, while the old man held grimly on to the bird's feet. I held my breath, wondering whether he was going to fly off over Amalfi's rooftops, never to be seen again, but the man swept the rooster down toward him, quickly wrapped the string around his legs, and shoved him, still squawking, under his arm. He ran toward my car. He thrust the bird in among the hens, who went suddenly quiet, slammed the door on them, then turned and held out his hand.

"*Va bene, signora,*" he said. "*Il dinaro.*"

I had it folded in my jeans pocket, the way I used to when I went shopping in the Campo de' Fiori market for Jon-Boy's supper. Thinking of supper, I asked him what chickens ate.

The old boy's walnut face dropped in astonishment. "They eat what chickens eat," he said. "They roam free and choose what they like in the hedgerows, the fields. . . ."

Of course, that's what *free-range* meant! "Right," I said quickly. "Right."

We shook hands again. I climbed into my chicken wagon and started the engine amid a great outcry of anger from my very own egg layers and their husband.

Mr. Rooster tried to flap his wings, crowing angrily. I glanced nervously into the rearview mirror, praying he wouldn't escape his bonds, because it would be Hitchcock's *The Birds* all over again. I could see the headline now: *American Woman Found Pecked to Death in Rented Fiat.*

I had to stop off in Pirata because I needed to buy them food at Umberto's. There was no way I could let these birds out to "free-range"—they'd simply take off and find a way to fly home, leaving me eggless and out of pocket. I would keep them in their new cage until they got used to the place and understood it was "home."

"Umberto," I said, still breathless from running from the parking lot above town down the *scalatinella* to the piazza, "I need chicken feed."

Umberto looked like an ex-boxer, with a nose that had been broken in his youth and never reset, shadowy black eyes, and a muscular physique. He was about fifty years old, and like most everyone in Pirata, he'd inherited his business from his father, as had his father had before him. In the murky depths at the back of his narrow store were all kinds of surprises, from horseshoes to curling irons. I only prayed he had chicken feed.

"*Ai, signora,* it's much better to let your chickens roam free," he said earnestly. "The eggs will be wonderful, sometimes with two yolks even."

I quickly explained my predicament and he thought for a minute, said, "*Scusi, signora, scusi,*" and disappeared into the back realms.

I stood in the doorway staring uneasily up the hill to the parking for any sight of escapee chickens. Of course, like any good mother, I had left the window open a little so they wouldn't get too hot.

Umberto emerged from the back, dusting off a large paper sack. On it I noticed was written: *Food for Parakeets.*

"This is all I have, signora," he said. "Perhaps it will do for now. Later you can call the feed store in the city and have them deliver some to you."

"But *parakeets?*"

Umberto shrugged. "Birds is birds, signora, is all the same," he said, smiling.

Hoping he was right, I paid my money and ran back up the steps to the car and my waiting chickens.

THIRTY-FOUR

L'amour

IT WAS ONLY WHEN I'D PARKED BY THE STATUE OF Saint Andrew that I realized I was going to have to carry the chickens down the *scalatinella* myself. I looked over my shoulder at them, still squawking in the back. There was no one around to ask for help.

Taking a deep breath—not a good idea in the now very chicken-shitty car—I coughed my way out and slammed the car door behind me. I took a few gulps of fresh air while figuring out a plan of attack. I decided it would be easier to carry one chicken at a time. I opened the back door a crack, shoved my hand in, and grabbed a bunch of feathers. She shrieked and pecked my hand hard. I let go and slammed the door. I stared at my reddened hand—the peck hadn't broken the skin, but still it hurt.

"Little bastard," I said, angry now, "you're not gonna get the better of this independent woman." I thrust my hand in again, grabbed a chicken, dragged her out, and in one swift move tucked her under my arm the way I'd seen the old boy do.

She was much stronger than I'd thought such a little thing would be. That chicken kicked and struggled and pecked all the way down the steps. I shoved her into her new pen, cut the string around her legs, slammed the gate shut, and latched it with a piece of bent wire. Nervous, I checked the improvised lock. The chicken sat, feathers ruffled, where I'd put her, not saying anything for once, so I quickly ran up the steps and grabbed another.

Four times up and down and I had four chickens in their pen, all sitting quietly, waiting for my next move. Or more likely waiting for their boss's move, because there was no doubt the rooster was the boss.

I hovered outside the car, looking at the rusty-colored bird flapping up and down at the window, still squawking angrily and still pooping regularly all over my car seat. I wondered angrily where it all came from. Deciding I could take no more, I flung open the door, grabbed the rooster's neck, and gave it a pull. He squawked loud enough to wake the dead, but I didn't give in. Nor did the rooster; he simply dug in his claws and hung on.

"Come on, you little bastard, get out of there," I muttered grimly, refusing to give in the tug-of-war.

"Can I help you?" a voice said. I turned to find Lorenzo Pirata standing behind me. An ugly white dog sat beside him, staring eagerly at my rooster. "I hate to see a woman struggle with a rooster," he said, with an amused little smile. "And anyhow, it seems to be a losing battle."

He was immaculate in blue shorts, a white linen shirt, and soft expensive-looking suede loafers. He looked like an ad from an Italian fashion magazine, *"What the older man should wear this summer,"* and I was hot and bothered and covered in feathers and chicken shit.

I pulled my wits together. After all, this was the man who'd forbidden his grown children to talk to me, the man with whom I was to have lunch tomorrow, when we were to discuss "my house." He was a man I definitely did not trust.

"Thank you, but I think I can manage," I said distantly, trying to look as dignified as a woman involved in a battle for supremacy with a rooster could.

"What you need to do is grab him by the wings," Lorenzo said. Edging me aside, he opened the door and put both hands fast over the rooster, trapping his wings. "That's where their power is," he said, pulling the now silent bird from the car. "Cut it off and they know they are beaten. Now, where do you want him?"

I gestured down the cliff. "At the back of the house. I've made a little coop."

He headed swiftly down the stairs, followed by the dog, with me running after them carrying the bag of food. I darted ahead to open the little wire gate. He took a knife from his pocket, cut the leg strings, then quickly thrust the rooster in. It settled amid a great fluffing of feathers, then retreated behind his clucking harem of chickens to rearrange his ego.

"You'll have trouble with that bird," Lorenzo Pirata said, standing, arms folded, looking at my new "family." "And what made you buy Rhode Island Reds?"

I looked, puzzled, at my chickens. They were just chickens to me. "I don't know about Rhode Island Reds," I admitted. "All I wanted were some nice fresh eggs."

"Much easier to buy them in the market," he said, sounding amused. "And the chickens will need a proper house to nest in, but anyhow, it's best if they run free."

"I have food for them," I said, hefting the sack, hardly believing I was having an actual conversation with the Pirate of Pirata.

This time he laughed. "Umberto sold you parakeet seed," he said. "Don't worry; I'll have some proper chicken feed sent down. You don't want to kill them off before you at least get some eggs."

"True," I admitted, blushing. This self-sufficiency game was more complicated than it seemed. "And thank you."

He stood, arms folded, looking at me. Nervous, I dusted a

feather from my cheek. I said, "I'm surprised you helped me, Signor Pirata. After all, you told your daughter not to speak to me."

He looked gravely at me for a long moment. I noticed how bright a blue his eyes were. He was a tall, broad-shouldered, powerful-looking man. A very attractive man and no doubt fully aware of that. Women must chase after him just the way they chased after his son.

"I apologize for that," he said finally. "It was wrong of me."

I nodded, still wondering what reason he could possibly have had for asking his children not to talk to me.

"I'm looking forward to seeing you at lunch tomorrow," he added.

I said I was looking forward to it, too, and he said, "Good luck with the chickens. I'll have the feed to you right away." Then he was running back up the *scalatinella* with his ugly dog, looking, I thought, just as good from behind as he did from the front.

Handsome is as handsome does. . . . I remembered the old saying Jammy's mother used to quote at us whenever we were moaning about the hot guys on the football team and how great looking they were. We figured it meant they had better be as good on the inside as they were on the out- and if they didn't behave well to us, Mrs. Mortimer would have something to say about it. I wished Mrs. Mortimer were here now.

Leaving my birds sitting in a sullen heap, I walked around to the front of the house. I felt hot, dirty, and tired, and I still had to go back up and clean out my wrecked car. I sighed. The hell with it. I was too exhausted.

I sank onto a chair, admiring the soothing blue vista below me. I heard the roar of an engine and saw the Riva dart into the bay with Nico at the helm. He didn't turn to look up at the house and I guessed he had already forgotten all about the older woman who had amused him for a few hours the other day.

Then on the table I saw a small package. The box said: ALBERTO E LINA, CAPRI. In it was the pretty coral bracelet I had admired the other day.

A smile lifted the corners of my mouth. Nico had not forgotten me after all.

THIRTY-FIVE

L'amour

I'D BEEN TOO UPSET TO VENTURE INTO JON-BOY'S room since that first evening when I'd found everything exactly the way he'd left it. Now, with my lunch with Lorenzo Pirata "to discuss matters" looming, I thought I'd better take another look around and see if there were any documents regarding the house.

I'd left the windows open, and the fresh air had dispelled the musty odors. Now it felt as though Jon-Boy might walk through the door any minute.

The floor-to-ceiling shelves were crammed with his books, and a beautiful writing table stood by the window. This time, with a clearer head and also in the clear light of day, I saw that the table was an antique, probably eighteenth-century Italian, and probably valuable. I had not seen it before and I was surprised.

On it was a bunch of papers and the coffee mug with *Souvenir of Sorrento* inscribed on it, in which he kept his different-colored pens. He used a new color for each day; he said that way he always knew exactly where he was in the narrative.

I went and sat in his chair, a straight-up simple dining chair borrowed from downstairs and never returned. I opened the top drawer and saw a yellow legal pad with several pages covered in his small closely written script. There were also a couple of reference books and a battered old dictionary from his college days. And a dark blue leather diary.

I stared at the diary. It probably told everything I needed to know, but I was loathe to invade my father's privacy—and God knows there is nothing more private than a diary. Yet I *had* to know what had been happening in the months leading up to his death. Guiltily I read the first entry.

Jan. 1. Rome, he had written in the small space provided for that day. *Up all night—and the night before. Snow fell at midnight, grand soft flakes studding the sky like crystal ornaments, blending with the fireworks, sparkling in the streetlights, melting on the tongue, like a chaser to the too-much champagne we had drunk. "C" in red chiffon, wrapped in fur, face peeking from the big collar like a pretty little fox . . . or vixen is more like it. We met at Orlando's overcrowded party at the Palazzo Rosati-Contini—nothing but the best for Orlando, including the women. Had gone there in a bad mood after the usual chaotic scene with "I," expecting nothing—and suddenly I found myself escorting the vixen home. We both knew what awaited at the end of our walk through Rome's now deserted streets—but after forty-eight hours without sleep, trying to avoid the usual rows and distractions with "I" and do some work, plus all the partying and all the drinking . . . I hoped I was going to be up to it.*

Jan. 2. Six P.M. "C" is an incredible woman, beautiful . . . she seduced even this tired writer and succeeded in making me feel I was the only man in her life. Would that that were true. Now I think I'm in love. What a note to start the new year on. Life is suddenly looking good.

I slammed the diary shut. I shouldn't have read it. I didn't want to know the details of Jon-Boy's love affairs. I sat for a moment, undecided. His *life* was in there. I *needed* to read it. I opened it again and I looked up the final entry. The date was October 30. The day he died.

"I" has been here; I know it. When I returned from the Amalfitano, I noticed things had been moved. The desk lamp was on, a drawer was open, the armoire door left ajar. She had not taken "C's" red chiffon dress, but I knew she had seen it. Who knows what conclusions she came to? I suppose I should keep the front door locked, but that's not the way around here, and besides, I would never lock her out. I've found out the hard way that love never really dies, and I still care about her, yet I'm crazy for "C." Perhaps the only really true love we have is the love we give our innocent children. This is a thought I must always keep in my mind. Maybe at Christmas I'll fly to Chicago and surprise Lamour, the true girl of my heart.

Jon-Boy's final words had been about me. I laid my head on the desk and closed my eyes, picturing my father sitting here writing this. "I love you, too, Jon-Boy," I whispered.

I put the diary back in the drawer and locked it. I couldn't bear to pry anymore; it just wasn't right. I went to the armoire, took out the red dress, and held it to me. Perfume lingered in its folds, a sophisticated scent I couldn't quite identify. It was silk chiffon, falling into a soft flutter at the hem. The hand-stitched label said GIORGIO VIVARI. It was the designer I had encountered in Rome, the one who had complimented me on my charming foot! I thought not only was "C" beautiful and sexy; she was also expensive. Way beyond Jon-Boy's means, I knew, because he'd gone through his royalty windfall from the first novel—his only novel—as fast as it came in.

I never knew quite what he'd spent it all on, though he'd rented a glossy apartment in one of those grand palazzi in Rome that we could never afford when I was a child. And of course, he'd bought this house, the refuge to which he'd intended to retreat and write his next opus. I wondered if "C" had put a stop to that? Or maybe "I"? I had fewer details on her, but I guessed she was the rejected lover, and jealous women did crazy things; everyone knew that.

Hadn't I felt those same pangs of jealousy when Jammy told me of Alex's betrayal, even though he was dead? I'd felt the humiliation of being cheated, the pain of being rejected for someone new. I had felt anger. Who knew what I might have done had I found out when Alex was still alive?

But I would never have killed him. More likely I'd have wanted to hurl *myself* off the balcony. *Failure* was a terrifying word, especially in love.

The shrill beep of the Italian phone service brought me back to reality. I dashed to my room and picked it up.

"So where were you?" Jammy's voice brought an instant smile to my face.

"Somewhere in the past. Reading Jon-Boy's diary."

"It's never a good idea to read other people's diaries."

"I know that. And believe me I feel guilty, but I thought he might mention what was going on, that there might be some clue. . . ."

"And was there?"

"Only that there was a woman in his life, beautiful, sexy, expensive. . . ."

"Sounds like par for the course, knowing Jon-Boy."

"Yeah, but there was also a second woman. He'd left her and I think she was jealous."

Jammy sighed again, a big, gusty sigh that I knew meant she had had enough of Jon-Boy's past. "So what's happening with *you*?" she demanded. "How's *your* love life with all those gorgeous Italian men around?"

"I assume you are talking about the Piratas?" I said. "I

went to Capri with one yesterday and I'm having lunch with the other tomorrow."

"Capri? That's exciting. Tell me all, girl."

So I told her all about my day with Nico, how charming I thought he was, how delightful a companion, and about the bracelet. "But . . . ," I said finally, and heard her laugh.

She said, "With men there's always a 'but.' Haven't you learned that by now? And what about the other Pirata? The painter who didn't want you to talk to his offspring?"

I told her the chicken story and how Lorenzo had come to my aid. "He apologized for telling Aurora and Nico not to talk to me," I said. "I kind of liked that he admitted he was wrong, Jammy. I mean a man in his position, he could have just told me to mind my own business and keep out of the Pirata family's way."

"That he could," Jammy said thoughtfully. "So I wonder what he wants?"

I told her he had invited me to lunch to discuss the house.

"Ha, the truth at last," she said. "And what do *you* think he wants, Lamour?"

I said I hated to admit it, but I thought he wanted the house back and me out of there and out of the Piratas' lives.

"You can always come home," Jammy said, sounding so unsympathetic I laughed.

I asked about Matt and the college kid and I promised to call immediately after the lunch and tell her everything that had happened.

Back downstairs I found a man standing outside the open front door. "Signor Pirata sent the chicken feed, signora," he said politely. He carried two huge bags into my kitchen and I thanked him and the signor Pirata and gave him a tip. He lifted his cap politely, then departed.

I quickly opened a bag, scooped the feed into a saucepan, then hurried out to my chickens. They were lined up, beaks sticking through the wire, looking irate. When I opened the gate the rooster came strutting at me. I flung in feed and slammed the gate shut. I filled the saucepan with water from the garden faucet, shoved it in, and clanged the gate shut again. I made sure the wire was wound securely around the makeshift latch and left them happily scratching and pecking at the food.

Perhaps they'd just been hungry, I thought. When they've eaten they'll be content and snuggle up on their straw nests and get to work laying.

I walked back around the house onto the terrace. The pretty coral bracelet was still on the table where I'd left it. I put it on, turning my wrist this way and that, thinking about Nico. He'd said it was meant for me, but of course I couldn't allow him to buy it. I'd write a check now and send it over to the Castello. Inside, though, I was secretly thrilled. Maybe I fancied Nico Pirata and maybe he fancied me. Love affairs have been based on less than that.

THIRTY-SIX

Lamour

I DRESSED CAREFULLY FOR MY BUSINESS MEETING with Lorenzo Pirata, because a "business meeting" was what it definitely was. I couldn't flatter myself I was being invited because of my charms. This Pirate captain moved in far grander circles than his forebears and was certainly out of my dating realm.

I wore a skirt I'd bought with Jammy in Rome. Actually I'd fallen for the color, a lovely apple green, more than the skirt, as I much preferred wearing pants. With it I wore a matching T-shirt and the raspberry-colored sandals I'd bought in Amalfi. I thought I looked a bit like a limeade Popsicle, but it was too late to change. I brushed my unruly hair into a tight knot because it looked more businesslike, added gold hoop earrings and a hint of Jo Malone's honeysuckle perfume. I'd already done my face, minimal as usual, just a little shiny pink blusher, lipstick, mascara. I wondered why I was going to all this trouble for a man who obviously didn't even like me.

I was halfway out the door when I remembered Nico's bracelet. I went back and put it on. After all, the Pirate didn't know his son had given it to me.

Mifune was waiting for me out on the terrace to accompany me on my walk up to the Castello. Adjusting my long-legged stride to his slower pace, I told him how much I was looking forward to seeing his gardens again.

"I am sorry I did not bring you to see them earlier, *cara*," he said, "but they do not belong to me and I could not invite you without permission."

I stared at him, astounded. "Mifune, do you mean to say you were forbidden to bring me to see your lovely gardens?"

"Not *forbidden*, Lamour. It was suggested to me that it might not be suitable."

That sounded like a Pirata euphemism for "forbid" to me. Fuming, I walked along the pathway lined with cedars, through the small grove of olive trees that provided the family with first-rate olive oil, also sold in stores in London and Rome. We stopped for a moment to admire the arched wooden bridge over the carp pond, where the orange fish leaped up at us, looking for food.

I remembered these gardens so well I could have drawn a map, but I was not here on pleasure and we walked quicker now, up the herb-lined gravel path. A helicopter sat on its pad below the house and I thought how rich the Pirate must be to own such a thing.

Mifune left me at the bottom of the wide stone steps. He said gently, "Do not take everything that is said today to heart. It is not exactly the way it seems." And with that cryptic remark he walked away, leaving me wondering uneasily what on earth he had meant.

A houseman in a white linen jacket was holding open the massive door. He told me his name was Massimo. I said, *"Buona sera,"* and stepped inside the Pirate's stronghold.

I looked around the lofty hall, painted that wonderful shade of ocher red you see in ancient frescos. There were cherubs and clouds on the pale blue ceiling and on the walls golden sconces that looked as though they could hold a hundred candles. The floor was tiled in black and white marble, and twin alabaster staircases rose to meet in a balustraded gallery in the middle.

Impressed, I followed Massimo through a pair of tall double doors into a formal living room. It was as large as the hall, with immense silk-curtained windows, and it had the air of a room long unused.

"Welcome to the Castello Pirata, Signora Harrington," Lorenzo Pirata said from behind me.

I swung round, startled. He held out his hand and I took it, because, friend or foe, I'd been brought up to be polite. He was immaculate as always, impressive with his leonine good looks, his piercing blue gaze, his thick silver hair. A *strong* man who I knew would make a formidable enemy. The ugly white dog stood next to him. She did not come over to say hello.

"You have a very beautiful home, Signor Pirata," I said.

He nodded. "Thank you, though I can't take much credit for it. The Castello was built by my family and I was lucky enough to inherit it. My wife was responsible for the decoration of this room, though, and I think she did a remarkable job, don't you?"

I wondered why I hadn't realized there must be a wife and quickly decided she must be some gorgeous blond trophy who right now was out spending his money.

"Absolutely remarkable," I said, looking at the high-backed brocade sofas and silk carpets, the gold lamps and little gilt tables filled with beautiful jeweled objects. Somehow it didn't quite match up with the first version of Lorenzo I'd seen, in the paint-spattered shorts.

"What can I offer you to drink?" he said, being the perfect host. "Perhaps a glass of champagne?"

Acting the perfect guest, I said, "Yes, thank you."

"I always think champagne is such a celebratory drink,"

I added, desperately making conversation, and the modern-day Pirate smiled and agreed there was nothing better.

I perched on the edge of a gold brocade chair and he sat opposite on the edge of a sofa. "And how are your chickens?" he asked.

"Oh, my goodness, I forgot to thank you for the chicken feed!" I exclaimed guiltily. "It's only thanks to you I didn't poison them all with parakeet food! They're doing well, I think. At least they're not protesting as much. I have to admit, though, I daren't go into that coop yet. I'm scared to death of that rooster."

He laughed, and I noticed how his eyes crinkled at the corners. He looked quite different when he laughed, more approachable. I thought he was probably a very interesting man, though I was never going to get the chance to find out.

"Cute dog," I said as she came over to inspect me. "What's her name?"

Lorenzo laughed. "Oh, come on now, tell the truth: she's the ugliest dog you ever saw, right? Her name is Affare—the Italian word for 'bargain'—because she cost me nothing and she's the best bargain I ever had. Apart from the vet's bills to fix her up. I found her on the street near my office; I noticed she was there every day, getting thinner and thinner. Then she must have been hit by a car, because one morning I found her bloodied and with a broken leg and ribs. Nobody wanted a dog this ugly. She looked at me and I looked at her. . . ." He shrugged. "What could I do? She was mine."

"And you were hers," I said, feeling unexpectedly touched by his story. I took another look at Affare, the bargain dog, sitting next to her master, her long white snout sniffing the air, her stump of a tail tucked under. She had the smallest eyes of any dog I'd ever seen, a long nose, rough white fur, and short legs. It would take a leap of faith to see beauty in her, but

I guessed it was her inner beauty that had captured the great Lorenzo Pirata.

"*Perdona, signore,* luncheon is served," Massimo said from the doorway.

We followed him into a dining room almost as big as the room we had just left. It was painted a faded gold, with a carved green marble fireplace at each end and a long series of French doors. Through them I caught a glimpse of a wide terrace with a row of extraordinary sphinx heads overlooking the wide vista of the coastline. The long dining table could seat at least twenty, and our two places arranged at the far end looked a little lonely.

Lorenzo held my chair and I took a seat. "This is like Buckingham Palace," I said, sounding like the dumb eight-year-old I used to be instead of the modern woman of the world I supposedly was. But the Pirate smiled and said perhaps it wasn't quite as grand as that and, in fact, the family rarely used these rooms, except for the holidays, Christmas and suchlike, when there were big parties. He'd thought I might like to see them.

"Thank you," I said. "I'm thrilled; I've never seen a place like this before—let alone eaten lunch in one."

Massimo was serving a pasta dish: tiny ravioli filled with crabmeat in a buttery sauce. They were delicious and I said so, enjoying the food despite myself.

"I'm glad to see you appreciate good food," the Pirate said, "though looking at you, I wouldn't have thought so."

"You think I'm too skinny?" I said indignantly, and instantly regretted it. But he laughed.

"I think you are quite beautiful, Lamour Harrington," he said, completely throwing me off. Of all the things he might have said, this was the most unexpected.

Somehow I got my wits back together. "My father always

told me that, though of course that was just a father speaking.
I never believed him," I added.

"Fathers always see beauty in their daughters," Lorenzo
said, and remembering Aurora, I told him I thought his
daughter was extremely beautiful.

"I only wish she were more aware of it," he commented as
a maid in a pale blue dress and a white apron came to take
our empty plates.

"You sound like every father there ever was," I said, smiling. "They never seem to want to lose their daughters to another man."

"That's probably true," he agreed, pouring more wine, as
Massimo appeared with the next course: a platter of delicious-
looking scampi, prepared with white wine and shallots and
garlic.

"This is heaven," I said, letting go of inhibitions and taking
another sip of the wine. I was beginning to enjoy myself. My
eyes met the Pirate's over the rim of the wineglass. He was
smiling.

I was on my third glass and feeling no pain. I leaned closer,
elbow on the table, chin in hand. "What's so funny?" I asked,
looking him in the eye.

"I've never met anyone like you."

I raised an eyebrow. "Man, woman, or beast?"

"Oh, definitely woman," he said, laughing out loud this
time.

The maid cleared our empty plates and Massimo appeared
again with a salad and a silver-edged wooden board with an
array of cheeses. I had the sense to turn down another glass of
wine, though I got the feeling it was too late. I thought guiltily
I had let down my defenses and we hadn't even gotten to the
"business" part of the meeting yet. I refused the cheese.

"Then shall we take our coffee out on the terrace?" Lorenzo asked. "I'd like to show you the view from there."

The terrace could have accommodated several of my little houses. It wrapped around the entire front of the Castello in a great sweep, shaded with stone-columned pergolas laden with honeysuckle and jasmine and hot pink bougainvillea. A narrow reflecting pool ran for a hundred feet or more along the rim of the terrace, with jets of water arching over it, exactly like the famous pool in the Alhambra gardens in Granada, Spain. Tables and comfortable chairs were arranged in the shade of striped awnings and under the leafy pergolas. Games, a backgammon set and an enormous chess set with silver pawns, and books were strewn around. The landscape architect in me appreciated the casual informality, achieved despite such a grand setting. It was like an outdoor living room, and obviously this was a place where the family spent a great deal of time.

I leaned on the balustrade gazing at the fantastical vista of the Bay of Salerno spread out for my pleasure, at the green indented coastline and the aquamarine sea blending into the azure sky. "I want to reach out and touch it," I said, smiling at Lorenzo Pirata, who had come to stand next to me, "just to make sure it's not a painted backdrop."

"Even Hollywood could not match this," he said, but his eyes were on me and not the view.

"And all these sphinxes? What did your ancestors do? Send a pirate ship to Egypt?"

He laughed and said that they probably had and the sphinxes had indeed come from Egypt and as far as he knew had been purchased by his great-great-grandfather, long before it became fashionable to loot Egyptian and Greek artifacts.

"There is a receipt in the archives," he said. "I forget exactly the sum paid, but it was certainly not what they were worth. So I suppose it was an act of piracy in a way."

Massimo poured the coffee and we took our cups and sipped it, still looking out across the bay in which my father had drowned in the storm. Now there was barely a flicker of wind and the sea was like a sheet of glittering blue glass.

"I've never seen a storm here," I said. "What's it like?"

He shrugged. "Very Italian. Dramatic, fierce; thunder, lightning, winds that swirl and moan all around, tearing out trees, blowing down roofs, wreaking destruction. Fortunately, they don't occur very often. And usually only in winter."

I was staring at the view but could feel his eyes on me. "My father died in a storm like that," I said.

"I remember. It was a great storm and it came early that year."

'Did you know my father?"

He nodded. "I knew Jon-Boy. We had a business arrangement about the house."

"Oh, of course, the house," I said, remembering it was the reason I was here.

"My wife also knew your father," he said. "She enjoyed his novel very much. I remember she said it was a window into the man's soul."

"Your wife was right. It was." I turned to look at him. I thought that under different circumstances I might be interested in this man. I might want to get to know him better, see what lurked beneath that smooth urbane surface. Find out if there were tempests and volcanoes burning inside or whether Lorenzo Pirata was a cool customer, a man always on the surface of life. Looking into his eyes, I didn't want to believe that. For some odd reason, even though I knew he was my enemy, I wanted to believe that the charm was his social facade and underneath was the real man, the one who liked nothing better than restoring his old fishing boat in the company of his dog.

"I'd like to meet your wife," I said.

"Marella died seventeen years ago. Aurora was only three."

I could have bitten out my tongue. "Oh, I'm so sorry."

"You couldn't know that," he said in a brisker tone. "And of course, Jon-Boy is one of the reasons I brought you here today."

"Only one of the reasons?" I asked mockingly, because I knew he was being polite, not to say charming, before dropping the bombshell and asking me to sell my house back to him.

"There were two," he said. "The first was that I wanted to have lunch with the woman whose ambition is to keep free-range chickens, and whose company I've enjoyed enormously. The second is more serious, I'm afraid."

"I'm afraid, too," I said. "I have no idea what you are going to say, but I have the feeling it's not good."

He held his arms wide, palms up in a shrug. "I have no choice. It's certainly not the end of the world," he added curtly, sounding quite different from the man of a few moments ago. "But I have to tell you, Lamour, you've made a grave mistake coming back to Amalfi. Of course I understand you wanted to see the place where you lived as a child, and where you were happy with your father. That's the reason I allowed you to stay and said nothing. Until now."

I held up my hands. "Stop! Stop! Did you say *allowed* me to stay? What right have you to ask me to leave? The house belonged to my father. Now it's mine."

We were face-to-face. "I'm sorry, Lamour," he said, "but the house did not belong to Jon-Boy. It was leased by him from the Pirata estate. That lease became void with his death."

My knees buckled and I sank into a chair. The house I considered my real home, *my true happy home,* did not belong to me. But Jon-Boy had told me it was ours, that he would always live there. Was Lorenzo Pirata trying to cheat me out of my home? And if so, why?

"It would be best," I heard him say, "if you enjoyed the rest of your little holiday, and then returned to Chicago, picked up your life there. After all, there's not much in Amalfi for a foreign woman alone."

I shot to my feet, suddenly angry. Who the hell did he think he was, talking *at* me, *the little woman,* telling me to go home to Chicago like a good girl? The hell with him! Besides, there was more to this than met the eye.

"You want me out of here," I said trying to keep my voice calm. "And I want to know *why*? What's your secret, Lorenzo Pirata? What are you hiding? Is it something to do with my father's death? The man who hated the water, who hated boats, who never set foot in one? The same man who supposedly sailed out into a storm and never came back? Did you have something to do with that, Signor Pirata? Or am I imagining things, the way we *women* so often do?"

Affare got to her feet, growling softly. "I'm very sorry, Lamour," Lorenzo said quietly. "But those are the facts."

"You're only telling me exactly as much as you want me to know," I said. "But I'll tell *you* something, Signor Pirata. I'm not going anywhere. I'm here to stay. And I don't care how many legal documents and fancy lawyers you throw at me."

I stalked from the terrace into the house, feeling his eyes on me. I turned at the door. He was standing where I'd left him, watching me. "Oh, and thank you for a wonderful lunch," I said, polite to the last. Mrs. Mortimer would have been proud of me.

THIRTY-SEVEN

I THREW OFF MY NEW SANDALS AND RAN DOWN THE *scalatinella* to the house. From now on I would go barefoot, the way I had when I was a kid. The soles of my feet would become tough again, and so would I.

I ran into the house, flinging off my smart lunch-party clothes as I went. Upstairs, I dragged on a pair of old shorts and a T-shirt. I glared around.

This was *my* room, *my* house, *my* home. Nobody would ever get me out of here. As if to prove it was mine, I pried open the can of apricot paint, grabbed the roller, and started on the walls.

It was seven o'clock before I took a break and a hot shower to get the aches out of my back. I wandered restlessly in the garden, making mental notes of things that needed to be done, promising I would delay no longer and that tomorrow I would begin its rescue.

I heard the rooster crowing—too loudly as always. Of course, dinnertime. The chickens were crouched on the ground, feathers fluffed, looking huffily back at me and Mr. Rooster flew threateningly at the wire fence. I took a quick step back. Did I really need a rooster? I still hadn't figured out if you got eggs without one, which just goes to prove how ignorant I am about the sex lives of poultry.

I opened the gate and flung in the feed. They leaped on it

like starving prisoners, making me feel guilty. I realized, not for the first time, that I knew nothing about chickens. And nothing about cows either, come to that. Yet weren't cows supposed to be placid, peaceful creatures? Maybe I should have started with Daisy instead of these wild birds!

With the chickens at least temporarily quiet, I went back to my painting, determined to at least finish *something* I'd started. It was after one o'clock in the morning when, with my arms one big ache, I finally did.

The room smelled of paint, so I showered, then went downstairs.

The old sofa fit my weary body as though it remembered me, and I dropped off the edge of the world for a few hours, not even thinking about Lorenzo Pirata. But he was with me when I woke up, right there at the forefront of my mind.

I wondered what Jon-Boy would have advised me to do. I hated to peek into his diary again, but I needed to know if he'd written anything about buying the house and where the deed of sale might be.

I threw on a robe, went to his room and took a seat at his beautiful desk. It was carved with pretty scrolls and shells and so perfect for a seaside villa. I imagined him finding it in some dingy antiques-shop window in Naples. Perhaps in one of those cobbled alleys where insolent mustached men lingered menacingly in the shadows ready to take on the unwary tourist who'd strayed off the prescribed route. Of course, Jon-Boy wouldn't have given a damn about them. We had wandered those backstreets together on many an evening, me with a gelato clutched in my hand and a great deal of it on my face and Jon-Boy with a cigarette in the corner of his mouth, peering into dusty doorways. I remembered the dim chandelier that had charmed him with its painted iron rosebuds and wreaths of laurel.

"It's perfect for your room, *tesoro*," he'd said to me, and I'd wrinkled my nose and said he was crazy; all I wanted was a green-shaded lamp, like the one he had on his table.

"Okay," he'd agreed, "but here's the deal. I get you a table and the lamp and you do some work for a change. After all, I can't have you going back to the Mortimers ignorant, can I?" My heart had skipped a beat at the mention of going back, but then he'd given me that sideways look and a grin so I knew he was only teasing. Nevertheless, I promised and he got me a table and the lamp. For a couple of weeks I sat there supposedly studying history and Italian verbs but mostly just staring out the window, dreaming dreams and longing to be free so I could go for a swim. Jon-Boy was working hard on his novel at his table downstairs, because then he still worked and he didn't yet have this fancy desk.

I opened the top drawer and took out his diary. Then I sat trying to get up the courage to read it, afraid of what it might reveal.

Stalling, sifting through the drawers, finding some rough notes for the never-written novel. Then, to my surprise, I found a whole chapter. It was about a child and her wonderment at everything she encountered on coming to live in a strange country. The child was obviously me and the father Jon-Boy.

In it, he described himself as kindly but irresponsible man, a nomad, wandering from place to place, always searching for something new to inspire him: a new city, a new wine, a new woman. The only constant in his life was the child without whom, he said at the end of the chapter, he was nothing.

I am a man without an identity. A failure, he wrote. *Children own us, and no matter how much we squirm and struggle, they will never let us go. That is true love.*

I put down the chapter. The man I had thought so strong,

so invincible, a man who owned his actions and his world, had confessed that at heart he considered himself nothing, except in the eyes of his child.

I sat for a long time thinking about him. I wished he were here so I could tell him he was not a failure—not in his work, nor in his life, nor in his love. I wanted to tell him he was the best father any girl ever had and I would not have changed my time in Italy with him for anything, that it was the event that had changed my life.

I put the chapter back in the drawer. I had no stomach to read the sad confessions in his diary, and instead I drove to Pirata, bought a scythe at Umberto's, then came back and attacked my garden.

I worked like a maniac for the next few days as though to prove to myself—as well as to Lorenzo Pirata—that this was *my* house and, as I'd promised, I was here to stay.

I cleared brush; I dug the earth and fertilized it; I dragged out weeds with my bare hands and got stung and prickled with thorns. I stood knee-deep in the cold rushing waterfall and cleaned watery weeds from under its banks. I stripped the belvedere of its layers of beautiful blue morning glory; then I hosed it down and got on my knees and up a ladder to scrub off decades of encrusted dirt.

I hadn't remembered how lovely the belvedere was, with its perfect proportions, its lovely columns and blue mosaic dome. I rushed immediately into town to buy a pair of delicate iron chairs and a little table for drinks. I put them in there and celebrated my handiwork alone that evening, with a bottle of Prosecco and a sunset to dream about.

Next, I tackled the great swathe of pink oleander and purple bougainvillea that had encroached several feet onto the terrace, hacking at it with my scythe, getting more blisters and sticking on more Band-Aids. And then I found a great surprise.

Hidden beneath all the heavy blossoms edging the terrace was a long tiled bench. The tiles were from Vietri, just along the coast. They were handmade, with pictures of branches of lemons against a cobalt background and of olive trees and sunbursts and blue waves foaming in silvery white. There was even a picture of the Castello up on its hill, its pirate flag flying as it always did when the family was in residence. And there was a picture of my charming little house, with its dome and arches, framed with cedar trees and pink blossoms. Everything was there, even the waterfall and the meditation stone.

It was breathtaking, a work of art, baroque and ornate with its elaborate curves and scrolls and its charming pictures. I recalled seeing a similar bench on a visit to the Hotel San Pietro in Positano with Jon-Boy. I also knew it must have cost a great deal of money and I guessed he bought it when the royalties from the novel were still flowing in. I was grateful that he had. Not only was it beautiful, but it confirmed my belief that the house belonged to him. Not even Jon-Boy would have commissioned something this expensive for a house he did not own.

I trimmed back the flowering bushes carefully so they would frame the bench without obscuring the view. Then I measured it for the cushions. I would have them made locally in sun yellow sailcloth piped in cobalt.

I sat on my bench with a feeling of accomplishment. I was claiming the house as mine. I had taken the first steps to restoring my garden. I had painted my bedroom and ordered a new bed. The refrigerator was also ordered, and the man from the propane storage place was coming to inspect my stove. I'd found an old-fashioned chimney sweep in Pirata and he'd promised to clean my chimney so I'd be able to have log fires in winter. I already anticipated the pleasure of listening to the crackling logs and watching the flames dancing and hearing the swoosh of the winter sea roaring against the cliffs.

But what I'd really achieved was that for an entire week I had put Lorenzo and his plot against me out of my mind. I'd gotten on with my life, on my own. It was the way I intended things to be.

And then Nico showed up again.

THIRTY-EIGHT

Lamour

"HOW ARE YOU, *CARA*?" NICO CAME BOUNDING down the steps to where I was sitting on my beautiful Vietri-tiled bench, taking a moment's break from my labors.

He couldn't have chosen a more inopportune time. I was hot, tired, and sweaty. There was dirt under my fingernails and Band-Aids over my blisters and my hair was dragged back in a limp ponytail. I looked about a hundred, or at least my age.

"I'm not sure how I am," I said shortly. "I'm too tired even to think about it."

"Poor girl." He dropped onto the bench next to me, but I kept my face firmly forward. I could feel him studying my profile and, self-conscious, I pushed back the escaping strands of damp hair. He snatched my hand in his, pressing it flat, examining it.

"But what's all this?" he cried, aghast. "What happened to you?"

I shrugged. "Nothing much, just hard work."

"But there is no need. Mifune has a crew of men working on our gardens. He would have sent someone over to do the hard labor. *Cara,* you were not meant for cutting down trees; there are other more suitable occupations for a woman as lovely as you."

I threw him a glance from the corner of my eye. He was so extravagantly ridiculous I wanted to laugh.

"Please let me arrange it for you," he said, but I shook my head and told him I wanted to do it alone.

"This is my house, despite what your father thinks, and I'll look after it," I said firmly.

Ignoring what I'd said about his father, he said cajolingly, "Then at least have dinner with me tonight. We can talk about your bracelet."

I relented a little—after all, he'd made such a charming, generous gesture, though I did wonder at the back of my mind what he expected to get in return. Telling myself I was being too cynical, I remembered my manners and thanked him. "But you really shouldn't have," I added, "and that's why I sent you the check."

"And here it is—back again." He put the check on the bench between us. "Please, it was a gift. Allow me that pleasure."

I met his pleading eyes. How could I resist? And damn it, why should I? Just because I was at war with the father didn't mean I shouldn't have fun with the son.

"Okay. I'll have dinner with you. On one condition: I pay."

This made him laugh uproariously. "Oh, American women and their independence!" he exclaimed. "*Cara,* no Italian woman would ever have dreamed of saying that."

"Take it or leave it," I said.

He nodded. "Very well. I'll take it."

I left him wandering through the garden, inspecting my week's work, while I showered and washed my hair and put on something reasonably pretty. I left my hair to dry in the wind, and this time we took Nico's lipstick-red convertible and with the top down drove at nerve-racking speed up onto the mountain road to Ravello.

We ended up at the gloriously glitzy Hotel Palazzo Sasso. Nico headed straight for the bar, where he was obviously well-known. It seemed to be a rendezvous spot for the glitterati,

and admiring the chic, bejeweled women I wished halfheart-
edly I'd made more effort to dress.

Nico greeted people as old friends, introducing me this
time and behaving quite properly, I thought. Then he escorted
me to a secluded table and ordered a bottle of champagne.

"Does your family always drink champagne?" I asked.

"What do you mean?"

"I had lunch with your father the other day. He served
champagne, too."

Nico's brows rose and for a moment he looked discon-
certed. "I hope you enjoyed your lunch," he said, but I could
tell he was restraining himself from asking exactly why I'd
had lunch with his father. I told him anyway.

He refilled our glasses. "That's none of my business," he
said quite curtly. "I know nothing about it." He looked at me
and then added, "All I know is that I want you to stay."

My spirits rose with the champagne bubbles. "Don't worry,
caro—I'm not going anywhere," I said, making him laugh.

"Do you like this hotel?" He gestured to the elaborate
marble halls, the gorgeous bouquets, the smart waiters in
white jackets, the glass elevators, and the waterfall.

I shrugged, "It's okay, I suppose," I said, and then we were
laughing again.

Taking my hand, he whispered in my ear, "It could be
yours, Lamour. We could take a suite; we could stay here together, you and I. I'll smother you in the luxury you deserve;
I'll shower you with rose petals and the kisses you need; I'll
make perfect love to you. . . ."

He was so outrageous I laughed. I said, "Thank you, but
perhaps not tonight, maybe some other time."

"Okay," he said briskly, as though he'd expected to be rejected and it was all part of the game. "Then you will take
me out for dinner." And he swept me back into his car and

down the hill to a simple cantina that had been around for more than three hundred years, called Cumpá Casimo.

The owner knew Nico—didn't everyone?—and though the place was packed found a table for us. We sat beneath lofty arches and were served veal with lemon and hearty home-made pasta. It was exactly the kind of meal that made me know why I so loved living in Italy.

"Where else could you eat like this?" I asked, helping my-self to another plateful, and Nico laughed at my hearty ap-petite until I was too embarrassed to eat any more.

"You're very sexy when you eat," he said.

"I've never thought of food as being sexy."

"But of course. What could be more sensual than food and wine? Even simple bread and cheese with a glass of Chianti at a picnic under the trees is sensual. *Carina,* you are too used to McDonald's and fast foods and eating only to satisfy immedi-ate hunger. Good food is also there to satisfy the senses."

I almost felt my bones melt as we gazed into each other's eyes. This man could charm birds out of the trees and women out of their minds. But not me, I thought, dragging my eyes away and my head back to reality.

We drove, slowly this time, thank God, back down the mountain to my parking spot by my guardian saint. Nico switched off the engine and we sat listening to the wind in the trees and the crickets chirruping. I felt like a high school girl out on a date with the hot guy with the red convertible. Nico's eyes were on me. He took my chin in his hand and turned my face to him. He leaned into me, eyes half-closed, his mouth seeking mine. I felt his breath soft on my cheek, smelled his light citrusy cologne. . . . I was falling . . . falling. . . . I snapped to my senses just in time. I put a finger on his lips, stopping the kiss.

He sighed. "You're a very contrary woman; you know

that, Lamour. You give a guy all the right signals . . . and then you pull back. Why, *carina*? It's only a kiss between friends."

"In that case, you may give me a friendly kiss right here," I said, tapping my cheek. And he did and we both laughed.

"I've had such a good time tonight, Nico," I said, meaning it, because he had made me forget all my problems.

He wanted to walk me to my front door, but I wouldn't let him. I wondered later whether it was because I wasn't sure that if I did I wouldn't succumb to that kiss after all and maybe another . . . and then . . . It was better this way.

THIRTY-NINE

Lamour

THE NEXT MORNING I CAME TO MY SENSES AND AD-mitted there was a possibility that Lorenzo was not lying and Jon-Boy had not bought the house. I mulled this over with my morning coffee while watching a small flotilla of sailboats skim the bay, bowled along by a brisk little wind that fluttered the leaves of the olive trees and sent my hair flying.

My only way out would be to offer to buy the house. I'd tell Lorenzo he could set the price and there would be no haggling. I sighed. I knew he would refuse. Lorenzo did not want me here and I was sure it had something to do with Jon-Boy, and much as I hated the idea, I knew the only way to find out might be through his diary.

It took another hour and a lot more caffeine before I could bring myself to mount the stairs, go to his room, and unlock the drawer with the diary. Even then, I couldn't sit at the desk where he'd written it. Instead I took it into the garden, hoping that sunlight and the fresh breeze would dispel any "ghosts."

In the peaceful belvedere, shaded from the sun, I ran my hand over the fine dark blue leather, imagining my father choosing his diary in some smart Roman shop. He'd always loved shopping for expensive things. Even when we were poor I remembered him buying the travel clock. "It's not sim-ply what you buy," he'd told me as we hovered over Cartier's gleaming glass counters. "It's the whole shopping experience.

Look how they treat us. Here you are always a *tesoro*, a little treasure, and I am automatically a 'gentleman.'"

I'd absorbed his words, the way I always did, smiling politely at the sales assistant, a gap-toothed "little treasure," chewing nervously on my pigtail, hoping Jon-Boy had enough money to pay for the clock. I suppose that day he must have, because that clock became ours. It's on his night table today, and I never forgot his lesson in the fine art of shopping.

Ruffling through the diary's gold-edged pages, I found that the entries became sparse after the first month, where he'd written about being swept off his feet by the beautiful "C" and about poor "I," the woman scorned. It picked up again with a single entry in April.

My life has changed, Jon-Boy wrote. *I'm like a man in a dream, a lover waiting for his woman to call. When she does not I'm cast into despair. How can this be? How can I allow her to rule my life? The answer is simple. I want her. I need her. I need to be around her, to catch her eye across the room at a party the way I did that first night, when we recognized each other and sought each other out. There was no hesitation, no waiting; we simply left and walked through snowy Rome holding hands until we came to the apartment and the bed where we could make love.*

I've always considered myself an honorable man, the kind who never chased after another man's wife, but this time I had no choice. This was destiny and my fate was already sealed. Of course "C" has her own busy social life with her rich husband that she will not give up, and so I am condemned to wait until she can see me. I prowl my apartment, imagining her with other men, flirting, seducing as only she can. My mind no longer functions in that separate way it did when I wrote my novel, when I could switch off reality, forget my surroundings, and simply immerse myself in the lives of the characters I was creating. There are no longer any fictional people in my head for me to make "real." They are gone, along with all rational thought.

My poor "I" is worried. I see it in her eyes, in the tiny frown con-stantly between her brows, in the way she tries too hard to be quiet when I'm sitting at my desk. She creeps around like a little mouse afraid of being stepped on by the big bad cat. And that's exactly who I have become. Do I still love her? I've asked myself that question a thousand times since January, and I believe the answer is yes, I do. I hold her in my arms, comfort her, sometimes we even make love, but it is over. I am helpless before the force that is "C." God help me, I think soon I shall have to face "I" and tell her good-bye, but I do not want to hurt her. Somehow it will be easier to take the coward's way out and let her come to the conclusion that it is finished, allow her the dignity of making the decision to leave.

Meanwhile, "C" has just called and I will see her tonight. She's throwing a party for a famous Italian author she would like me to meet. I asked why, since she obviously knew there was to be a party, she hadn't invited me earlier. Without saying that the author was a prizewinner and far more distinguished than I, she merely told me she hadn't thought I would enjoy it. And besides, her husband was giving the party, not her. Would I still go? Lured by the promise of what might come after, of course I would.

My father was obviously madly in love with "C," though I wasn't sure it was reciprocated. That is, until I read the entry for the following day:

"C" acted so jealous last night, hanging on to my arm and keep-ing me carefully away from other (beautiful) women, in spite of the fact that her husband was there, observing as always. I suspect this is not the first time "C" has strayed, though she swears that's not true. The famous Italian author was lionized, praised, applauded, while I kept to the background with my constantly filled glass of vodka ("C's" drink, to which she has now turned me on), getting quietly smashed. I felt ashamed to show my face because I'm not working at my craft, not pursuing my dream, not going anywhere. . . . I asked myself how this could go on, told myself it would have to end, that

tomorrow I would be back at my desk with all thoughts of "C" ban-
ished, with only work and the still-to-be-created characters of my
next novel awaiting their souls. There is definitely something godlike
in what I do, birthing people whose destinies only I control. Would
that I had the same control over my own.

In the end, when people finally began to leave the party, "C"
caught my eye across the room, the way she always does. She nod-
ded and smiled, and taking my cue, I said my good-byes and walked
quickly through the rainy streets to the small apartment I'd rented
nearby. An hour later, she arrived in a rustle of silk taffeta and a scat-
ter of raindrops, her luscious mouth already smiling. Cole Porter was
playing on the radio and her scent invaded the room and candles
flickered. She was in my arms and I could ask for nothing more.
Everything was forgotten except "C" and the moment.

I closed the diary, keeping my finger in the page, because I
knew I needed to read more. My sigh came from the depths
of my heart. Jon-Boy had been lost to love or infatuation or
whatever the emotion was he'd felt for the mysterious woman
"C." His mind was fragmented. His work had been the most
important thing for him. Writing was what he did, who he
was. Without it he'd become a pawn in "C's" grasping and
beautiful hands. And what of the poor "I," the woman who
was about to be dismissed from his life? She was no longer
important. Only "C."

I flicked through the other pages, most of them empty. It
seemed Jon-Boy had not been able to write his journal, either. But yes, here was another entry. In October, the month
he had died. And in it, I was startled to see my own name.

If it were not for Lamour, he wrote, *I could say that happiness has*
completely deserted me. But I get her letters, or I hear her familiar voice
on the phone, I get that old tug at the heartstrings and I find myself
smiling. Perhaps I was wrong to leave her. I never asked her how she
felt; I thought she was okay with the Mortimers, who love her like

their own. What I never fully understood was, no matter who else loves her, I am her father and my love counts most. All those early years, it was just Lamour and me against the world. With success I moved out of that world, and now I regret it. How simple life was then, how easy and rational. Now I'm confused, unable to write. . . . I'm only able to find a remnant of that old happiness when I remember being with her at the house in Amalfi. Maybe next week, or the week after . . . or the one after that . . . I'll call and say, "Hey, Lamour why not come out and join me? Let's catch up on our lives; let's be the way we used to, just you and me together, here at our house." For a while at least, that is, because I know ultimately I'm going to lose her to some handsome young guy who'll make her a whole lot happier than her fucked-up father. And so be it.

It was the final entry. I closed the diary and went back upstairs and locked it away in Jon-Boy's desk. I was devastated that he had never made that call. How different our lives might have been if he had.

FORTY

Lamour

I DECIDED TO SEND A POLITE NOTE TO LORENZO, via Mifune, apologizing for being rude and explaining that I'd been shocked and upset. I said that I hoped it might be possible for me to buy the house where my father and I had been so happy and that it would mean a lot to me. Then, remembering Lorenzo didn't seem to want me around, I added that I would have to be in Chicago several months a year, for my business. Fingers crossed, I waited for his response.

A week passed. Mifune told me Lorenzo was not at the Castello and Nico didn't seem to be around, either. I missed him dropping in to see me, taking me out of myself and out on the town, making me laugh.

Meanwhile, I was in house limbo. But I wasn't defeated, and to prove it to myself I drove to the marina in Sorrento recommended by Mifune and bought myself a boat. She was ten years old—a mere child in boat terms, I told myself confidently, and just big enough to hold me and one passenger and the shopping. The outboard motor was a bit balky when first tried, but then it sprang to life with a satisfying noise and I positively flew across the crowded marina, receiving warning honks and glares from other sailors. I commissioned my little boat to be painted my favorite shade of blue, with the name "The Lady Lamour" in gold shadowed in black so it would stand out.

I had burned my financial boats, but remembering Jon-Boy's shopping tips, I enjoyed every moment of the transaction. I even enjoyed paying for it. I told myself I'd just have to go to work again and make more money. Meanwhile, I had my nest egg from the sale of the apartment, which I hoped would cover the cost of the Amalfi house. That is, if Lorenzo Pirata would ever get back to me and agree.

FORTY-ONE

ANOTHER WEEK WENT BY AND STILL NO RESPONSE from Lorenzo. I said nothing to Mifune. Working in the garden with him, I knew he was watching me, saw that he felt what I was feeling. He understood why I needed the house and what I was searching for and I was comforted, knowing somehow he would help me find it.

"Patience, *cara*," he said to me as I prowled restlessly. "One day all will be resolved." I wished I could be as sure.

Meanwhile, my new refrigerator was not delivered. Nor my washer and dryer. Then came a strong note from *il architetto*, stating that there was erosion of the cliff that would have to be dealt with—at great expense. Plus the septic tank would have to be replaced. And perhaps also there might be some structural problem at the rear of the house, where it abutted the cliff. Enclosed was an astronomical bill, far exceeding the amount I had been quoted for the inspection.

Plus my chickens had yet to lay a single egg. They ate in a frenzy, then disappeared into their expensive new wooden coop to snooze on their nests, while Mr. Rooster patrolled the perimeter of the cage like a prison guard, crowing every now and then to let me know he was boss.

I was going to have to give the little buggers their freedom, then see if they laid. But the thought of facing Mr. Rooster out in the open was daunting, and I put off the freedom ploy until later.

No progress was being made on any front. I was on hold until Lorenzo gave me an answer.

Still, my little golden house wrapped its old charm about me as I struggled to get it back in shape. Then one fine blue morning, the truck with my new appliances arrived. Two burly deliverymen in blue boilersuits appeared at the top of the *scalatinella,* one clasping the washer in his arms, the other the dryer.

I stared, unbelieving, at them, edging crabwise down the steps, vast arms wrapped around the appliances. I saw the second man miss a step, wobble frantically sideways, then still clutching the dryer fall forward onto his friend, who in turn lurched forward. He flung his arms out to save himself, letting go of the washer, which crashed onward down the steps. Bouncing nicely, the dryer followed.

The two men sat in a heap, dusting themselves off, while my washer and dryer, now a mangled heap, lay useless at the bottom of the steps.

"Scusi, perdona, signora," they said, getting up and inspecting themselves for cuts and bruises, "but do you have a Band-Aid?"

"A Band-Aid," I yelled, getting my voice back, because previously they had rendered me speechless. "You want a *Band-Aid*? Just look at my new washer! It's ruined. They're both ruined!"

They turned to stare at the mangled heap. "*Calmo, calmo, signora,* is nothing that cannot be fixed," one said soothingly.

"Fixed? You want to *fix* this heap of junk? No, I'll have to call your boss."

They marched back up the steps while I paced, wondering gloomily who was going to end up paying for this, suspecting it was myself. Five minutes later, they appeared at the top of the *scalatinella,* this time holding my refrigerator between them.

"Stop! Stop!" I waved my arms frantically. "Don't you have a dolly or something to get the refrigerator down the steps?"

"Ah, sì, sì, signora," they said, and muttering under his breath, one man abruptly abandoned his end, leaving the other straining to hold the refrigerator alone.

I closed my eyes. At this rate I would soon be ruined.

The other deliveryman came back with a too-small dolly. Amid more muttering they heaved the refrigerator onto it. I held my breath as they edged it step-by-step down the cliff side and onto the terrace. I breathed again. Okay, so at least I would have a refrigerator. I led them to the front door, carefully pointing out the step. As they maneuvered over it I saw my new refrigerator tilt to the left. Then the right. Then left again. . . . I flung myself against it, desperately trying to stabilize it. It was no good. It came crashing down. Only this time on my foot.

"Jeez," I gasped, hopping backward, my face contorted with pain. "Now look what you've done."

"Perdona, signora," the larger one said solemnly, "but it was your fault. You should not have grabbed hold of it; we had it perfectly under control. . . ."

It didn't pay to argue; I knew I would have to face that with the owner of the store where I'd bought the appliances. Meanwhile, my injured refrigerator was maneuvered into place in the kitchen. It stood there, chipped and battered, but at least when it was plugged in it worked. I was almost happy to settle for that.

I said good-bye to my trusty workforce, then hopped upstairs to the bathroom to soak my injured foot in a tub of cold water, because of course I did not yet have ice. Bitterly I inspected my swollen foot. Nothing, *absolutely nothing*, was going right in my life. And this time even Nico wasn't around to commiserate with me.

But Aurora Pirata was.

FORTY-TWO

SHE WAS SITTING ON THE BENCH OUTSIDE MY DOOR, legs crossed, head flung back, arms spread along the curved tiles, looking like a photo in a fashion magazine. That this girl didn't know she was beautiful staggered me. She could have been a *Vogue* model any day.

I said a cautious, if surprised, hello. She nodded her head and said *"ciao"* back.

"I'm surprised to find you here, Aurora," I said, because she made no attempt to start the conversation or to tell me why she was here.

"I thought I'd tell you I'm asking my father to give me this house," she said in that fast voice she used sometimes. I thought it meant she was nervous, but there was also something manic about her at times like this. "I'll tell him I want it so when I get married I'll have my children here. Of course you know he'll give it to me, Lamour. He can't refuse me anything."

Anger flared. I'd had it with Aurora and her father. "Great," I snapped. "Then you can also have the new washer and dryer. They're lying at the bottom of the stairs, or didn't you notice? And you can have the damned chickens as well."

"What chickens?" she asked so sweetly she stopped me in my angry tracks.

I looked suspiciously at her, but she seemed suddenly genuinely interested.

"I kept chickens when I was a little girl," she said, all quick enthusiasm. "My mother and I together. They were white and the babies were adorable. I know all about how to look after chickens."

"Terrific. Then you'll have no problems with these," I snapped, unmoved by her new sweet tone.

"Oh."

She looked so downcast that despite my anger I felt sorry for her. The girl was like a ball of mercury, splitting in a dozen different directions at once. I couldn't keep up with her moods. But I still knew that she didn't like me and didn't want me around.

"Anyway, I'm sure you're right about your father," I added. "I doubt he'll deny you anything."

She got to her feet, a swift, graceful movement that took my breath away. I thought she should have been a ballet dancer, standing there so slender and elegant, looking sadly at me now.

"Thank you for listening to me," she said with a subdued kind of dignity. I watched her go, saw her stop and stare at the broken refrigerator. Then she walked slowly up the *scalatinella*, back, I supposed, to the Castello. She seemed to have forgotten all about the chickens.

I thought my ownership of the little house was in even more jeopardy than before.

FORTY-THREE

I COULD WAIT NO LONGER FOR LORENZO'S ANSWER.
I decided to go see him. Massimo answered the door. "I'll
find out if the signore is available," he said.

I lingered in the Pompeian red hall, checking out the
paintings, until Massimo came back and told me the *signore*
was home. Instead of leading me into the *salone*, Massimo
took me back down the steps and around the terrace to the
stone tower.

I found myself alone in a room lined floor-to-ceiling with
shelves of books, with tall, narrow windows set high in the
stone walls. The ugly dog came and licked my hand. She
wagged her tail sweetly and I melted. At least one of the Piratas was friendly.

Lorenzo came down the stairs. "Come, sit down, Lamour,"
he said in a friendly tone. He was wearing his old paint-
spattered shorts and a red polo shirt and I thought he looked
like an ad for Ralph Lauren, one of those classy guys who in-
habit old mansions on Long Island's North Shore, where
Gatsby lived. Lorenzo was too handsome to be believed. But
believe him I did when he said, "I know why you are here,
Lamour. I'm sorry not to have replied sooner, but I was away
on business—New York, then Paris. . . ." He shrugged. "I'm
glad to be back home again."

He sat back in his leather chair behind his desk, twirling a pen in his fingers. "I appreciated your note," he said quietly. "But I'm afraid I cannot change my position. I cannot sell you the house."

Seeing my stricken face, he said, "I'm sorry, Lamour; it's simply not possible. But I hope you will enjoy the rest of your stay."

I was a fool ever to have put myself in this position. We stood a foot apart, each searching the other's face. I felt a pang of regret that I had to be on the wrong side of this man, because he was interesting in a way I had never encountered before.

"I don't know when I'll leave," I said. "If ever. And if that makes me your enemy, then so be it."

Lorenzo bowed his head in acceptance. He walked me to the door.

"Good-bye, Lamour Harrington," he said.

I thought I saw a glimpse of sadness on his face, but it was gone so fast I couldn't be sure. "Good-bye," I said in a choked voice; then I strode back down the path to the little house that was mine no longer.

FORTY-FOUR

Lorenzo

LATER THAT EVENING, ALONE IN HIS HOUSE, Lorenzo Pirata wrestled with his conscience. Lamour's stricken face was imprinted on his memory. He hadn't expected her to be so vulnerable, nor had he anticipated how much she would be hurt.

He saw Mifune tending the garden, half-hidden under his conical straw hat that now seemed too large for his delicate frame. As always, Lorenzo was struck with a pang of tenderness for the old man who probably knew him better than anyone ever had except for his wife, Marella. In fact, there was nothing Mifune didn't know, and that's why Lorenzo sought him out now.

"*Buona sera*, Mifune," he said. "Will you come sit with me for a while? I need to talk to you."

Mifune took a seat next to him on a stone bench at the side of the path. Affare lay at Lorenzo's feet, alert for his next move.

"I told Lamour I couldn't sell her the house," Lorenzo said. "She was devastated. I hadn't realized how much she cared."

"Lamour remembers only happiness there, signore," Mifune said. "The house brings back memories she treasures. It was a shock when she heard Jon-Boy did not own the house, but she still believed you would let her have it. And ask yourself, signore, if Jon-Boy were alive, would he not, after all, still be living there?"

Lorenzo acknowledged that he would.

"Then you must see that the idea that she could live in her father's house is valid," Mifune said. "You and I both know the reason why she should not, signore. But so much is forgotten in the flow of water in the river of time, surely now you could bend just a little and allow her this small happiness."

Lorenzo heaved a deep sigh. "Mifune, you always manage to put things straight in my mind," he said. Getting to his feet, he bowed to the old man.

Mifune smiled. "It is merely a process of logic and meditation," he said calmly. "Everything has a solution. You must let it float into the clear mind, then grasp it while you are able."

"I'll do that, Mifune," Lorenzo promised, and with Affare at his heels, he strode back to the Castello.

He thought that unlike him, Lamour had nothing to hide. She was simply an innocent woman searching for happiness. He had no right to keep her from that.

FORTY-FIVE

Lamour

AFTER A RESTLESS NIGHT FACING UP TO THE TRUTH that I could no longer live in my little house, I was wakened with the dawn by Mr. Rooster, bellowing fit to bust, and right outside my window, it seemed.

I leaped out of bed and ran to look. There he was sitting on the tiled bench, pecking at the bougainvillea. His harem shuffled around him, messing on my new cushions and squawking contentedly.

Obviously I hadn't latched the gate securely last night after I'd fed them. Damn, oh damn, damn, damn! . . . I'd never get those stains off the cushions. I didn't stop to think that it wouldn't matter anymore anyway, nor would the battered washer and dryer sitting at the bottom of the *scalatinella,* like in a white-trash-family backyard.

I flung on an old gray T-shirt and shorts and ran downstairs barefoot. The hens glanced up, then went back to their pecking, but Mr. Rooster tilted his head sideways and gave me a nasty one-eyed glare. He left no doubt in my mind that war had been declared. It was him or me.

Ignoring him, I grabbed the first hen, tucked her wings under, and held her fast. The nasty little creature still managed to give me a series of hearty pecks as I ran to the coop and shoved her in, slamming the gate and securing the loop of wire that held it shut. I ran back to the terrace. One down, four to go.

The hens were smarter than I'd thought. They'd gotten wise and scattered throughout the garden. Only Mr. Rooster still perched angrily atop the bench, Lord and Master of all he surveyed.

I picked out hen number two, herding her in front of me in the direction of the coop. All was well until she made a sudden sideways swoop and I swooped right after her. I landed in the dust, clutching the screeching hen by her ankles—if hens have ankles, that is; anyway it was the bit above her horrible yellow feet.

"I hate you too," I yelled as she flapped and struggled, "but you're going back in there if I have to kill you to do it."

I heard laughter. I looked up and saw Affare bounding toward the chickens, yelping in delight, and Lorenzo standing on the *scalatinella*, watching me. It was all I needed!

Lorenzo called Affare off, and she sat hungrily watching the chickens. "Still haven't gotten the knack of corralling those hens, huh?" he said.

I scrambled to my feet still clutching the furious hen. "They escaped," I said icily. "But there's no need to worry; I'll have them back in there in no time." I was lying of course, but I wasn't about to allow him to get the edge on me again. I was the independent woman, right?

Lorenzo grabbed the chicken from me. He tucked in her wings and held them down, and dammit if that mean piece of poultry didn't just sit there in his arms, as though she had never squawked and pecked at me in her too-long life.

"I wouldn't even *eat* that damned chicken," I said, disgusted.

There was a smile in Lorenzo's eyes as he looked at me and I remembered I was straight out of bed, hair uncombed, face unwashed, teeth unbrushed. I wasn't even showered, and now I was covered in dust and feathers. It was the story of my life, having him see me at my worst and just when I needed to present a strong image, the cool, perfect woman.

Tears of frustration lurked behind my eyes, but I was damned if I'd let them flow. I was drained by the past few months, exhausted and ready to admit defeat. I couldn't do battle with the Pirata family; the house was theirs, and with it went all my dreams. Had it not been for Mifune, always there to offer advice and consolation, to regenerate my spirit, I would have called it quits long ago. Now I had no choice.

I watched Lorenzo pen the rooster. "So why are you here?" I demanded. "I thought you'd never want to see me again, now you've finally managed to get rid of me."

Lorenzo put the last two chickens in the coop and latched the gate. "I've come to make peace, Lamour," he said quietly.

"What d'you mean, peace? You expect us to be friends now?"

Lorenzo pulled a sheaf of papers from the pocket of his shorts. I stared suspiciously at what looked like a legal document, sealed with red wax and stamped with the Pirata crest with the battlemented tower and the skull and crossbones. I looked warily at him.

"This is your new lease," he said. "The Amalfi house is yours for as long as you wish to live in it."

I gasped. I didn't believe him. It was some kind of joke. "It's not true," I said, sounding childlike instead of like the smart cookie I prided myself on being.

"It's true."

I grabbed the document and skimmed it quickly. It really was a lease, and in my name. It was signed by Lorenzo *and* witnessed. "But why?" I asked, puzzled.

"It's for you—in memory of your father," he replied, suddenly serious. "But it comes with one condition."

My hackles rose; surely he was not going to play the old-fashioned squire and say what I thought he was going to say.

"That you agree to have dinner with me tonight, at the Castello," he said.

I laughed with relief that he wasn't going to pull the old squires' rights thing on me. "I'd love to. And thank you. Thank you, thank you, oh, *thank you*." I was brimming with gratitude; I'd have done anything for him at that moment. Well, almost *anything*.

"Then tonight at eight," he said, walking away, with the ugly dog running after him.

He turned at the *scalatinella* to inspect the wreckage. "Some new form of modern sculpture?" he asked, and I could hear him laughing as he ran lightly back up the stairs, like the young man I knew he believed he was in his heart.

FORTY-SIX

IT WAS A PERFECT NIGHT, SOFT AS CASHMERE, WITH a pale sliver of a moon and stars like sequins sewn onto the dark blue sky. I took my time dressing for dinner with Lorenzo Pirata. This time it wasn't to be about "business"; we were moving from enemies to cautious friends. I wondered what we would talk about now that we were no longer fighting over the house.

I slipped into my pretty coral dress, my *only* dress, the one I'd bought with Jammy in Rome. My skin had acquired a peachy glow from the sun, and checking in the mirror, I thought I looked pretty good. A spritz of the Jo Malone honeysuckle and I was ready.

Carrying my expensive red-suede mules so as not to get them dusty, I walked up the hillside, through the trees, and along the sandy path, lit by perfect Art Nouveau iron lamps in the shape of lilies. I was thinking about the man I was about to have dinner with. He was interesting and definitely attractive, older and experienced. Lorenzo knew his way around the world and was sure of his place in it.

Massimo was waiting by the open door and this time he smiled as he said, *"Buona sera,"* and ushered me through the hall onto the terrace. Lorenzo was there, with Affare at his side.

Smiling, he came toward me, arms outstretched. He took both my hands in his. "Welcome," he said, and he looked deep into my eyes. I fluttered my eyelashes, embarrassed; then he offered me a glass of champagne. We strolled to the edge of the terrace, looking at the coast, strung like a queen's necklace with diamond lights. There was only us and about a million crickets, a tree frog or two, and the twitter of a late-to-bed bird.

"This is the kind of 'silence' I remember from when I was a child," I said. "It's the most beautiful sound in the world."

"To me, it means home," he said.

Soon Massimo came to tell us dinner was ready. We sat across a table draped in pale green linen with rustic burnt orange chargers, amber goblets, and tiger lilies in a silver urn. Lorenzo poured the wine, a Barolo from Tuscany, while Massimo served.

I was so caught up in the magic of the setting, the perfect starry night, and the man opposite me, I hardly noticed the food. I drank my wine and smiled at Lorenzo.

"I've met you before," he said. I raised my brows in a question. "When you were a child."

"Really?" I didn't remember him at all.

"Of course then, I didn't really know Jon-Boy. I'd see him occasionally in the village, usually at the Amalfitano."

I leaned an elbow on the table, cupping my chin in my hand, interested. "So how did we meet?"

"It was on a hot summer evening. I was climbing down the steps to the cove when something out at sea caught my eye. At first I thought it was a dolphin, but then I realized it was a head bobbing in the water, far out in the bay. I looked through my binoculars and saw it was a child. I raced down those steps and fired up the speedboat—"

"It was silver," I remembered, laughing, "and faster than a speeding bullet—just like Superman. And there was always a yellow rubber dinghy with an outboard motor moored next to it at the jetty. I used to take that out when no one was around."

"Then I'm only glad you didn't also have a go at the speed-boat," Lorenzo said drily.

I grinned. "So what happened that day?"

"I circled you in the boat, yelling what did you think you were doing, alone in the water, so far from shore?"

I could remember the coolness of the evening sea and how infinitely strong I had felt, strong enough to swim to Pirata and back if I'd wanted. . . . I was queen of the sea. . . .

But Lorenzo didn't think so. He said, "You were yelling at me to go away. 'Can't you see I'm trying to swim across the bay?' you yelled back at me. I thought you were filled with way too much sass and self-importance for such a skinny lit-tle whelp of a girl."

"I put my thumbs in my ears and wiggled my fingers at you." I snickered, remembering.

"You also stuck out your tongue. But by then I was so mad I just grabbed you by the arm and hauled you in like the dumb little fish I told you you were."

"Of *course*! I remember you now!" I saw him clearly as he was then: young and handsome, with dark hair and blue eyes. "I remember your eyes," I said. "They fixed me like two lethal steel points. They haven't changed," I added.

"And I remember your ratty red bathing suit; it was full of holes."

"That was my favorite," I said indignantly. "I'd had it for a couple of years, it was way too small, but I wore it every day that summer."

"The holes showed your skinny bottom," he said, and I groaned.

"My entire wardrobe consisted of a pair of shorts, a couple of T-shirts and a pair of sandals that were too small, so I just went barefoot. I can't even recall any underwear," I added without thinking.

He laughed and I blushed.

"Jon-Boy never had much money," I explained. "Of course when he got some he'd spend it in style: dinner at good restaurants in Rome, wine and grappa for everyone at the Amalfitano. I guess he just didn't think too much about my clothes as long as I seemed happy. And I certainly didn't care. After all, there was no mother there to complain about the way I looked."

Lorenzo nodded; he knew all about Jon-Boy. He said, "Anyhow, I fished you out of the water and got you back to shore, with you protesting all the way that you were going to tell Jon-Boy and that he'd soon put me straight. You said besides, you were a darn good swimmer and could easily beat me if I cared to race across the bay."

"Now I remember I asked you who did you think you were anyway? King of the world? Little did I know," I added with a glance at our surroundings, "that you *truly were*."

"Remember how I hauled you along the jetty? Your eyes were red and your hair was full of sand, and you looked like an unkempt mermaid." He was laughing at me now. "I got the hose and turned it on you. You yelled loud enough to wake the dead."

"That water was *icy*!"

"You looked like a little gypsy. Skinny and brown and big eyed. A waif with no clothes." He looked at me. "You haven't changed much; I still see a bit of the waif there."

I brushed back my hair with an exaggerated sigh. "I was hoping for more of a retro, Audrey Hepburn look."

He leaned closer, his face near mine. "I see a bit of that, too, now I look."

Our linked eyes sparked little flames of reflected candlelight.

"Why did you really come here, Lamour?" he asked, suddenly serious.

I didn't have to think twice about the answer. I told him that because of Jon-Boy and the free way he'd lived I'd become a free spirit, too. And that all those years in Chicago I'd been holding myself back. When I finally came back here, to the Amalfi house, I knew there was hope of finding "freedom" again. "Freedom," I said. "And happiness."

"And have you found them?"

"I'm still searching. Sometimes happiness eludes you because you're not looking in the right place," I said. Then I smiled. "I think I must be quoting Mifune."

"A wise man."

"Tell me what you know about Jon-Boy," I said.

"I'd rather talk about you. Who you are, what you are?"

"I suspect you already know all about me."

"But only you can tell me about the *true* you, Lamour." He was very serious now. "And believe me, I want to know everything about you."

No man, not even my husband, had ever been this curious about me. My relationship with Alex had always been about him. It was I who'd asked the questions, I who had found *him* fascinating. In fact, I was so unused to talking about myself, I didn't know quite where to begin.

"So, you know about me and Jon-Boy—," I finally said, but Lorenzo cut me short.

"I know you loved your father and that he loved you. Tell me who else you loved, Lamour?"

My mouth tightened; I didn't want him to know about Alex and how vulnerable I really was. "It's too personal . . . ," I protested.

"But you are a person and I am another person and we are talking to each other as new friends, are we not?"

I stared down at my nervously clenched hands. "Okay, so I was married once," I said. "He died a couple of years ago in a car crash." I heard Lorenzo's shocked indrawn breath but went quickly on. "Alex was rich, selfish, handsome. I thought he loved me, and oh, how I loved him. But all the time he was cheating on me, planning on divorcing me to marry another woman." I shrugged away the old wound, but the scar was still fresh and I knew it showed. "So, that's who I am. A thirty-eight-year-old woman too dumb to know her husband had fallen out of love with her and that she was no longer wanted."

He waited for me to continue.

"I suppose I came here in part to get over it," I added. "You see, I didn't know about Alex until my friend told me just a few months ago."

"And why did she tell you, after all this time?"

"Because I was still mourning Alex. I'd put my life on hold. There was just my work . . . and . . . well, nothing else really."

He reached sympathetically across the table for my hand. "You were right to mourn. After all, you loved him. The fact that he wasn't worthy of your love was his loss. And now, look at you, here in Amalfi, starting a new life."

I liked the way his hand felt on mine, hard, like a working-man's, warm and comforting. "I'm looking for happiness again," I said quietly. "The kind of happiness I knew when I was a little kid, here with my father."

We talked late under the moonlight on the terrace. Lorenzo was a good listener. I knew he understood about my life and my need to change. Looking at him, so strong, so handsome, so wise, I felt a pull of attraction for the older man. He was everything a woman could desire. But not for me. For me, he would just be my friend.

"Hey, hey, hey, what have we here? A romantic tryst by candlelight?" Nico's mocking voice cut through the still night, followed by a burst of laughter as a bunch of smart young people came running up the steps. They stood on the terrace, looking at us.

I snatched my hand guiltily from Lorenzo's.

"Papa, who are you with?" Aurora was breathtakingly lovely in a deep turquoise dress and flat Grecian sandals with thin satin straps that wrapped around her slim legs. Her long dark hair was pulled back in a high ponytail and her brown eyes blazed with jealousy.

"I'm having dinner with a friend," Lorenzo said calmly. "Lamour, allow me to introduce my daughter, Aurora. I believe you already know my son, Nico."

"Hello, Aurora. And yes, I do know Nico," I said, but the girl simply turned her back and walked away.

"How are you, Lamour?" Nico dropped a kiss on my cheek as though to show his father we were more intimate than he knew.

I pushed back my chair, aware of the group of beautiful young people, still watching, still giggling. "It's getting late," I said.

And taking my elbow, Lorenzo escorted me back through the house and down the front steps to the garden.

"Don't get into any trouble now, you two," I heard Nico shout after us, followed by more gales of laughter.

I strode angrily along the sandy path down the hill to the cliff. I couldn't wait to get home.

"I'm sorry they embarrassed you," Lorenzo apologized. "They are just children playing."

"They are too old to behave like children. How dare they be so rude?"

He took my arm and turned me to face him. "Nico was

wrong. Of course he shouldn't have said what he did. Because of him, my daughter misread the situation. She was jealous."

"She just doesn't want to see her father with any other woman, no matter how innocent it is," I snapped.

"You're right: she doesn't; she's afraid of losing me. But you, of all people, should understand that."

And of course I did. I sighed, suddenly sympathetic to Aurora, who after all was only twenty-one years old and motherless.

Lorenzo put up his hand and gently stroked my hair back from my hot face. He was so handsome in the moonlight, so strong looking. I was sure Lorenzo would never be afraid of anyone; he would never let any woman down, including his daughter.

"Poor Lamour," he said gently. "You've been through so much."

"There's no need to feel sorry for me," I said coldly.

We walked in silence until we came to the cliff. Below us the sea purred softly, its briny scent mingling with the perfume of the gardens. From his pocket Lorenzo took a small gold key on a black satin cord.

"It's a key to the elevator," he said, and taking my elbow he walked me to a pair of doors set flush into the rock face, flanked by a pair of pointed cypresses in white wooden tubs. "I couldn't bear to think you might fall on the worn old steps," he said, "so in future I want you to take the elevator. Please," he added as I began to protest. "Do it as a favor to me, Lamour. Even though they are lit, the steps could be dangerous at night."

Suddenly shy, all I could think of to say was "thank you."

I was suddenly weary. I wanted to be back in my little house, alone with my thoughts.

As the elevator doors closed on me, Lorenzo inclined his head in a brief good-bye. I looked wistfully back at him, like the wide-eyed waif I had been all those years ago, the first time he met me. When he had been a young man, not much older than his son, Nico, was now.

FORTY-SEVEN

NICO SHOWED UP THE NEXT MORNING. HE GLANCED at the broken appliances, then at me. "Having a good day?" he said with a grin.

"Not so far," I snapped. "And especially since you arrived."

"Whoa, whoa." He held up a protesting hand. "So what did I do wrong?"

"Why don't you ask yourself that question?"

He walked toward where I was sitting on the tiled bench, but I turned away.

"Come on, Lamour; it was just a bit of teasing." He put his hand on my arm, where I felt it burn like the hot coals of sin.

"You embarrassed me and you certainly were disrespectful to your father," I said. I went on to tell him angrily that I thought that he was a spoiled rich kid who'd always had everything and knew nothing of the real world. "Surely your mother taught you good manners," I finished heatedly.

Nico sighed. "She did. And I apologize. And you're right, she would have been ashamed of me and of Aurora, though Aurora always has an excuse. But I have none."

I caught his eye and I laughed. "You're outrageous; you know that, don't you?" I said, still laughing, and he admitted yes, he did, and I agreed to go with him to the Amalfitano for lunch.

We powered across the bay in his Riva, hair flying, drenched with spray, arriving at the jetty laughing. I didn't laugh, though, when I saw the same bunch of chic young people from last night already taking up several tables. And of course I was in old shorts and a T-shirt, windblown and wet from spray.

"I think I've just changed my mind," I said, but Nico gripped my arm firmly. It was too late to escape; we were there by now. "This is my good friend Lamour Harrington," he said. "She's a famous landscape architect and daughter of the even more famous Jon-Boy Harrington, whose novel you have, of course, all read."

Fifteen young faces stared at me, surprised. Fifteen young voices said, "*Ciao,* Lamour," and, "Was he really your father?," and, "How do you become a landscape architect?" Soon I found myself sitting in the crowd, talking about myself and Jon-Boy. I also found I was enjoying myself, eating salad and pizza with the twenty-year-olds, though I knew from the respect they gave me—deferring to me, letting me lead the conversation—that I was not one of them.

Still, by the time I got home, I was feeling better about last night. Nico lingered on the terrace obviously dying to stay. I told him I was going to take a siesta.

"Why not a siesta for two?" he suggested, but I laughed and pushed him away. There was something very endearing, though, about Nico Pirata. He walked away, shoulders drooping with feigned sadness, making me smile.

FORTY-EIGHT

LATER, LORENZO PIRATA CAME BY. PLEASED, I SAID, "It's my turn to welcome you. And to say thank you for last night. It was . . ." I searched for the right word. I came up with "perfect." And I meant it.

"It was my pleasure." He hesitated, and I thought, surprised, he looked suddenly shy. Then he said, "I came to ask if you had ever visited the gardens at the Villa Cimbrone, in Ravello."

I thought of my barhopping dinner in Ravello with Nico but decided against telling him about that. "They're famous," I said, "but I've never seen them."

"Then why don't I show you? And you can impress me with your knowledge of the exotic plants and trees."

Secretly flattered, I pretended to think it over. "What else do I have to do today?" I asked. Then I beamed at him. "Absolutely nothing more important than seeing the Cimbrone gardens. With you," I added.

"Then let's go," he said, pleased.

So I grabbed a straw sun hat, a bag, my camera, and my lipstick. Ignoring the elevator, we climbed back up the cliff together. He held out his hand to help me up the last few steps and hauled me, laughing, to the top. We were as easy together as two old friends. Of course he hadn't yet told me what he knew about Jon-Boy, but I would work on that.

He drove a BMW convertible sports car, small enough to maneuver through the narrow medieval streets, but he kept the top up because, he said, he didn't want me to burn my beautiful skin, which somehow made me feel pampered. He handled the car well, not driving like a maniac the way Nico did, cornering smoothly with no screeching of tires. I watched Lorenzo's hands on the wheel, strong golden-brown hands with long fingers and a sprinkling of dark hair. I wondered what those hands might feel like running through a girl's hair, on her naked back as he held her close. I sat up straighter. What was I *thinking*! I started talking knowledgeably about the gardens we were to visit.

"I know they were designed by an Englishman, a Lord Grimthorpe, in the early nineteen hundreds," I said. And they're said to be the most beautiful in Italy. Though of course personally I'm prejudiced in favor of the Castello's gardens."

"Ravello has been a refuge for many famous people," he told me. "Greta Garbo ran away here with the conductor Leopold Stokowski. Jackie Kennedy took private vacations at the Villa Rufolo, and many writers came here, Tennessee Williams, Gore Vidal—"

"And Jon-Boy Harrington?"

He threw me a quick glance. "And no doubt Jon-Boy Harrington," he added.

We walked up a hilly pathway and stopped at an old wooden door set into a high wall. Lorenzo rang the bell and an ancient attendant let us in. We stood for a minute, looking at the lovely fifteenth-century Villa Cimbrone, restored by the same man who'd designed the gardens, and now a small, quiet hotel.

We took in the beautiful vaulted cloisters and the ruined chapel, allowing the peaceful atmosphere to soak into our souls. There was a special stillness to the air here that seemed to cut out the rest of the world. Impulsively I took Lorenzo's hand, wanting to share the moment with him, the feeling that anything might be possible and the ghosts of the past might appear to show us around their earthly paradise.

The Cimbrone gardens were a half-tamed wilderness that combined the exotic with the charming. There were climbing roses and palm trees, cyclids and cimbidiums, pools and tea pavilions, wild grasses and towering cedars. Perfumes hung in the air, butterflies alighted on perfect blossoms, and humming-birds sipped an abundance of nectar. We strolled down the Grand Allée, a majestic tree-lined path scattered with foun-tains and statues, through the garden to the Belvedere of In-finity, a grand terrace, breathtakingly suspended over the turquoise sea.

Limp with pleasure, I leaned my head against Lorenzo's shoulder. He put an arm around me and we stood silently ab-sorbing the staggering vista, breathing in the perfumes, hear-ing the stillness. Other visitors wandered by, but it was as though we were alone.

Being in the Villa Cimbrone gardens was like being in a great museum: there was so much to see it was only possible to get an overview. Overwhelmed, we strolled back down the shady *allée,* admiring the towering forests of chestnut and ash on the hillsides above and the terraced groves of lemon trees and vineyards. The man whose lovely vision these gardens had been had lived only twelve years to enjoy them, and out of respect we paid a visit to his grave. Lord Grimthorpe is buried beneath a temple of Bacchus, and I thought that this garden, suspended between sea and sky, was the perfect final resting place.

We strolled back down the steep footpath, ending up in the charming little Piazza Duomo, at the Villa Rufolo. Boccaccio wrote about it, that it was built in the thirteenth century in the Moorish style then fashionable from trading with the Moors and the Saracens. There was a Norman tower thrown in for special effect, as well as lush flowery terraces and another view of the Bay of Salerno beautifully framed by twin cupolas of an ancient church shaded by an enormous old umbrella pine.

To our delight we stumbled upon a chamber music concert in the courtyard below the Norman tower and we sat for an hour listening to Bach played exquisitely in a magical setting. Afterward we wandered back through the little town.

"Did you enjoy your day, Lamour?" Lorenzo asked.

I was so happy I wanted to hug him. "I loved every minute of it," I said. "And thank you." I laughed. "It seems I'm always saying thank you to you these days. I'll have to do something for you in return."

"Then have me over for dinner one evening." He was serious. "I'd like that very much."

I told him I was a terrible cook, but he said it didn't matter. "I just like watching your face when you're really interested in something," he said.

"Next Friday. At seven. We can catch the sunset," I said.

"And now we'll have dinner here," he said.

At the Palazzo della Mare, over Bellinis and plates of red-pumpkin seafood risotto, cooked with sage leaves, he told me about his wife.

"We were both so young," he said, smiling as he remembered. "She was the sister of a good friend. He invited me to stay at their house near Genoa. I found three sisters there, each more charming than the other, but Marella was special. There was a simplicity about her that was endearing. She's the only woman I knew who never coveted anything. Not jewels, not clothes, not yachts, not cars or houses. All she wanted was children.

"She loved the Castello and insisted we be married there and not at her family home. We liked all the same things, music, food, our dogs.

"In a way, we grew up together," he said. "I am who I am today partly because of Marella. She tempered my youthful wildness. I always say she civilized me, but she said she wasn't so sure she'd ever quite achieved that."

"Were you like Nico?"

He lifted a surprised eyebrow. "No, never like him. I fell in love young and I stayed that way. Nico is wild. He needs a woman capable of taming him. Right now he's dissipating his talents, his intelligence. Nico is wasting his life. He doesn't understand that youth disappears all too quickly. It's time he started thinking about the future, but I can't get him to change." He shrugged. "Once children are grown, they make their own choices. I have no more say in the matter.

"But Marella and I had an idyllic life together, centered around the Castello. We had a small yacht and in the summer we'd take the children and our friends and sail along the coast, to the south of France, or over to Capri or Ischia." He smiled regretfully. "I count myself lucky to have such happy memories."

He asked me about my life and I told him how I'd lived with the Mortimers and that they were my true family. We talked about music, my work, and his, about food and wine. Time flew by and before we knew it the waiters were hovering, anxious to close.

Lorenzo and I drove back down the mountain to Pirata in comfortable silence. There was an ease between us now that I liked. When we arrived, impulsively I reached up and touched his handsome face. "Good night, friend," I said, and I kissed him lightly on the cheek.

As I ran down the *scalatinella,* I heard him call after me, "Good night, friend." I felt that little thrill, the signal that tells a woman she's interested. *Oh my God,* I thought, *could I be falling for both of them?*

FORTY-NINE

THE FRIDAY MORNING OF MY DINNER WITH Lorenzo, I sailed *The Lady Lamour* to Amalfi. I was pleased with my simple little blue boat; it was basic, but to me it spelled freedom, and unlike Jon-Boy, I loved being on the water.

I purchased a couple of small sea bass right from the fishermen. I bought a melon and raspberries and some fresh cannoli that were so tempting I ate one walking down the street. I bought thin peppery *grissini* and cheeses, Arborio rice, and a bunch of small-leaved arugula. Loaded down, I hurried back to my boat and home.

Jon-Boy had never been much of a cook, and I had inherited his lack of talent. Besides, as a working woman I'd eaten out a lot; there was never time to shop and prepare meals. I found only two knives in the kitchen drawer: a large, serious one and a small serrated one. I took the serious one and attacked the sea bass. I cut it up its stomach and laid it out flat in the butterfly position I vaguely remembered from Mrs. Mortimer's Julia Child cookbook as the best for filleting a fish. I picked tentatively at the bones with the tip of the knife, then impatiently shoved it under the spine. To my astonishment, it slid smoothly out. I never knew what a messy business scraping scales off a fish could be, but I did it, then washed the fish under the tap and patted it dry. I thought it looked quite professional, like fish in a restaurant.

I put the arugula in a pretty cobalt glass bowl I found at the back of a cupboard. I cut the melon into cubes and doused them in Amaretto liqueur; then I added the raspberries. I sautéed the rice in sweet butter, added white wine, then stock, stirring often as the recipe instructed.

In between stirs, I hurried to set the terrace table with my collection of mismatched plates and glasses, pausing only long enough to take in the view. I rushed back to give my risotto more stirs. I read the recipe again. At the last minute, stir in more butter and fresh-ground Parmesan cheese, it said.

I galloped upstairs, took a quick shower, flung on a loose white linen shirt and pants, tied up my hair in a ponytail, put on lipstick and mascara, and was ready for action. Oh, I forgot something. I dashed back for a dab of honeysuckle scent.

Promptly at seven, Affare, bouncing down the steps with happy little yelps, announced Lorenzo's arrival. He handed me an enormous bunch of pink peonies. They were already opening in the heat and promised to be as big as saucers. I thanked him and we smiled, delighted with each other.

I put the flowers in a big blue china bowl—the only thing I could find big enough to hold them—and set them on the table. I had champagne chilling in a galvanized iron garden bucket—Jon-Boy never had fancy silver and I hadn't yet gotten around to buying such luxuries.

Lorenzo popped the cork and poured the wine and we toasted each other, clinking our glasses. I beamed at him. "I'm not a cook," I warned. "This will not be like dinner at the Castello."

He didn't care. "I'll enjoy it because I'm with you," he said.

We wandered down to the belvedere to watch the sunset in its usual fiery glow, which was always followed by a tranquil pink haze; then we came back to the terrace.

He sat at the table and Affare settled next to him on the

yellow cushion. I rushed back to the kitchen just in time to snatch my sea bass from the oven before it became completely charcoal. Dismayed, I sprinkled it with fresh lemon juice and the local dark green olive oil. I stirred butter and Parmesan into my risotto, but somehow it had all stuck to the bottom of the pan, so I just scooped it into a yellow serving bowl and hoped for the best. I dressed my salad with the same oil and a little balsamic, added salt and black pepper, and carried my culinary attempts out to the table.

Lorenzo laughed when he saw me, hot from the stove, hovering nervously over my first home-cooked dinner.

"There's no one I'd rather be sharing it with than you," I said honestly. "I can never thank you enough for . . . all this. . . ." I flung my arms wide. "For my own little paradise."

"No more thanks," he warned. "All that is behind us. We have the future to look forward to."

He poured more wine as I wondered what he meant by that. Then I watched anxiously as he tasted the risotto.

He raised his brows, looking surprised. He said it was as Italian as any Italian could have made it. But when I tried it, it stuck to my teeth. I knew he was only being polite. And my sea bass had burned to death.

I groaned, embarrassed. "It's awful, isn't it?"

"Just a little overcooked. Nothing to worry about. Perhaps next time you should try leaving the bones in," he said. "Fish stays moist that way."

Humiliated, I carried the plates back to the kitchen, and I came back with the cheese and fruit and the cannoli. "I didn't cook any of this, so it's all edible," I said despondently, making him laugh.

"You're an honest woman, Lamour," he said.

I said, nibbling on a cannoli, "Don't you know a woman can't be all things to all men?"

"*Lamore* is a very evocative name." He pronounced it the Italian way. "Tell me how you got it."

So I told how I was named for Jon-Boy's great-grandmother, a beautiful but flighty woman with an iron will and very little money. "She lived alone outside New Orleans," I said, describing the big decrepit old house with its filigree balconies and trellises covered in passionflowers. After she died, the house and land were sold off for what amounted to peanuts. Now there's a middle-class development there, filled with young marrieds, three-car garages and baby strollers. All that remains of her is her name. Thanks to Jon-Boy, who called me after her."

"I can think of no other woman who deserves it more," he said.

The little hurricane lamp I'd lit flickered on the table between us, and the deep blue night settled all around. Crickets tuned up, and small flying creatures, tiny bats, pretty little things with webbed wings, whizzed fast through the air. The scent of damp earth wafted up from the garden, mixed with the sweetness of jasmine and the sharp odor of lemons. And as always, there was the scent of the sea.

"I'm back in Paradise," I said. "Do you think Jon-Boy would approve?"

"I believe he would want you to be happy."

"All fathers seem to want their daughters to be happy."

"I suppose with our sons, we feel they are able to take care of themselves. With our daughters, a father always feels it's up to him to make sure she is happy."

"Until the right man comes along and takes her away from you," I said, and he nodded and agreed that was true.

I fixed coffee and we played a few games of backgammon, which I purposely lost because I felt so bad about the ruined dinner. I don't think Lorenzo noticed, though, and besides, men always like to win. We played in silence, concentrating on the game, but it was the comfortable silence of friends.

Affare was snoring gently, but when Lorenzo rose to leave she was up in an instant. "That dog loves you very much," I said, watching her dance excitedly on her hind legs.

"I find love is a very good commodity to have," he said.

"Me, too," I said. We stood looking at each other. Electricity trembled between us, sending responsive tremors through my body. He held out his hand and I took it. It was warm, hard, but his lips were gentle as he bent and kissed it.

"Thank you," he said as our eyes linked again.

"You're welcome," was all I could think of to say, but my voice was deeper, throatier.

We walked silently to the elevator.

"I'm sorry about dinner," I said, apologizing all over again. He held up a hand to stop me.

"It was wonderful," he said.

Then with a smile he stepped into the elevator. The doors closed and he was gone.

FIFTY

I ALWAYS KNEW WHEN LORENZO WAS HOME. I'D hear the helicopter clattering low over the cliff, and if I was in the garden I'd wave and see Affare's inquisitive head pop out and I'd laugh, knowing that soon I'd be seeing Lorenzo. He'd turned out to be a good friend, and I could imagine no nicer evening than one spent in his company, playing backgammon on the Castello terrace, or at an evening concert in Ravello, or sharing a simple meal on my terrace, mostly, I admit, takeout from Umberto's. I'll never make a great cook, but I know what's good, and fortunately for me, Umberto usually has it.

It was different with Nico. He would drop in and take me to lunch in Amalfi or Sorrento.

Then one Friday evening as I was pouring Nico a glass of Pellegrino—he had a hangover and was temporarily on the wagon—I heard the helicopter overhead.

"Your father's home," I said.

He gave me a long, smoldering look. "Ha! Not that he's there much anymore. He's always here with you."

I looked at him, brows raised. "So?"

"So is he planning on seducing you? Or you him?"

"Nico! How dare you say that?"

He shrugged. "Jealousy, I guess."

"You're behaving like a child," I said sharply.

He threw me another smoldering look. "You've got it all

wrong, *cara*," he said softly. "I'm no child, and I'd like to prove it to you."

I turned away, ignoring what Nico had said. "Come on, Lamour," he said. "Why are you holding out on me? Haven't I proven my feelings for you?"

I laughed then. "What feelings? That you enjoy flirting with me? Oh, come on; you flirt with every woman, Nico. It's second nature, as easy as drinking this water." I slammed the glass of Pellegrino on the table with a hand that shook.

He got up and came round the table. He stood next to me, fixed me with his eyes.

"Nico, stop this," I said angrily. "You're going to spoil our friendship."

He heaved a frustrated sigh. "What's all this nonsense about friendship? I want you. Don't you understand that?"

"I don't want to hear this. . . ."

"Yes, you do; you feel the way I do, Lamour. You just don't want to admit it. Come on, *cara*; tell the truth now."

I edged away, back around the other side of the table. "Stop it, Nico; please stop this," I said, afraid of the hot look in his eyes.

"No, you stop," he said, reaching out and grabbing hold of me. "I want you, Lamour, and you want me. . . ."

"Get off me!" I tried to push him away, but he had his arms wrapped around me. I felt him tremble, felt his excitement. . . .

"Nico!" Lorenzo was standing in the doorway. His face was so tight with anger, even Affare slid, subdued, behind him.

Nico looked at his father. "Perfect timing, Pa," he said bitterly. "Just before Lamour and I made it upstairs to the bedroom."

"Nico! You know that's not true." I threw an anxious glance at Lorenzo. His face had turned to stone. He moved aside to let Nico pass. Nico did not look back or say anything more. He'd already caused enough trouble.

I sank into a chair. Lorenzo came toward me. He laid his hands flat on the table and put his face close to mine. "You are too good for my son," he said quietly. Then he walked to the door.

He turned. His eyes burned into mine. "And besides," he added, *"I want you."* Then he walked away.

My breath caught in my throat, I couldn't speak. It was the sexiest thing any man had ever said to me. And I knew I wanted him, too.

FIFTY-ONE

I COULDN'T SLEEP THAT NIGHT AND I WAS UP AT first light. Pulling on a bathing suit, I headed to the cove.

I waded out, enjoying the cool water against my thighs; then I dived. Eyes open, I let the sea slide past me. I burst to the surface, laughing with the sheer physical joy. Then I drove through the water, feet kicking up little puffs of spray, sleek as any seal. My worries were temporarily forgotten. This was my idea of heaven.

I swam for about ten minutes, then trod water, looking up at the flawless sky, pale blue tinged with rose, and at the green cliff side that hid my little house so well there I could catch only a glimpse of its blue and green tiled dome. I looked at the shoreline with its secret inlets and villages accessed only from the sea, where fishermen had lived for centuries. And at Pirata across the bay. I thought of Lorenzo and his story of how he had rescued the silly little girl who had swum out too far, and I laughed out loud.

After a while I swam slowly back to shore and was surprised to see Lorenzo waiting on the jetty, with the dog. I waded out of the water, feeling ridiculously like Ursula Andress in the Bond movie. Dashing droplets from my lashes, I shook out my hair, then stood, arms folded across my breasts.

"What are you doing here?" I asked, knowing I sounded sulky.

"Looking for you," he said.

"Oh." I shook out my hair some more, sending more drops flying.

"I see you still like red bathing suits."

I glanced suspiciously at him. Was he laughing at me? He was wearing bathing shorts and he looked pretty darn good in them. A lion of a man, hard bodied, powerful. I busied myself with a towel. "Why did you want to see me anyway?"

"Unfinished business."

He walked toward me. I stood my ground, though my heart had shifted its rhythm and was thundering hard. "Oh," I said again, for the good reason that I couldn't think of anything else. "What business?"

"I needed to kiss you."

I gaped at him, like a fish caught on his line. He came closer, put a finger under my chin, tilted my face up to his. I closed my eyes, waiting. Then his lips were on mine.

It was a gentle, sweet kiss. I slid my arms around his neck and moved closer. He pulled me to him and we were locked in an embrace I wanted never to end. Everything was forgotten with that kiss. There was only Lorenzo and me in the world. My knees began to tremble.

"Cara," he murmured, *"Lamour, cara."* And he kissed me some more. "I wanted to come back to you last night," he murmured. "I wanted to kiss you; I wanted to be lost in your eyes, in the sound of your voice . . . in your laughter. I wanted to hold you like this, *mia carina;* I wanted to feel your softness next to me, to touch you. . . ."

His hand on my naked back sent a shiver the length of my spine. His eyes asked a question and mine gave the answer. Taking my hand, he led me to his old fishing boat. There was a tiny cabin down below with a simple couch. It was small but plenty big enough for a pair of eager new lovers. For that was what we were about to become.

I stopped asking myself how or why or even whether I should be doing this. I no longer cared. I wanted him. And he wanted me. Rocked by the gentle swells, we made love.

We must have made love for a long time, because when we finally came to our senses the sun was riding high in the sky. Lorenzo pulled me to my feet. He stared admiringly at my long, lean body with its new "pasta" curves and then he kissed me hard. "I'll race you across the bay," he said.

Of course he beat me, because by then I was limp as a newborn kitten and still abuzz with pleasure. It had been a long time since I'd made love, and anyway, I'd never felt this overwhelming passion, where nothing else mattered, not even the risk of being caught red-handed in the old boat. All I'd wanted was Lorenzo.

After he'd beaten me easily, we swam back to shore. Wrapped in a huge towel, I told him I'd make breakfast, and we climbed back through the garden to my house. I sent him upstairs to shower while I fed Affare an odd breakfast of leftovers, and busied myself in the kitchen, fixing coffee and French toast. I arranged everything on a round wicker tray and turned to call him. He was standing in the doorway, watching me.

"Oh," I said, blushing, something I hadn't known I could still do. "I didn't know you were there."

"I enjoy watching you," he said, with that slow smile of his, the one that started in the crinkles at the corners of his eyes, then the corners of his mouth, and traveled until it lit up his whole face. I thought Lorenzo Pirata was a good smiler.

I ran upstairs and put on a robe; then we ate breakfast at my kitchen table, like an old married couple. I poured more coffee.

Elbows on the table, Lorenzo said, "So what would you like to do today?"

"I'd like to be alone with you," I said honestly.

He knew I meant I didn't want to be around the Castello with Nico and Aurora and their friends, not now when it was so obvious we were lovers. "Then we'll go to Positano," he said. "It'll be quiet at this time of year, and I know a place where we can be absolutely private."

An hour later, with Affare tucked behind us in the helicopter, we flew to Positano and the Hotel San Pietro. Lorenzo had taken the penthouse suite with the private pool and the loggia with the fabulous view that even beat the one from my own terrace. Affare had her own bed, and we had ours. It was so big Lorenzo said he had to shout *"hallooo"* to me across the great white divide of linen sheets, but we soon found our way to each other.

We didn't leave that suite for three days and three nights. We ordered room service and champagne, and someone came to walk Affare. It was the most wonderful, passionate three days of my life and I wanted it never to end. Though of course it did.

FIFTY-TWO

THE WEEKS THAT FOLLOWED PASSED IN A HAPPY haze. Fortunately for me, Aurora was back at the university and Nico stayed in Rome, which meant Lorenzo and I had the Castello to ourselves. Not that we meant to keep our love affair a secret; it just worked out that way, and for the moment it seemed easier.

I was glad that the tower bedroom had not been Marella's and I had no need to feel uncomfortable there. It was completely ours, the place we retreated to at the end of the day— or in the afternoon or, in fact, any old time we could—to fall into bed, lost in the pleasure of our bodies. Lorenzo was a beautiful man. In his arms there was no difference in our ages. We were simply one.

Of course I e-mailed Jammy to tell her all this. Worried that she might think I'd gone crazy, I asked her did she think I was doing the right thing? *Jammy, I'm in love with him*, I said. *Help! What shall I do?*

I got a one-line answer: *Do what you always do, which is whatever you like.* Jammy knew me too well. I wasn't asking for advice, simply confirmation that since I was doing it anyway, it had to be all right.

She called me later and we had a long heart-to-heart. I told her how happy I was and that I believed Lorenzo was, too. "But I worry he thinks he's too old for me."

"He is," Jammy said. "Or else you are too young for him. Think about it, Lamour: when Lorenzo is in his eighties, you'll only be in your fifties. That's when the difference comes in."

I knew it was true, but surely love overcame things like age. Love conquered all. I wanted so much to believe that, but now I had a little niggling doubt. I told her it didn't matter anyway, because there was no talk of marriage or a future together. Lorenzo and I were living for the moment.

And anyway, there was another major obstacle between us: Jon-Boy. I thought Lorenzo knew the truth about what had happened to him and was keeping it from me. I didn't want to believe that the man I loved might in some way be involved in my father's death, but the thought lingered ominously at the back of my mind.

I sought out Mifune. "I've fallen in love with Lorenzo," I told him. He nodded; of course he already knew. "Mifune, I still think he had something to do with Jon-Boy's death, but when I asked him about it, he told me it was all so long ago, it's best forgotten."

Mifune was sitting cross-legged on the meditation stone. His lined parchment face was lifted to the sky, his eyes half-closed. He seemed surrounded by an aura of tranquillity, and I longed to share that.

"The past has faded into infinity," he said. "Isn't it time now to proceed toward the future without Jon-Boy?"

But the future seemed very hazy to me. I was Lorenzo's mistress; there had been no talk of marriage. "Besides," I said, "there's the age difference."

"Age is of the senses," Mifune said. "We are not constrained by our years; we gain by them. Eventually our bodies give in to time; some of us die young, some old. Time is what we possess, not age. And what you and Lorenzo have is time."

Of course, he was right.

Then Aurora and Nico came home. They arrived together, in Nico's red Porsche. Lorenzo and I were playing backgammon on the terrace. Affare ran around barking and Lorenzo immediately got up to embrace his children, but Nico came over to me. He offered me his hand and I took it.

"*Bitch,*" he said, bending to kiss it.

I looked at him, shocked, but he grinned and said, "I haven't given up hope yet, lovely Lamour, so don't you forget that."

I glared at him, but he turned away. Then I heard Lorenzo say to Aurora, "Lamour is here."

"Of course she is," Aurora said, and I knew that the grapevine had already reached her with the news that her father and I were "an item."

"*Buona sera, Signora Harrington,*" she said coldly, following her brother into the Castello.

A short while later, Massimo came to tell Lorenzo he was needed on the telephone. I was alone on the terrace, strolling among the sphinxes, looking at the glittering coastline, when I heard Aurora's quick high-heeled footsteps. I turned round and found her immediately behind me, practically breathing down my neck. I took a quick startled step backward.

"Why do you come here?" she said, speaking so rapidly the words seemed simply to spill out of her. "Go back where you came from; leave us alone. The Pirata family doesn't want you. You and your father bring nothing but bad luck. Go home now; leave us in peace. . . . My father is too kind, too good; he's only being nice to you because he's a gentleman; don't you understand that—"

She stopped her raving as suddenly as she had started, staring at me with those huge dark eyes. "Go!" she commanded.

I recognized she wasn't acting rationally; she was manic,

consumed with her fears about her father. Of course she loved him and he'd spoiled and protected her, but there was something more, something deeper I didn't understand.

"I'm not here to harm anybody, Aurora," I said as calmly as I could, because right then she looked ready to strike me. "I'm simply a friend, nothing more. I've come here to be where my own father lived, where I have happy memories. That's all it is."

"Ha!" She obviously didn't believe me, and she shifted her gaze, looking out to sea, as though she saw my father's ghost there, though of course she had never known him. As though reading my thoughts, she said suddenly, "It seems Jon-Boy Harrington will haunt the Piratas forever."

Shocked, I caught my breath. How could she say such a thing, knowing my father had drowned right here, that I had lost him so tragically? What was *wrong* with the girl!

All of a sudden her anger dissolved. Like a collapsed balloon her shoulders drooped and her head fell to her chest. "Forgive me," she said, in a quiet little-girl voice. And with that she turned and walked slowly back along the terrace. She stumbled as though she couldn't see properly. I thought she was crying and wondered why the outburst and then the sudden deflation, the drop into a kind of despair I didn't understand.

I didn't tell Lorenzo about the incident when he returned because I didn't want to be responsible for any strain in his relationship with his daughter.

That night set the tone for my relationship with Lorenzo's children. They resented me and I was angry at them. I refused to go to the Castello when they were there, and instead my little house became our rendezvous. Lorenzo and I spent those long, silky summer nights in my newly apricot-colored bedroom, on my hydrangea-embroidered sheets, naked in each other's arms. Every morning we would leave Affare sitting anxiously on the beach while we raced each other across the bay, though I had yet to beat him, and when we came back I would make him my special French toast. We put the problems with Aurora and Nico to the back of our minds and simply got on with living and loving. I was a happy woman.

And then on the spur of the moment, Lorenzo decided to throw a party.

FIFTY-THREE

Lamour

MASSIMO DELIVERED HIS HANDWRITTEN INVITA-
tion to me personally, saying the *signore* had wanted to make
sure I received it.

The party was to be the following Saturday, commencing
with cocktails at nine in the evening, followed by dinner and
dancing. "Black tie" was written discreetly at the bottom of
the vellum page. It threw me into an immediate panic. My
wardrobe contained nothing more exotic than the pretty,
summery dress I'd bought with Jammy in Rome, and that
certainly couldn't be counted as "evening dress." There was
no time to shop. What was I to do? I thought of the Vivari
red chiffon hanging in Jon-Boy's closet and knew I might
just be skinny enough to fit into it.

I dashed upstairs and dragged it off its hanger. I gave it a
good shake, sending dust motes flying, but there was nothing
a good airing out on the terrace wouldn't take care of.

I slipped the dress over my head, thinking about the woman
who'd last worn it. A trace of her perfume still lingered, an
exotic, almost Oriental scent, and I remembered Mifune's
story of the beauty with the long black hair. A shiver ran up
my spine, but then when I looked in the mirror I saw a trans-
formed woman.

The dress fit as though it had been made for me. The
neckline swooped from narrow straps to a deep V. Draped

tightly under the breasts, the soft chiffon fell in a straight col-
umn to the floor. It was truly a gown for a goddess. Not only
was Giorgio Vivari an artist; he was also a man who knew his
craft—and who understood women. And I would wear his
masterpiece to the party.

On Friday evening at dusk, I heard Lorenzo's helicopter
flying low on its way back to the Castello. A short while later
he came running down the steps and I ran to meet him. We
stood in each other's arms, hugging and saying how much
we'd missed each other.

"Will you stay with me tonight?" I asked, kissing his left
earlobe, but he said he could not; people were already arriving for the weekend and he had to get back. "I would ask
you, too, Lamour," he said, "but it will be chaos with everybody arriving at once, including Nico and Aurora's friends.
Tomorrow will be better."

I kissed him good-bye and watched him walk away, feeling
like a child told she couldn't go to the grown-ups' dinner. I
told myself of course I was being silly and guessed that obviously Lorenzo didn't want to upset Aurora in front of his
guests. She was a problem and there was nothing I could do
about it.

The following night I prepared carefully. I pulled my hair
into a shiny chignon, anchoring it at the nape with inexpensive coral pins I'd found in Amalfi. I put on the sexy red dress
and the pretty high-heeled red mules I'd bought in Rome. I
wound my yard of diamonds around my neck like a choker
and added diamond hoop earrings, though these were fake. I
wore no rings, no bracelets. When I looked in the mirror I was
pleased. I could definitely keep up with the Joneses tonight.

I rode up the elevator, looking out at the sea sparkling under a full moon. Trust Lorenzo to get it right, I thought with
a smile, because the Castello never looked more beautiful

than by the light of the moon. I took off my shoes and carried them, as usual, so as not to get them dusty. I could see the Castello through the trees, aglow with lights, and heard snatches of music.

When I got in sight of the front steps, I put on my shoes. Cars were out front and people were milling around in a flurry of "*ciao*s" and bursts of laughter. Massimo in a formal black jacket stood at the top of the steps to greet them. Behind him, I glimpsed white-coated waiters hurrying through the hall with silver trays loaded with canapés. A bar had been set up on the terrace, and globe lights hung from the trees. The birds had forgotten to go to bed and were chirping excitedly, along with the usual chorus of crickets.

An attack of shyness hit me suddenly. I hovered uncertainly in the shadows. I didn't know anyone, and these people came from a different world.

"*Perdona, signora,* but don't I know you?" a voice said.

I turned and looked at Giorgio Vivari, the man who had designed the very dress I was wearing. The man who had complimented me on my charming instep at the restaurant in Rome.

"Of course I remember you," I said. "We met briefly in Rome, at Da Fortunato."

"Ah, now I remember." He bowed over my hand oh, so charmingly. "How could I ever forget your pretty foot."

We laughed together; then he said, "I am Giorgio Vivari."

"And I am Lamour Harrington."

He asked why I was all alone out here in the shadows, and I admitted I was shy and knew no one.

"But I, too, am alone," he said. "Please, allow me to escort you to the party." And feeling like Cinderella at the ball, I floated into the Castello on Vivari's arm.

Lorenzo came hurrying toward us. I thought he was so

incredibly handsome, so darn elegantly man-of-the-world-gorgeous in his tuxedo, my knees went weak and I was seized with a mad desire to kiss him all over. But to my astonishment he stared at me like a man who had just seen a ghost.

He gathered himself quickly. Kissing me politely on both cheeks, he said, "Lamour, welcome. You look beautiful. And with Giorgio, I see."

I was taken aback by Lorenzo's coolness. "Actually, I'm surprised to find myself with the man who designed my dress," I said. "Though it must have been years ago. You probably don't even recognize it," I added, turning to Vivari.

"But I remember it well," he said. "It's a couture dress designed specially for a famous client. Only this one was ever made. But on you it looks perfect. *You* were made for this dress, instead of the other way around."

Lorenzo excused himself abruptly and went off to greet some new guests.

"I have a confession to make," I said to Vivari. "I found the dress hanging in the closet at my father's house. I wondered who it belonged to, but it's been there so long, I thought anyhow she wouldn't mind me borrowing it tonight."

Vivari put an arm around my shoulders. "Let me tell you Cassandra Biratta would be furious if she saw you, because it looks better on you."

My pulse leaped at the sound of her name. "Cassandra Biratta?"

"The Contessa Biratta. Do you know her?" I shook my head, and he told me she lived at the famous Palazzo Biratta in Rome. "But of course Cassandra has houses in many places," he said. "And don't worry about it, *cara;* this dress was made for her when she was much younger. She would not look good in it today."

He escorted me out onto the terrace, got me a glass of

champagne, and introduced me to some people, but I soon wandered away.

At last I knew the name of my father's lover. I knew where she lived in Rome. From what I knew of her from Jon-Boy's diary, I felt in my heart she had killed him. And with a sinking heart, I realized that Lorenzo knew. Shocked, I made my way indoors in search of the powder room.

The large bathroom and adjoining bedroom had been decked out like a fancy hotel in debutante-ball days, with a plump lady in black and a starched white apron ready to supply fresh towels, tissues, face powder, and perfume, to pin a broken strap or stitch up a ripped hem.

"*There* you are." Aurora appeared suddenly, slamming the door behind her. The attendant looked up, startled, and so did I.

"Oh, hello, Aurora. This is a lovely party," I said, though in fact I was here to take time out and gather my shattered dreams. I wasn't even really thinking about Aurora. My thoughts were all of Lorenzo. What did he know? What was he hiding? Why hadn't he told me about Cassandra?

"Lamour!" I glanced quickly at Aurora. I thought she looked odd. She was pale and her hands were shaking. She sank onto a couch, staring at me with her dark, unreadable eyes. Of course she looked beautiful in a pale lemon-colored gown that clung softly to her young body. Her long dark hair hung in a sleek fall past her shoulders, but now she pushed it wearily back.

Suddenly worried, I went and sat next to her. "Are you all right?" I asked. I wanted to take her hand to stop it from shaking, but I was afraid because I didn't know what she might do.

"I hate this," she whispered so I had to bend my head to catch what she was saying. "I hate all these people. I hate the

Castello. I hate *you,*" she said loudly. Her blank eyes met mine. "I hate myself." Then she got up and ran from the room.

My eyes met the attendant's, but she turned quickly away. Her business was only to tend to the cosmetic worries of the guests, not the fears of their minds. Still worried about Aurora, I made my way back out and onto the terrace. But I had more than Aurora's tantrums on my mind.

Later Lorenzo found me in the shadow of a sphinx head at the far end of the terrace. "You look magnificent," he said quietly.

"In the Contessa Biratta's gown," I said. "Of course you recognized it."

He nodded. "I'd seen her in it with your father. She was a legendary beauty. But now, *cara,* let's forget about that. Come; join my guests. The evening has only just started; soon dinner will be served, and then there's dancing."

He looked pleadingly at me, but the magic had gone out of the night. He'd known all along about Cassandra Birrata. I didn't understand why he couldn't tell me the truth about what had happened that night. Instead he'd left me to flounder along alone, searching, wondering, never knowing how my father had died. I knew I could never trust him again.

"I'm sorry, Lorenzo," I said in a choked voice, and kicking off my shoes, I sped back down the terrace into the night. Lorenzo did not follow me, and I did not want him to.

I ran back down the *scalatinella,* unzipping the gown as I went. I couldn't stand the feel of it against my skin. I hated it. I never wanted to see it again. Ripping it off, I hurled it into the bushes and ran naked into the house.

I paced the *salone,* shaking like a frightened cat. The hair on the back of my neck was standing on end. *I had found her. I'd found Jon-Boy's killer.*

I went into the kitchen, opened a bottle of wine, poured

myself a glass, and drank it with a shaking hand. Finally, wrapped in my old white cotton robe, I went to sit on the terrace. Huddled on my lovely bench, I could hear the music wafting down the hill from the party, see the lights glowing against the sky, and later the fireworks, and hear the cheers that accompanied them.

I decided that tomorrow I would ask Mifune about Cassandra Biratta and then I'd decide what to do.

To the whisper of music and the croak of a tree frog I fell into a restless sleep on the old blue sofa that had cradled me safely so many nights since I came here.

FIFTY-FOUR

Lamour

THE NEXT MORNING I SOUGHT OUT MIFUNE IN HIS vegetable garden, an orderly paradise with beds of herbs and tomatoes and tall green beans. Zucchini blossomed bright yellow on their fat green stems and peach trees formed a perfect symmetrical pattern espaliered against a sunny south-facing wall.

I ran down the sandy path toward him; I had no time to waste. "I've found who my father's mistress was," I said. "The Contessa Cassandra Biratta. Was she the woman with the long black hair, the beauty you told me about?"

Wearing his battered straw coolie hat, Mifune was on his knees tending a recalcitrant row of pea shoots, a vegetable he had introduced to the Pirata gardens from his own country. He liked things orderly, and since pea shoots were not amenable to orderliness, they offended his aesthetic sensibilities.

He got up and dusted off his knees. "She was, *piccolina*."

"And was she here the night he died?" I almost couldn't bear to hear his answer; I already knew that Cassandra Biratta had killed my father.

Mifune went to sit on the stone bench at the edge of the path, and I sat beside him.

"I have searched my conscience many times, *piccolina*," he said, and his voice was so soft that I had to bend my head to catch his words. "I made a solemn promise, one that I cannot break. But I cannot stop you from doing what you must do to find the truth about your father's death. You have that right. Cassandra Biratta was here often, at the little house. And she was here the night your father died. Beyond that I can say no more."

I mulled over what he'd said. I knew that where there was a love affair there was often also jealousy. And knowing my father, I'd bet there was also another woman . . . another mistress. The one with the initial "I" in his diary.

"Were there two women fighting over Jon-Boy?" I asked.

"You are a woman and you sense it in your bones," Mifune said. "Her name was Isabella Mancini. She was your father's lover before the *contessa*."

"You knew her?"

"I knew her." His eyes met mine. "I can say no more."

"I'll find Isabella," I cried, "and I'll go to the *contessa*. I'll ask her how she killed Jon-Boy. I'll tell her she was seen here the night he died, out on the cliff in the storm . . . that there are witnesses. . . ."

Mifune held up a warning hand. "Be careful, Lamour. Cassandra Biratta is like an elegant white crane, the kind you see in old Japanese watercolors. Graceful, beautiful, and with a heart of steel."

I still didn't know why Mifune had taken a vow of silence about Jon-Boy's death and I thought I probably never would, but I thanked him from the bottom of my heart for what he had told me. I had finally solved the mystery of my father's death. And now I was about to confront his killer.

I e-mailed Jammy, giving her all the details. Early the next morning I was in my car and on my way to Rome before I had time to rethink Mifune's warning.

FIFTY-FIVE

Lorenzo

LORENZO PROWLED HIS TOWER ROOM. HANDS BE-
hind his back, head down, he was thinking about Lamour and
the events at the party. When he'd seen her in the red dress
with her dark hair pulled back, for a second he'd thought she
was Cassandra. He'd been so shocked, he'd simply left her
there with Giorgio, and when he'd come to his senses, it had
been too late.

Glancing out the window, he noticed that dusk was falling.
The olive trees rustled, fluttering like silvery coins in the evening breeze. Lorenzo thought there was little more beautiful
on God's earth than an old olive tree, with its gnarled knotted
trunk and its twisted branches. Mifune had planted these trees
for Lorenzo's grandfather. He had created all this beauty that
Lorenzo's family enjoyed now. Mifune knew everything there
was to know about the Pirata family, and it was to Mifune that
he now decided to go in search of some answers.

The old gardener heard his footsteps on the gravel. He stood
waiting by the open door. "Signor Pirata," he said with a low
bow. "I am honored." He stepped back to allow Lorenzo to
enter and asked if he would care for some green tea.

While Mifune busied himself with the preparations,
Lorenzo looked around. He never failed to be amazed by the
simplicity of his old friend's surroundings. A Zen-like aura
of peace permeated Mifune's simple dwelling, and thinking

of his own complicated, too-busy life, Lorenzo envied him that.

Mifune carried in an old enamel tray with two thin porcelain tea bowls. Cross-legged on the tatami mats, the two men faced each other across the low table. Mifune poured the tea and, with a small bow, presented a bowl to Lorenzo. "Signore," he said, "to what do I owe the honor of your visit?"

"Do you remember the promise I made, many years ago?"

Mifune nodded. "I remember, signore."

"You also made that promise, but for me it was a sacred vow. It's one I can't break, though now I am tempted." Mifune's pale eyes narrowed. Surprised, his wild eyebrows spiked upward, but he said nothing, letting Lorenzo say what he had to say.

"I'm in love with Lamour," Lorenzo said, "but our relationship is built on a lie. My friend, I cannot go on like this. I'm torn between two truths—one from the past and one from today. What can I do? Can I ask her to share her life with me, knowing what I know about her father? I see no way out. The vow was a sacred trust. How can I possibly think of breaking it when it might damage everything I've worked to achieve all these years?"

"It is simple, signore," Mifune said at last. "You have always respected your promise, but now there is another person to consider. Ask yourself, is it fair to keep the truth from Jon-Boy's daughter? Does she not also have rights?"

"I hadn't thought of her rights," Lorenzo admitted. "But I see now I must consider that, too."

"Do not leave it too late. Lamour found out that Cassandra Biratta was Jon-Boy's mistress. She came to me and asked some questions. I gave her the answers as honestly as I was permitted within the limits of our vow. She is already on her way to Rome to confront the *contessa*. Lamour is a headstrong woman, signore. She will not take no for an answer. She is determined to find out the truth about her father's death." His eyes met Lorenzo's. "And after all, can we blame her?"

Of course Lorenzo couldn't blame her. He, of all people, understood a daughter's love for her father.

"I'm in love with a woman I have no right to love," he said to Mifune. "Not only am I too old for her, but I have my family to think of. I see no way for a future together. How can I ask her to share the last part of my life when she is still young and with all her good years in front of her?"

Suddenly looking tired, Mifune said in his quiet voice, "It is a question of the heart. I have always believed that a man must follow his best instincts. Meditation isolates the thoughts and focuses the mind until only the spiritual remains within you. Try it, my signore, and may it help you in your troubles."

The visit was over and Lorenzo thanked his old friend. He said he was sorry to have burdened him with the past as well as the future, and Mifune bowed and said humbly that it was his honor to help in his small, insignificant way.

Lorenzo went back to his tower. He did not switch on the lamps but sat for a long time at his window, looking out into the soft, dark night. He closed his mind to other matters and channeled his thoughts to the past, to his wife, Marella, to whom he had made his vow. Before too long, the way became clear. There was only one thing to do. And he must act immediately.

FIFTY-SIX

Lamour

I WALKED THROUGH A LOVELY PIAZZA, UNDER enormous plane trees that cast a delightful shade, passing the Palazzo Biratta twice before I realized that the grandiose building half-hidden behind ornate iron gates was it.

The palazzo took up the entire southwestern corner of one of the most romantic squares in Rome. Built of pale carved stone embellished with rose-colored marble pediments and architraves and set in a courtyard behind immense iron gates, it towered an impressive five stories. The steeply sloped roof was edged with carved griffins and the heraldic devices of the Biratta family, which went all the way back to the Renaissance era. I'd done my homework; I knew the Birattas had started out as merchants, climbing through wealth and bribery and manipulation to a position of great power, culminating in the bestowing on them of the title of "Count." The Birattas were still immensely wealthy, still involved politically, through banking and the Vatiçan, and they were still one of the most powerful families in Italy. They were a formidable enemy.

And yet when I'd telephoned, Cassandra Biratta had agreed at once to see me. Now I wondered why. Was she afraid that I was about to make her affair with Jon-Boy public? Was she afraid that I knew the truth about his death and was about to tell the world?

And there would go your reputation, *contessa,* I thought bitterly as I pressed my finger on the bell and heard it ring in the stone gatehouse. I'd expected some little old lady in black who'd been with the family for half a century to answer, but instead a uniformed security guard appeared, his hand ready on the gun at his hip. Obviously his family did not mess around, and I suddenly felt nervous about what I was going to do.

I gave the guard my name and told him the *contessa* was expecting me. He went back to check his list; then he opened the electronic gates and signaled me to enter.

A houseman in a white jacket and black pants stood waiting at the top of the impressive flight of stone steps leading up to the front door. He ushered me into the hall, offering to take my jacket, but I said I preferred to keep it on, thank you.

There was something decidedly chilly about the Palazzo Biratta, a coldness that had nothing to do with the temperature but emanated all the way from its forty-foot arched ceiling to its marble terrazzo floors, via the sweeping staircase and lofty corridors and its tapestry-hung walls. It was filled with the over-the-top overstuffed things money had bought over centuries and reminded me of Grand Central Station, with antiques. I shivered, thinking you would be hard pushed to find a cozy spot to curl up in on a winter's eve here.

I followed the houseman down one of the long corridors, past marble statues ensconced in spot-lit niches, past gilded consoles and formal flower arrangements fit for the lobby of a grand hotel. We ended up in what I guessed was one of the palazzo's more modest sitting rooms, obviously suitable for a talk with a more modest, everyday person like myself.

"The *contessa* will be with you shortly, signora," the man said. "Would you care for some refreshment? A cool drink or an espresso?"

I thanked him but said no. I preferred not to accept anything from the woman who had killed my father.

Left alone, I inspected the ornate furnishings, the great swags of silk brocade at the windows, the bibelots and silver-framed photos. It crossed my mind that this place must be hell to dust, and I wondered if it was worth it; living here would be like living in a museum. I had a sudden longing to be back in my simple house with its magical view the only ornament needed. I wished I was out on my terrace having dinner and sharing a glass of wine with Lorenzo.

Lorenzo. My heart sank. Lorenzo had guarded his secrets and I was about to let those secrets out of the bag. *Oh, Lorenzo, Lorenzo,* I thought, and I could almost hear the sound of my heart cracking. *I believed you were my enemy; then you became my friend, and then my lover. . . . And now you'll never want to see me again.*

The door opened behind me. I swung round and looked at one of the most beautiful women I had ever seen. Jon-Boy's description of her in his diary flew instantly into my mind: *"C" . . . wrapped in fur, face peeking from the big collar like a pretty little fox . . . or vixen is more like it. . . .*

That face was a pale, perfect oval, her mouth a full, sensual scarlet. Her dark eyes tilted at the corners over the high cliff of her cheekbones. Beauty like this did not occur often, and at her age it definitely did not come cheap. She was, I guessed, in her sixties, slender and lithe as a girl, her long legs displayed by elegant high heels and a skirt that hit just above the knee. She was not the kind of woman to wear stilettos; these shoes were just high enough to show off her ankles and yet remain within the bounds of good taste. In fact, "good taste" was what the Contessa Biratta was all about, from her Mabé-pearl earrings, to the creamy ropes of very large South Sea pearls at her neck, to her armful of gold bracelets and the discreet gold watch.

She was so absolutely lovely, I had no wonder Jon-Boy had been unable to resist her. But then I also remembered Mifune's description of her: *Like an elegant white crane, the kind you see in old Japanese watercolors. Graceful, beautiful, and with a heart of steel.* Shaking Cassandra Biratta's hand and looking into her cold, dark eyes, I understood what Mifune had meant.

"Please have a seat, Signora Harrington," she said in a low voice, cool as the air-conditioning. She motioned me to a formal pale brocade sofa and took a seat on a matching one on the other side of a glass table scattered with more priceless Biratta artifacts.

I watched her taking me in. I was an alien being in her rarefied existence, yet I knew she had been born into an impoverished peasant family in Apulia, one of the poorest parts of Italy, and that she had ascended to all this grandeur via her beauty. In fact, Cassandra Biratta epitomized the term *courtesan,* now more often known as "trophy wives," because these days rich men marry courtesans instead of merely keeping them as pampered mistresses.

"You resemble your father," she said, surprising me, because I'd thought she would deny ever knowing him. "So, signora, why don't you tell me why you are here?"

"I came to ask you about Jon-Boy's murder," I said, and saw her stiffen.

"Then I cannot help you. I know nothing of your father's death, other than what I heard."

I nodded. "The great storm, Jon-Boy out alone in a boat, Jon-Boy presumed drowned, his body never found . . . that's the way the story goes, Contessa Biratta. But you and I know better."

Eyes narrowed to slits, she didn't looked nearly as beautiful as she said, "That is what I was told. I have no reason to believe otherwise."

"Then what if I ask you about Isabella? Surely you remember her? The young woman you replaced in my father's bed?" I heard her hiss with fury, but I continued regardless, inventing as I went, somehow knowing what this woman would have done. "You were *jealous, Contessa*. You went to her; you told her Jon-Boy cared nothing for her. You made sure she didn't get near my father until that night when she showed up at the house in Amalfi."

Cassandra sat back on the hard sofa. Her tightly knotted fingers betrayed the look of calmness she had arranged on her face.

"My dear Signora Harrington," she said quietly, "this is all hearsay. You were a child when I knew your father. You were not even living in this country. How can you believe all this nonsense?" She shook her head. "No, no, no, you are wrong. Your father had a 'relationship' with Isabella Mancini for a while, I knew that, but it was over by the time—"

She stopped abruptly but I knew she had been about to say "I came on the scene. . . ." But of course, that would have been an admission that she had an affair with Jon-Boy, and she wasn't about to fall into that trap.

"I met Jon-Boy here in Rome," she said instead. "I admired his talent. My husband and I have a policy of helping artists, as this family has since the days of the Renaissance. The count took a great liking to *il dottore*. They spent many pleasant evenings together discussing literature, especially Hemingway and Dos Passos and other writers of that era, who have always fascinated the count. As have the great classic Italian poets whom Jon-Boy was apparently studying for his new novel. The two men got along very well and Jon-Boy came often to the palazzo."

I tried and failed to imagine Jon-Boy at ease in this rarefied atmosphere, lounging against these hard sofas and discussing

Dante with the count over a glass of vintage port. Jon-Boy was of the earth and he would never willingly have spent more than ten minutes in a place like this.

"There was a dress of yours, hanging in his closet," I said to her. "A red chiffon. The designer was Giorgio Vivari."

She shrugged. "Many women have dresses by Vivari."

"Not this one," I said, watching closely for her reaction. "I showed it to Signor Vivari. He told me he designed it specially for you. There was only ever *one* dress like that made, *Contessa. Your dress.*"

She took a deep breath, obviously gathering her thoughts, and also, I guessed, her wits. I was on my mettle for whatever she might throw out next, but then she surprised me.

"So what do you want me to say?" She spoke in a low, quiet voice, as though afraid she would be overheard. "You want me to admit I had an affair with Jon-Boy? And why should I, *cara*? So you can tell my husband what he already suspects was true? So you can wreck my marriage and I'll end up in the divorce courts? And all for a man who is already dead?"

I hated her for the sheer callousness of that last remark, but trembling, I held myself back. "I have no interest in wrecking your marriage," I said coldly. "I simply want to know what really happened to my father. And how you killed him."

Her face dropped and her eyes flew wide open. She got to her feet. "I told you I know nothing. I was not there that night. . . ."

"You were seen," I said. "You were out on the cliff that night, with the rain and the hail pelting down and the wind blowing up from hell. You *know* what happened to my father, and now you must tell me."

She stalked angrily to the window, where she stood, arms folded across her chest, staring out at the tall plane trees shading her beautiful courtyard.

"There were witnesses," I said softly. "If you wish, I can bring them here, so you can ask them yourself what they saw."

She was silent for a long moment; then she turned. "I did not kill your father," she said simply, "and that is the truth."

I looked into the beautiful face of my father's lover, the woman I had considered evil, a murderer. Her eyes met mine and I saw the tears in them.

And to my astonishment, I believed her. And I believed she still loved Jon-Boy.

FIFTY-SEVEN

L'amour

FRAMED BY THE TALL SILK-CURTAINED WINDOW, Cassandra might have been a portrait by Sargent: moneyed, titled, timeless, and ever graceful.

When I told her I believed her, her lovely face seemed to crack just a little, showing the faint stirrings of emotion. She came to sit next to me on my hard sofa. Her eyes searched my face.

"You are so like him it's uncanny," she said at last. "When I walked into this room and saw you standing there, I was suddenly swept back to a place and time I had hoped to forget." She shrugged. "Of course I should have known better. Your father is unforgettable."

She pressed a bell to summon the houseman and I thought she was going to tell him to show me out, but instead she asked if I would care for a drink. Surprised at her hospitality, I asked for water. She requested a vodka and tonic on the rocks, and to tell the truth, I thought she looked as though she needed one. Her face was suddenly drawn, her eyes locked off from me.

The houseman was back in minutes with our refreshments. She sipped hers gratefully while I sat wondering what she was going to tell me, because it was obvious that something was on her mind.

"Thank you for believing me," she said at last. "Yes, I had

an affair with Jon-Boy, and yes, I was in love with him, in my own way. I enjoyed him." She shrugged. "You know *il dottore,* charming, handsome, irresistible." She thought for a moment. "Of course Jon-Boy was more than just that. He was a man of deep feelings, of heightened emotions, a sensitive man, and his own worst critic. He was mercurial, wanting peace and solitude one minute, parties and people and lovers the next. I wasn't faithful to him and he knew it, *and* knew why. He was too in love with me and I couldn't allow that. I know that sounds contradictory, but after all, I was a married woman. I had my own life and I was never going to give that up. Jon-Boy knew it when he met me, knew it was to be nothing more than a wild flirtatious affair. But for him it became more. He was obsessed by me; I felt smothered by his love. Finally I could stand no more, and besides, I knew it was dangerous and that he might go to my husband. I told him it was over and he begged me to come one last time to the house in Amalfi." She lifted her shoulders again in a shrug. "I said yes."

She gulped the vodka. Her hand was shaking so much, the ice cubes rattled against the glass.

"I'm grateful to you for telling me this," I said in a low voice, because I didn't want to disturb her confessional mood. I wanted to encourage her to tell me what happened next.

"Jon-Boy asked me to bring the red dress. 'Wear it for me one last time, Cassandra,' he said. 'I want to remember you the way you were the night we first met at the New Year's Eve party.'

"So I wore the dress for him at dinner that night, and the perfume he liked on me, Shalimar. I no longer use it; it's too associated with him. He was his usual happy-go-lucky self, talking about his new book, the new restaurant in Capri we had to try together. . . . He was talking like a man making plans for a future and I reminded him I was there to say good-bye. He refused to accept that. I was a little sad to be leaving him, but I needed to get on with my own life. I was a woman with a social position to think of, my responsibilities, my husband. It was very much over for me."

She drained the glass and set it firmly on the small table next to her. Her mouth had left a scarlet stain on the rim, and she dabbed at her lipstick with a tissue.

I hunched forward, hands tightly clasped over my knees, willing her to go on.

"So, Jon-Boy's daughter," she said, "now you know all I can tell you. There is nothing more to say."

"Oh, but there is," I cried. "You were there that night; you were part of what happened. . . ."

She rose to her feet, calm and collected again. *"Understand this,"* she said, and now her low voice was full of menace. *"I was not there the night Jon-Boy died. And none of the so-called 'witnesses' you claim saw me will ever testify that I was. I will not allow you to drag me and my family name into a long-ago death in which I had no part. Are you quite clear about that, Signora Harrington?"*

"Contessa . . . ," I began, but she was already striding toward the door.

"My man will show you out," she said, dismissing me. "Good-bye, Signora Harrington." She turned at the door. Her eyes searched my face and I knew she was seeing Jon-Boy again in me. "It was nice meeting you—for old times' sake," she said. Then she closed the door behind her.

FIFTY-EIGHT

Lamour

I RETREATED TO THE HOTEL D'INGHILTERRA AND immediately picked up the phone and called Jammy.

"Well?" she said as soon as she heard my voice.

"She's still just as gorgeous as Jon-Boy described her," I said, sounding as dispirited as I looked. "But there's something inhuman about that kind of beauty. Y'know what I mean, Jam? It's like she's frozen inside and all her efforts go into preserving that beautiful facade."

"Well, after all, it's her stock-in-trade," Jammy said. "It's what got her where she is. She loses that, she's in trouble. The good old count will be on to the next, and Cassandra'll be hoping she never signed a prenup."

"I don't think they had them in those days," I said. "But anyhow, her pearls alone would keep us comfortably for a good few years."

"Maybe I'll have Matt buy me some," Jammy said thoughtfully, "sounds like a good investment. Ah, but then there goes the mortgage and the vet bills, to say nothing of the college fund," she added, making me laugh. "So then what happened?"

I described the palazzo and the security guard and the houseman and the room where the *contessa* and I had our "meeting."

"I felt as though I'd stepped back in time," I said. "I should have been wearing a powdered wig and hoopskirt and flirting with a silk fan instead of sitting on that stiff brocade sofa asking the *contessa* if she murdered my father."

"And did she?" Jammy's voice was tense.

"She told me she did not."

"And . . . ?"

"I believed her."

One of Jammy's familiar gusty sighs blasted down the phone line, and I added hurriedly, "She didn't kill him, Jam, but she did finally admit she had an affair with him."

I told her the details and she listened until I got to the part with the *contessa*'s veiled threat about me not harming her family name, and the witnesses who wouldn't testify.

"She called my bluff," I said, "because although I'm sure Mifune knows, his lips seem to be sealed. As are Lorenzo's. And anyhow, I'm never going to see Lorenzo again."

"Wait a minute; *wait just a minute!*" Jammy yelled. "Why are you not going to see Lorenzo again? What's the *contessa* got to do with him?"

"The two families are old friends; they go back centuries, I guess. Of course the *contessa* will tell Lorenzo I went to see her. I believe Lorenzo thinks she killed Jon-Boy and he's protecting the count's family name. Knowing that, how can I possibly see him again, Jammy? Even if he wanted to see me, which of course he won't because I went behind his back and accused the *contessa* of murder."

"So where does *love* figure in all this?"

"Love?"

"Yeah, you know, that good old emotion you and Lorenzo were feeling for each other. All that heady, winey soul-mate stuff, the kisses and the touching and . . . ohh, you know, *sex*. . . . All the *good* things. What about all that, Lamour?"

"I don't know," I said sadly. "I think I've burned my bridges,

Jammy, and now there's no going back. And the awful thing is, I still don't know what happened to Jon-Boy."

"Lamour." She said my name gently. "Don't you ever ask yourself if it's worthwhile? It's all so long ago. Is it worth unraveling the tangled strands of time to find the answer when in doing so you lose the chance of real true happiness? *Please,* Lamour, I'm *begging* you . . . think about it. Go to Lorenzo; apologize for stirring things up; tell him you love him and that nothing else matters. Then go live with him, marry him . . . whatever. . . . Just get *on* with your life. *Please,* honey, tell me you'll do that."

Suddenly Matt's voice came down the line. "I hate to admit it," he said, "but she's right. Put yourself first for once, Lamour. Grab that happiness while you can. Trust me, it's the best way—the *only* way—to go."

I promised to think about it, then said good-bye. I sat on the edge of the bed looking defeat in the face, and not for the first time in my life. They were right, of course, but it wasn't so easy to let Jon-Boy's death go like that. I *owed* that to him, in return for my happy childhood memories. And besides, I loved him.

The phone trilled and I picked it up. *"Pronto,"* I said listlessly.

"Lamour."

My numb heart did a little revived blip at the sound of Lorenzo's voice. "I'm downstairs in the bar," he said. "Could you please meet me there?"

I couldn't decide whether it was an order or a question, but I said yes. I combed my hair and put on some lipstick. I wondered how he knew I was here, then realized Mifune must have told him I'd gone to Rome and he knew I always stayed at the Inghilterra.

I took the tiny elevator down, thinking that a bar was hardly an appropriate place to seal one's fate. But then I hadn't expected to be doing that quite so soon.

Lorenzo was sitting alone at a table by the window. He got up when he saw me. With a catch in my throat, I thought how handsome he was, how strong he looked. An invincible man . . . a man who because I had exposed his secrets I was sure was here to say "Good-bye; it's not been so nice knowing you. . . ."

"Lamour," he said, taking my hand and brushing it with his lips.

A kiss on the hand wasn't exactly the way a man passionately in love usually greeted his woman, and I knew that he knew.

"This is a surprise," I said, taking the seat he held out for me. "What are you doing here?"

He signaled the barman and ordered two glasses of champagne. It had always been our celebratory drink, but I knew not today.

He turned to look at me. "I'm here for you," he said simply, and this time I swear my heart gave an extra little thump. "I've already spoken with Cassandra," he added, and this time my stupid heart, working overtime, sank. I could actually *feel* it somewhere in my stomach, which now began to churn with fear.

The champagne arrived. He picked up his glass and to my absolute astonishment said, "Here's to Jon-Boy, Lamour. May his memory live with you forever."

"I had to confront Cassandra," I said. "She said she didn't kill him. And I believe her."

He nodded. "I know. And I'm sorry you had to go through that." He smiled for the first time. "Cassandra Biratta is not an *easy* woman."

"She told me about her affair with Jon-Boy," I said, "and

then she gave me a sort of veiled threat about not demeaning her family name. I got the feeling she could pull strings and have me out of this country and no questions asked before I could even turn around."

"And I have no doubt she could," Lorenzo agreed calmly. "But you are not going after her, or her family. You are not going to pursue the matter any further, Lamour."

"Oh? And why not?" Anger made my voice rise.

"Because I am going to tell you exactly what happened," he said. "I'm going to tell you the truth."

I stared at him, sitting so calmly next to me. *"Really? Truly?"* I sounded like a little kid promised some great treat.

"Truly. But not here." He got to his feet and took my hand. "Come, Lamour," he said. "We need privacy. I'm taking you to my apartment."

Still holding his hand, I walked meekly to the waiting car. The driver held the door for me to get in. Lorenzo sat next to me and we were whisked through the crowded street to the home I had never seen.

FIFTY-NINE

Lamour

THOUGH IT, TOO, WAS AN OLD PALAZZO, LORENZO'S coolly modernistic home came as a culture shock after the excesses of the Palazzo Biratta. He had not let go of my hand since we left the hotel, and still clutching it tightly, he led me into an airy, almost loftlike space. I sat on a black leather sofa, smiling as I remembered Jammy's disparaging comments about Italian leather sofas. I believe she would have approved of this one's deep comfort, though. I was aware of soft neutral colors, of beautiful hand-loomed modern rugs, the spare simplicity of the furnishings, and the muted lighting, and I immediately felt at home. But I wasn't here to comment on Lorenzo's interior décor.

Sitting opposite me, he looked very serious. He leaned forward, hands clasped loosely between his knees. I was suddenly afraid of what he was going to tell me. Could *he* have killed Jon-Boy? I felt the blood drain from my face.

"I'm breaking a solemn promise by telling you what I'm about to tell you," he said, "but there is no other way, and I must hope that the person to whom I gave the promise will be able to forgive me. You are a determined woman, Lamour, and I can't blame you. In your place I would probably feel the same."

"I owe it to Jon-Boy," I said, feeling a sudden icy calm

overcome me. Whatever Lorenzo had to say, I was ready for it. Good or bad.

"Seven people knew what really happened that night," Lorenzo began, "and three of those are now dead. Jon-Boy, my wife, Marella, and one other woman. As you might have guessed, those still living—myself, Nico, Mifune, and the *contessa*—will never testify to what they saw. There is a reason for that, as you will see as the story evolves.

"Let me first tell you that Jon-Boy was loved by everybody. He was the kind of man who brought joy to daily life; just to sit with him talking of books and writers, of wine and music and travel, was a pleasure. Somehow you went home with a smile on your face and a lighter heart for having been in his company. Of course women flocked to him; how could they not? He treated them like rare treasures, even though he might know them only a few days or weeks. There was, however, one special woman in his life. Her name was Isabella."

"The 'I' in my father's diary," I interrupted. "I think he must have loved her very much."

Lorenzo nodded. "Indeed he did. The trouble was, he loved another woman more."

"Cassandra."

"Of course. Cassandra."

"She told me he loved her *too* much. She said she was smothered by his love."

"She lied," he said. "Cassandra was obsessed with Jon-Boy. She took over his life. He became a changed man; he didn't even attempt to write—and to me this was the greatest tragedy of all. I've never forgiven Cassandra Biratta for dissipating your father's talent. He'd already written one great novel, but he counted that in his past. He talked to me about his ideas for the next, about his philosophy of life, about children—and believe me, Lamour, when I tell you he loved

you probably more than you'll ever know. Sometimes it's easier for a man to talk to another man about his love for his
child than to talk to the child herself. And I admit, when I
heard that you were at the Mistress's House, I was curious to
meet this paragon. But I had my own world to protect. And
that was the cause of all the trouble."

I waited for him to tell me what he meant by "my own
world to protect." Could he mean Nico had something to do
with the murder and he had to protect his son?

"Jon-Boy's relationship with Isabella had been going on for
a couple of years," Lorenzo said. "She was a lovely girl, simple, sweet, earthy like him. She came from a poverty-stricken
background and she expected nothing beyond his love and attention. She worked in the bakery in Rome where he went
every day to pick up a slice of white pizza—"

"It was his favorite," I interrupted, smiling, as I remembered us walking through the Campo de' Fiori together, with
the hot pizza—more like focaccia crust sprinkled simply with
olive oil and salt—burning our hands and our tongues. We
could never wait long enough for it to cool before we ate it.

"Isabella moved into Jon-Boy's Rome apartment," Lorenzo
said, "but she still kept her job at the bakery, going off very
early every morning, leaving him alone in bed. She told me
her father was a true peasant of the old school. She said he'd
probably kill Jon-Boy if he knew about them. That's the reason she kept her job, as a sort of sop to her conscience; that
way at least she kept her independence. And she never took
money from Jon-Boy. Not a cent."

"Was she beautiful?" I asked wistfully, wishing I had
known the woman who loved my father so much.

He thought about it. "Not in the way Cassandra is beautiful, but she had great charm, and yes, she was quite lovely in a
softer, rounder way. She reminded me of the old Federico

Fellini movie stars Claudia Cardinale, Sophia Loren, Monica Vitti—those lovely, earthy, gutsy women. She was a pleasure to know."

Hands shoved deep in his pockets, head down, he began to prowl the room. "It's important you know about her because of what happened later," he said, and I nodded; I understood.

He stopped and looked at me. "Their relationship was drifting; Jon-Boy told me he felt pressured by his inability to work, and by Isabella's desire to be loved. And then he met Cassandra and he became a changed man.

"Jon-Boy thought of nothing but her. He no longer cared about his talent or his work, or even Isabella. He was a man deeply, tragically, in love with a woman who wasn't worth it. She drove him crazy and he took it."

Lorenzo stopped his prowling and came to stand in front of me. Looking down at me, he said, "Of course Cassandra knew about Isabella and she had her out of Jon-Boy's life so fast the poor girl hardly knew what hit her. Without Jon-Boy knowing, she moved Isabella's clothes out of his apartment, changed the locks, told her she was no longer wanted and that she should go back to her peasant family in Liguria.

"Cassandra kept guard over Jon-Boy like a pit bull. She allowed no one near him. She fancied herself his muse; she wanted to be the one who would guide his new novel, then present him to society as the world's most famous writer and her 'trophy.'

"Isabella called me, begging for my help. Of course I did what I could. I talked with Jon-Boy, but he was like a man in a dream. 'I love Cassandra, Lorenzo,' he said to me. 'There's nothing I can do about it, except send Isabella some money.' I was angry with him for treating her like that and told him that sending money would only add insult to injury. Of course, I sent money myself, trying to help her out, and she was grateful. But what none of us knew was that Isabella was pregnant."

I stared at him, dumbfounded. He came to sit next to me and took my hand in his.

"Lamour, this is what happened that night," he said. "It will be painful for you to hear, but it's the truth." And looking into my eyes, holding tightly on to my hand, he began to tell me.

SIXTY

Lorenzo

"THE STORM HAD BEEN BREWING SINCE MORNING," Lorenzo said. "Giant cumulus clouds crowded the sky, like ships under tight sail, scudding before the wind blowing in from the northeast. The sea was sullen, with little whitecaps, nothing important, but still I was uneasy. I told myself it was only October, too early for anything serious. Nico was just seven years old. He was home from school because of an epidemic of measles and I took him down to the cove with me to check on the boats.

"Nico had been a sailor almost since birth, when I held him on my knee at the helm of my old fishing boat as a baby. He was as at home on the ocean as he was on land, and right then his ambition was to be a speedboat racer.

"Down at the jetty, I tightened the lines on the three boats: a twenty-foot Chris-Craft; my fishing boat; and the small yellow tender with the outboard motor my wife used when she went shopping in Pirata or Amalfi.

"I checked the horizon, noting the black line that seemed to divide sea from the sky, and which I knew forecast trouble. Yet how bad could it be this early in the year? I thought about getting some men and beaching the boats but decided to take my chances.

"By afternoon the seas were swelling, great slow surges that slammed powerfully against the cliffs without breaking. The wind had picked up and was blowing trees sideways, flattening the grasses and shrubs, sending all the small wild creatures scurrying for shelter. But I'd seen it all before and was confident everything was battened down and made secure. I wasn't too concerned.

"By five o'clock the skies were already dark. I thought about Jon-Boy and how exposed his house was. I didn't know if he was there, but anyhow, Mifune and I decided we'd better check everything was securely shuttered.

"We found Jon-Boy out on his terrace, admiring the turbulent sky and the surging sea. 'Hi there,' he shouted over the wind. 'Have you ever seen anything like it? It's like the end of the world is coming.'

"'And it will, if you don't come inside.' Cassandra was at the open window. 'Tell him he's crazy, Lorenzo, and then come in and have a drink with us.'

"Mifune and I helped Jon-Boy close the shutters, latching them with the iron straps; then Mifune went off to check on the old cedar by the waterfall. The tree was his pride and joy and I knew he was praying it would be spared from the storm.

"Jon-Boy had lit a fire and now he threw on another log, then poured me a glass of wine. Cassandra was sitting on the sofa, smoldering with pent-up anger. Surprisingly, she was all dressed up in the red chiffon gown. I wondered why, because Jon-Boy was in his usual shorts and T-shirt. I assumed she had wanted to look glamorous and sexy for him. She got up to refill her glass and I thought how beautiful she looked. I also noticed that she was a little unsteady on her feet. She was drinking vodka neat and it was obvious this wasn't her first. I had the uncomfortable feeling they'd been having a fight, and I was right, because then Cassandra started getting on Jon-Boy, goading him about him losing his talent. I decided I'd better leave, but I now knew we were in for a big storm, and because the little house was so exposed I was worried for their safety. There might be a mudslide or a fallen tree, a broken chimney. Anything might happen.

"'If this storm gets as bad as I now think it will, you'll be safer staying with us at the Castello,' I said, but Jon-Boy laughed and said they'd be fine.

"As I walked back up the steps, I was surprised to see a car at the end of the road. I couldn't see who was driving because it backed up suddenly, made a quick turn, then took off. I thought nothing more about it and walked back up the hill to the Castello.

"When I told Marella about Cassandra, all dressed up in her red gown, drinking too much and needling Jon-Boy about his writing, or lack of it, she said she thought Cassandra was a fool. 'Jon-Boy's too in love with her,' she said. 'He's given up a good woman for her and now she wants to turn him into her puppet. She wants to be the muse to the great writer so she can show him off at parties. She thinks nothing of the terrible hurt she's done to poor Isabella, or to her own husband, the count.'

"I doubted if the count even knew what his wife was up to. Whenever I saw him socially there was never so much as a hint of a rift in his marriage. But Marella said that the fool's ego was so big he would never stoop to think any woman could cheat on a member of a family as prestigious as the Birattas.

"Dinner was eaten to the accompaniment of the howling of the wind and the rattling of windows. Nico kept on about how we should have beached the boats and I knew my seven-year-old was right. I had to tell him it was too late to do anything about it now." He smiled ruefully. "But you know Nico: he was never a boy to take no for an answer, especially from me, and that Chris-Craft was the current love of his heart. He was determined not to let anything happen to her. After dinner he sneaked out of the house. Ten minutes later we discovered he was missing and I knew immediately where he'd gone. I went after him.

"By now the rain was torrential, mixed with hail, hard like nails, driven sideways by the wind so you could hardly see. Lightning lit the horizon and I was terrified thinking of Nico on those slippery *scalatinella,* terrified he would get swept off the jetty by a wave, terrified for my son. . . . And when I got down there, Nico was nowhere in sight."

He paused and looked at Lamour. "I can't tell you what went through my mind in those few minutes, looking at the empty jetty with the three boats lurching up and down on the swells, slamming into the pilings, and no sign of my son. A hundred different scenarios played through my brain, each more terrible than the last. . . . And then I heard his voice.

" 'Papa, Papa.' He came running down the steps toward me. 'Come quickly,' he yelled. 'Come quickly, Papa.'

" 'What is it?' I grabbed him by the shoulders. 'What's wrong, Nico?'

" 'Come, come. Jon-Boy . . .' He tugged frantically at my arm and I followed him back up the stairs to the Mistress's House. He'd been there to ask Jon-Boy to help him with the boats, seeing what was happening.

"The door was open, slamming back and forth in the wind, sending the fire in the grate sparking and smoking. Cassandra, looking like a beautiful baleful devil in her red dress, was standing in front of a heavily pregnant Isabella. I had only a moment to think about it, but it seemed to me Isabella looked like a poor little waif, a child herself, soaking wet from the rain, her long hair straggling, and her huge belly . . .

" 'Get out of here, you cheap nothing woman,' Cassandra was screaming at her, going on and on.

"Isabella ignored her. She spoke only to Jon-Boy. 'I called you,' she was saying in her sweet, low voice. 'I left you messages, Jon-Boy. I tried to tell you about the baby. . . . I found where you were living, but they wouldn't let me in. . . . You didn't even try to find me; you didn't want to know me anymore. . . . You didn't want to know I was carrying your child. But she knew . . . and now I thought you should know, too, despite her. . . .'

"Cassandra slapped her face. Jon-Boy grabbed Cassandra. He hurled her away. He had eyes now only for Isabella. 'I swear I didn't know,' he said. He was desperate. 'I would never have left you alone. . . .' He reached out for her.

"From the corner of my eye I saw Cassandra pick up the paper knife from Jon-Boy's writing table. She hurtled across the room, but I grabbed her before she got to Isabella. 'She's lying,' she screamed. 'And anyway, Jon-Boy knew all along you were pregnant. He didn't care. He knew it wasn't his.'

"I twisted Cassandra's arm, though it was her neck I really wanted to twist, and the knife dropped to the floor.

"Jon-Boy seemed afraid to take Isabella in his arms and comfort her. He held out his hands tentatively and for a long moment she stared into his face. Searching for what? I wondered. An answer, I suppose. . . . And she didn't find it."

Lorenzo turned to Lamour; he took her hand as he said, "I swear to you, Lamour, in that moment I saw that something inside Isabella had snapped. I saw it in her eyes. She grabbed the knife and rushed at Cassandra. I heard Nico yelling in the background and Jon-Boy shouting, 'No, no.' He caught the knife by the blade. Blood dripped from his wounded hand.

"For once Cassandra was silent. Isabella looked at the knife as though she had never seen it before, then at the bleeding Jon-Boy. Her face contorted with pain. She held her hands over her belly and moaned.

"I spotted Mifune hovering in the doorway, saw Nico run to him and Mifune put his arms protectively around him. For seconds all was silent. The wind gusted through the house, sending the smoke curling from the fire. I said, 'Isabella, let me help you. I'm going to take you to the Castello; we'll get a doctor. Everything is going to be all right. You and Jon-Boy can talk about this later.'

"She looked at me with those big brown eyes, but I swear it was as though she wasn't there. Suddenly, filled with a kind of furious energy, she pushed past Mifune, and she was out the door, running down the slippery flights of steps, heading for the cove.

"Jon-Boy ran after her, but Cassandra grabbed his arm and clung to him. He thrust her away. 'I'll never forgive you for this,' he said, and then he was running down the steps after Isabella.

"Cassandra slumped into a chair. Tears ran down her face and she put up a hand to brush them away, leaving traces of Jon-Boy's blood on her cheek. But I had no time or sympathy for her right then.

"'Mifune, come with me,' I yelled, heading after Jon-Boy. 'Nico, you stay here; you'll be safe now.' But Nico ran after us, followed us down to the cove.

"The rain slashed down so we could hardly see, but I knew those steps like the back of my own hand, knew where they were too worn, where to jump. Lightning flashed and I saw Isabella take a tumble and Jon-Boy run to her. Somehow she struggled to her feet before he reached her. She ran onto the jetty.

"He caught up to her, reached out for her, pulled her into his arms. As he did so, she went limp. Dear God, I thought, pan-icked, she's dead. I heard Mifune and Nico on the steps behind me . . . heard also the sudden rattle of rocks and stones as the cliff began to slide, sending mud and rocks onto the jetty.

"Jon-Boy laid Isabella down. He bent over her, talking to her. I was running down the last few steps now. . . . Suddenly she sprang to life, fighting him off. He got to his feet, slipped in the mud, lost his footing again, crashed down next to her. He lay still. I was running toward them now, almost there. . . . Isabella knelt over him. I saw her put her face over his and kiss him. I saw her lift a large rock over his head. And then she let it drop. Even over the roar of the wind I heard his skull crack. Then she slammed his head down on the jetty. Again. And again.

"I pushed her away, lifted Jon-Boy in my arms. But he was already dead.

"I looked at Isabella. She just stood there, panting like a small scared animal, her hands over the child in her belly.

"I looked back for Mifune, but Nico had slipped and fallen and he was helping him up. I ran back to the steps to make sure he was all right, yelling for Mifune to come help me. When I turned around, somehow Isabella had rolled Jon-Boy's body into the small boat. She'd cast off the lines and got in next to him. The boat spun round and round in the turbulence, and even as I watched, it was picked up by the gi-ant swells and carried swiftly out to sea."

SIXTY-ONE

Lorenzo

"INTO THE DARK, DARK NIGHT," LAMOUR SAID, HER voice thick with tears.

"That's the way it happened," Lorenzo said gently. "I'm sorry, Lamour; I never wanted to tell you this. But now you know the truth."

He wanted to help her but knew he could not. At this moment, she was alone with her pain. "There was nothing I could do," he said quietly, "except wait for the storm to abate and the sea to send them back to us."

He fetched her a glass of water, waiting until her sobs had lessened before he continued his story.

"Early the next morning the coast guard spotted the yellow tender a couple of miles offshore. There was only one person in it. Isabella. And she was half-dead. As was the baby she had given birth to, alone at sea in the storm."

Lamour gasped. He put his arms around her and held her to him. "Isabella died, Lamour. But her daughter lived."

He felt her stiffen. *"Jon-Boy's daughter,"* she said.

Lorenzo took her face in his hands, thinking he had never loved her more than he did at this moment, when, because of what he was about to say, he might lose her. "*My* daughter now, Lamour," he said. "Aurora."

Her stunned eyes met his.

"Marella and I were filled with pity for the baby. How

could things be worse for her? Her mother had murdered her father, and now she was an orphan. I looked at my wife holding that poor little scrap and I knew we had to keep her. It was the right thing to do. But Marella made one condition. That Aurora would never know the truth about her real parents. We agreed there was no reason an innocent child should suffer because of them. Three years later, when Marella knew she was dying, she made me repeat that vow.

"So you see," he said finally, "when I heard you were coming and that you were determined to find out exactly what had happened to Jon-Boy, I had no choice but to try my best to dissuade you." He smiled ruefully. "Of course it didn't work, because you had already charmed your way into my heart. I should have known any daughter of Jon-Boy's would have that capacity."

"Like Aurora," Lamour said.

"Like Aurora," he agreed. "But now you know the truth, and why I've spoiled her, and why she's wary and uncertain that she is loved and always will be. There's a fear, a kind of deep despair, in Aurora that I can never get rid of, no matter how I reassure her. Of course when Marella died, it only got worse. Psychologists blame it on the circumstances of Aurora's birth, exposed to the elements, alone with her dying mother. She was born in the cold and the rain with no one to hold her; there was no mother–daughter bonding. Aurora is damaged. She's manic-depressive; some days she can hardly bear to breathe, to live. And I, of course, live in fear for her— for what she might do to herself. . . . Perhaps our love came too late for her." He shrugged. "I will always hope not."

He handed Lamour the glass of water. She took a sip, looking big eyed at him over the rim of the glass. "Poor, poor Aurora," she said, really understanding her for the first time.

"And thank you for telling me. I know Marella would forgive you, under the circumstances."

"I hope so. Of course, Aurora still knows nothing about Jon-Boy and Isabella. Now I'm wondering if we did the right thing. Perhaps, after all, it would have been better to tell her right from the beginning."

"At least then she would have known she had a sister," Lamour said, suddenly waking up to the fact.

A smile broke across Lorenzo's face. "Did I ever tell you why I love you?" he asked, and then they were in each other's arms, each finding comfort in the other.

SIXTY-TWO

Lorenzo

AURORA HAD ALWAYS KNOWN SHE WAS ADOPTED, but she had never questioned Lorenzo about her birth parents. He believed it was because she didn't want to know, but now he felt he owed it to her to tell her the truth, and her psychiatrist agreed. But remembering Aurora's fragile psyche, Lorenzo wanted to avoid the tragic details. He needed to make this as easy and untraumatic as possible for her. He'd discussed this with Mifune, who of course knew the whole story and who had known Aurora since the day she was born.

"Tell her she was always loved," was what Mifune had said. "For Aurora, love is everything."

That afternoon Lorenzo went in search of his daughter. He combed the grounds for her, but in the end it was Affare who found her, up in the tree house where she and Nico had played as children.

Lorenzo tugged on the bell-rope they had rigged up to warn of interfering grown-ups. Affare barked and the bell jangled, and Aurora's head popped over the side of the tiny balcony.

"Just like Juliet," Lorenzo called, smiling.

"But with no Romeo," she answered with that bleak note in her voice that, he knew only too well, signaled that she was having a bad day.

"Come sit with your papa for a while," he said, settling on

a stone bench in the shade of the grove of umbrella pines whose lovely rounded shapes never failed to remind him of the fifteenth-century paintings by the Florentine artist Paolo Uccello.

Aurora came slowly down the ladder. Her face looked pale, her long hair was uncombed, and she was shoeless in cut-off denim shorts and a rumpled T-shirt. She looked as though she'd just stepped out of bed, and in fact she had, because she had spent the night in her old refuge, the tree house. Lorenzo wondered if she was taking her medication, but he knew if he asked it would provoke her. He'd have to get Nico to check on her.

Affare gave Aurora a few enthusiastic licks, finally bringing a smile to her face, for which Lorenzo was grateful. He hoped the sunny mood would last.

"*Carina,* I've often wondered why you never wanted to know about your birth parents," he began. "You've expressed no curiosity, but now you are twenty-one years old."

"I never asked because I didn't want to hurt your feelings, Papa," she said.

"I understand." He took her hand and held it between both his. "And I know you can never call anyone but Marella Mother, nor anyone but me Papa, because that is who we will always be. But in fact, *carina,* I knew your birth mother. Her name was Isabella. She was a lovely girl, not much older than you are now, simple, sweet, loving. But Isabella was not married. One day she and her lover had a fight over another woman and Isabella ran away. She was eight months pregnant with you when she set out to sea in the storm."

"You mean that legendary storm, when Jon-Boy Harrington died?"

"Yes. In fact, Jon-Boy tried to save her. Sadly, he perished, too. When the coast guard found the boat you had just been born and Isabella was still alive. Barely. There was nothing anyone could do to save her. She died a few minutes later. But when I saw Marella holding you, a tiny scrap of a girl with huge eyes and a mop of dark hair, I knew that out of this tragedy we had been blessed and that you were ours to love." He gave Aurora's hand a squeeze, looking anxiously at her.

"We called you Aurora, after the goddess of the dawn, because you came to us with the dawn. You were our destiny and we yours. Aurora, you are the daughter of my heart, just the way you would have been your birth father's."

Aurora's sudden cry of anguish set Affare howling. The girl flung herself into Lorenzo's arms trembling. He patted her back soothingly, the way he had when she was a child, afraid to go to sleep because of the nightmares where "bad things" always lay in wait for her.

"It's not your fault, *carina*," he whispered. "It was no one's fault. Isabella was dying even as you were born. Her reckless act killed her—not you. Not her baby. Believe me, Aurora, it was not your fault."

"Then whose was it?" Her head shot up and she stared wildly at him. "Who got her pregnant? Who was this lover? Who *is* my father?"

"He was a fine man. A good man, beloved by everyone who knew him. He would have been a good father to you."

"How do you know?" she demanded.

"Because I know his other daughter," Lorenzo said, knowing the die was finally cast but not knowing what kind of Pandora's box he might be opening. Aurora was staring at him, openmouthed. "He was Jon-Boy Harrington," he said.

Aurora frowned, bewildered. "You mean *il dottore*?" Like everyone else, she'd heard about the legendary writer. Then she added, shocked, *"Lamour's father?"*

Lorenzo nodded. "Lamour is your half sister."

Aurora turned her head away, staring off into space. "I don't like her," she said at last.

"You don't know her," Lorenzo said, "but now you have a chance to find out."

"You are in love with her," she said accusingly.

Lorenzo understood she was jealous, and he told her that one day she would understand that love between a man and a woman was a different thing from that between a father and a daughter. "Ask Lamour," he said, "because no girl ever loved her father more."

To his surprise, Aurora did not cry. She sat up, straight backed and perfectly composed. It was as though the shock of knowing who she really was had come as a relief.

"Thank you, Papa, for telling me." Getting up, she added, "I think I'll go for a walk alone. I need some time to think."

He got quickly to his feet and put his arms around her in a hug. "I understand, *carina*," he said gently. "But I want you always to remember that you are my daughter, the daughter of my heart. Nothing will ever change that."

Aurora was smiling as she walked away, and Lorenzo thought she seemed at peace with herself.

SIXTY-THREE

MIFUNE WAS WORKING NEAR THE SWIMMING POOL when he saw Aurora coming down the path after her talk with her father.

She was walking slowly, her head held high, seemingly unconcerned, yet as soon as she knew she was out of sight her shoulders and her head drooped. She sank to the ground and lay there curled into a ball, knees under her chin, arms clasped over her head, tight as any babe in the womb, signaling anguish from every bone in her body.

At first Mifune thought she was crying, but then he realized these were not sobs. Aurora was moaning, ghostly sounds that came from the desperate hidden part of her over which she had no control. The beautiful young woman he had known since she was a child had reverted to the wild, a small, hurt animal who did not know what to do.

Mifune went and sat beside her, but Aurora was so consumed with her own angst she did not even notice him until he spoke.

"Little one," he said gently, "there is no reason for all this pain. Shock, yes of course, but not this pain. Your father still loves you the way he always has, right from the moment he first saw you. As did your mother."

Aurora's head shot up. She glared at him from under a curtain of dark hair. "My *mother*? Even you knew who she really was, Mifune. Everyone knew except me. I was the dope no one could bring themselves to tell the truth to. The bastard child of Jon-Boy Harrington and a worthless woman. . . ."

"Never call Isabella worthless." For once Mifune's voice was sharp. "Your birth mother was a lady; she was gentle, kind; she was a pleasure to know. . . ."

Aurora's laugh was bitter. "What a combination I am, Mifune. And all the while I thought I was the daughter of Lorenzo and Marella Pirata. I made myself believe I counted in life because of them, that I was somebody instead of the nobody I've somehow always known in my heart I really was. Do you know what it feels like to *know* that, Mifune? To wake each day with a question on your lips: *Who am I today? The good or the bad, the light or the dark?* Saying, *'Please, God, let me be the "happy" one today; don't let me fall into that black pit of depression again. . . .'* No, of course you can't know that. Only those who suffer from this handicap, this giant black dog that beats you down one day, then reprieves you the next, can know. Sometimes he deludes you into believing you could be a whole person, not some poor torn soul searching for herself, striving to get out of bed in the morning, to find a reason to go on living and behave 'normally.' Ahh, Mifune, you know something? I'm twenty-one years old and I still don't know what 'normal' is."

Mifune did not touch her because he knew she would draw back into herself and he wanted her to keep on talking, to try to talk herself through this bad moment. He wanted desperately to help her, but he knew she needed more than his small words of wisdom.

"Little one," he said gently, "I, too, had to search for the person who was 'myself.' I was left an orphan at the age of two. I never knew my parents. I was farmed out to an uncle and aunt while they lay ill in the far northern reaches of

THE HOUSE IN AMALFI 313

Japan. First my parents died; then my aunt died. There was
Japan. First my parents died; then my aunt died. There was
no money for an education. I was a poor peasant and I went
to work alongside my uncle. I was forced to come to terms
with that and find my own kind of peace. There was no love
in my life. I was not as fortunate as you, Aurora, to find a family to love me."

"A secondhand family," Aurora said bitterly.

"What the Piratas gave you was not secondhand love. It
was pure love, and you must never forget that. I have watched
you struggle with depression, Aurora. I know how hard it is
for you, but I am begging you now to understand, to know
that Lorenzo and Marella loved you as much as they loved
Nico. There was never any difference, not just in the way you
were both treated but in their acceptance of you as their own
child, and in the gift of their love. Do not throw away that
gift, Aurora. Let your father find the help you need to overcome those days when the black dog doesn't want you to get
out of bed, when he allows you no pleasure in life, when he
sees no reason for you to live. Your father has always helped
you; you know he will do anything for you. He will help you
now."

Curled back in that tight fetal ball, Aurora retreated from
Mifune's all-knowing eyes behind her curtain of hair. She
didn't speak for a while because she was thinking and she
didn't want Mifune to know those thoughts. The black dog
weighing down her shoulders had gone as suddenly as he appeared. Now the path was clear, the way rosy as a sunset. She
knew exactly what she must do. And she knew who she
wanted to accompany her on that final journey.

She got unsteadily to her feet. "Thank you, Mifune, for
your advice," she said, bowing to him. Then sweeping her
long dark hair out of her eyes, she walked slowly along the
path leading to the cliff and to the sea where Jon-Boy and her

mother had died and where she had been born. She took the *scalatinella* leading to the Mistress's House and to her half sister, Lamour Harrington.

Unnoticed, Mifune followed at a discreet distance. There was something in Aurora's sudden change of attitude that sent out warning signals. Her too-careful body language made him sure she was hiding something. Aurora was unpredictable and right now she was dangerous. He did not know what she might do.

SIXTY-FOUR

Lamour

AS HAD BECOME MY HABIT, I WAS SITTING IN THE belvedere with my glass of wine, watching the evening sky turn astonishing shades of pink and orange. The silvery sea reflected the hot colors until I felt I was in the middle of a giant kaleidoscope where every angle shimmered and shone, changing every second.

"*Mia sorella,*" a quiet voice said.

I looked up and saw Aurora standing by the belvedere. She had called me her "sister" and I knew that Lorenzo had told her, but I couldn't tell from her tone whether she was being sarcastic or pleasant.

"Don't get up," she said. "I'll just sit here, if I may?"

"Please." I waved an arm at the empty chair and asked if she would like some wine. When she said she would, I poured her a glass, and we sat together in uncomfortable silence, staring out to the sea, avoiding looking at each other.

"So we are sisters," she said at last.

I nodded. "Lorenzo told me, too."

"Did you love your father very much?" she asked, rather wistfully, I thought.

"Very much. I've learned that he wasn't perfect, but then, who of us is?" I shrugged. "Certainly not I. But Jon-Boy was a good man, a kind man. And you know what else he was, Aurora?" I smiled, remembering. "Jon-Boy was *fun*. We had such good times when I was a little kid, especially after he brought me here to Italy. All my good memories are of our times together in Rome, and then here at this house. That's why I came back. My personal life was falling apart and I wanted to try to recapture the feeling of true happiness I remembered from then."

She stared curiously at me with those huge dark eyes that seemed to reflect no light. "And how did it feel, that kind of happiness?" she asked.

I looked at her, shocked. This child of love and privilege was asking me, the kid who was shunted from house to house, who was dumped on the Mortimers and who rarely saw her father. . . . Could this girl *really* be asking me what true happiness felt like?

She waited seriously for my reply. "It took me a while to find this out, Aurora," I said finally, "but I believe happiness is to be found in the small things of life. Don't go searching for the holy grail, for goodness' sakes; just take any happiness you can, right there at that moment you find it. It's in small things like when you're dunking a chocolate chip cookie into a glass of ice-cold milk, anticipating how it will taste, the chill and the chocolate, the melting texture on your tongue. It's in the purr of a cat who curls herself up on your lap, giving you her warmth and sharing her contentment. It's even in Affare's joyful bark of greeting, and her settling comfortably at your father's feet while you play an evening game of backgammon together. It's when you dance with a man and his eyes smile at you, telling you you look wonderful and that he's thrilled to be with you. . . . It's in the pretty new dress that makes you feel good. . . . It's in the softness of the bed that envelops you after you've exhausted yourself working in the hot sun. It's even here, right now, Aurora. It's you and I, two newly found sisters, sharing a glass of wine and together watching the sun set."

Her black eyes were fixed on me. "Is that all there is?" she asked sadly.

I was in too deep here; I couldn't handle this kind of despair, this soul's worth of sadness. "It's not all, *carina*," I said gently, "but it's a start, don't you think?"

"And did you find it then? The happiness you were looking for here?"

"Now I have. Thanks to my lovely Amalfi house and its garden. And to my old friend Mifune. And of course to your father."

"You two are in love."

I caught the flicker of resentment in her voice. "I love Lorenzo," I admitted. "But then as you know, he's an easy man to love."

"He told me you look like your father. *Our* father."

"He told me that, too. I have pictures of Jon-Boy, if you'd like to see them."

A mask of caution descended over her face. "I think I'd like that," she said, but I could tell she was apprehensive. After all, it wasn't easy being presented with a birth father and a sister you had never known about until that day.

I said impulsively, "Look, Jon-Boy was as good a father as a free spirit like him could be. You would have liked him, but I think you were better off with Lorenzo for a father." She looked surprised, but I wanted her to know the truth as I now knew it.

I brought out the leather case containing the old snapshots of Jon-Boy and me, most of them taken right here in Amalfi. There was also a clipping from *The New York Times* praising his novel, with a photograph of him looking handsome and amused, a lock of black hair sliding over his eyes.

Aurora looked at the photographs in silence. She read the article, then folded it carefully up again. She stared for a long time at a snapshot of Jon-Boy and me standing on this terrace, holding hands, beaming into the camera. She ran a gentle finger over it and said, "I can see you were happy together, Lamour. I'm sorry you lost him."

I pushed down the lump in my throat. "And I'm sorry you never knew him. But we both gained something, Aurora. You gained a wonderful father in Lorenzo."

"And you gained a lover."

We were on tricky ground again; I heard it in her suddenly steely voice. I didn't answer, busying myself replacing the photos in their case.

"Lamour . . . ?"

I glanced up, wondering what was coming.

"I really need to get to know you. I think I *need* you. I've never had a real woman friend, not even in school. I was always so . . . different . . . you see. . . ."

Oh God, the poor girl was damaged and here I was judging her. None of us could cure Aurora. We could only in our simplistic way try to encourage her. I had to be there for her. "Of course I'll be your friend, Aurora," I said eagerly. "After all, that's what sisters are supposed to be."

She held out her hand to me. "Then come with me. Let's be alone together for a while, Lamour. Just you and me. Let's go for a sail; I'll take you to my secret place, a cave I discovered. Not even Nico knows about it. But now I want to share it with you."

It was a bit late to go sailing, the sun was already setting, but I leaped at the chance to become her confidante, keeper of her secrets. After all, she was my half sister and I was also about to become her stepmother. Bonding was a priority.

"Let's go, *sorella mia*," I said with a new lilt in my voice, and we walked together down the flights of rocky stairs to the jetty where the boats waited.

From his position at the top of the cliff, Mifune saw them go. He saw Aurora on the jetty untie the mooring lines of her father's old fishing boat. He saw Lamour bound gaily on board, then hold out her hand, laughing, to help Aurora make the leap from the jetty. He saw Aurora fiddling with the controls. He knew she had never sailed her father's boat before. She scarcely knew what she was doing, but of course Lamour was unaware of that.

Every nerve in Mifune's body warned him of danger. He turned and made for the Castello and Lorenzo as fast as an old man could.

SIXTY-FIVE

Lamour

I HAD FOND MEMORIES OF LORENZO AND ME MAKING love on this old fishing boat, but this was the first time I had ever sailed on it. Smiling, I watched Aurora guide us out to sea. I thought, relieved, she seemed calm, almost contented, and I wondered if knowing about Jon-Boy and Isabella might be some kind of turning point for her and now she might be able to face her future without the fears that had plagued her all her young life.

She turned the boat south, then came to lean companionably on the rail next to me. I don't know much about sailing, but I'd always thought somebody should be at the helm, even in a little baby-type boat like my own. "Hey," I said, a touch nervously, "shouldn't one of us be doing the driving?"

But Aurora just laughed, a rare sound. "Oh, this old ship knows exactly where it's going," she said. "Don't worry, Lamour; it's on automatic pilot."

I hadn't realized boats could have automatic pilots and I wasn't sure I believed her, but she seemed unconcerned, so I took her word for it.

"How interesting," she said, suddenly animated. "See that cloud on the horizon, Lamour? I'll bet you that in a few minutes it'll be joined by another, then another. This must have been exactly the way the storm blew up that killed Jon-Boy and Isabella."

I stared at her, shocked. She was smiling happily, her eyes fixed on the horizon.

"See, what did I tell you!" she exclaimed. "There's another cloud. I know the weather around here better than I know my own mind. We're in for a storm, Lamour. Isn't that exciting?"

I groped around in my mind for what to say. I knew next to nothing about boats and sailing or about bad weather at sea, except that my father had disappeared in the kind of storm she was predicting now. Afraid of provoking her, I said as calmly as I could, "We'd better turn round, Aurora, head for home. Your father will be getting worried."

"No, he won't; he doesn't even know we've gone. Nobody does."

She was right. I stared at the receding shoreline. It was too far to swim, and anyhow the sea was already surging into a swell, lifting our little fishing boat, then letting it slide down again in a way that churned my already nervous stomach. Aurora was now up in the bow, hair streaming in the wind. And then I realized Aurora had lied to me. There was no automatic pilot and this boat was sailing into the swell and the oncoming storm, unguided.

I lurched along the deck to the little cockpit. I stared blankly at the control panel. At least there was an old-fashioned wheel; maybe I could turn us around, head back to shore.

"Lamour."

Aurora was standing next to me. She put her hands over mine. "Don't do that, Lamour, please," she said softly. "I need you with me. You said you would be my friend. I didn't expect this storm, but it's wonderful, isn't it? It's just so perfect I can't believe my luck." She laughed, a joyous, lovely sound that made me think everything was going to be all right after all.

And then she said, "Don't you see why it's perfect? It's just like the night I was born. And now I'm going to die. I was going to do this alone, *mia sorella,* but now I think maybe you will have to join me. And I promise you, it will be lovely, beautiful, just the way it was for your father." She gripped my hands tighter, staring deep into my eyes. "We'll join him now, Lamour, in his lovely resting place. . . . What could be nicer than the family together at last?"

Oh God, oh God. . . . She was crazy. . . . She had planned all along to kill herself . . . and now I was going to join her. . . .

"Aurora, *why?*" I struggled to get my hands free, but she pressed them down on the wheel so hard I yelped with pain.

"Don't you get it?" she said. "I wanted you to witness my death; then you would have to be the one to tell Lorenzo. And I wanted you to see the way your father died . . . so you could feel the kind of pain I feel. You who are so pure and se-cure, so independent and calm, so . . . so *real.* . . . "

The boat gave a sudden lurch as a wave hit broadside. Au-rora let go her grip and staggered back, smacking her head against the metal lantern. Her eyes rolled in her head and she slid to the floor, just as the boat rolled again, sending me crash-ing on top of her. Somehow I scrambled to my knees. . . . There was blood on my hands, on my shirt . . . and blood trickled thick as old wine from Aurora's head. I took off my shirt and put it under her. She did not move.

Terrified, I grabbed the wheel again, staring out through the little cockpit window. The edge of the horizon darkened, then blurred, moving quickly toward us, as though night was creeping up out of the ocean. The boat lifted over another swell, rocking deeply. I glanced from side to side, assessing the sea. Even I knew that in weather like this I would have to tack, that is, sail the boat first one way, then the next, in short angled spurts, heading back to the shore. Only trouble was I didn't know how to do that. I looked at the horizon creeping closer and with dread in my heart knew I had no option but to find out. And right now.

I looked anxiously at Aurora, still unconscious on the floor, and thought of my father. History was repeating itself. There was nothing I could do for her; I tried to concentrate on keeping the boat afloat. Sudden bitter tears flooded my eyes. I choked them back. "Jon-Boy, oh, Jon-Boy," I yelled bitterly into the wind that was slamming into us, just as the rains came, "don't let it be this way; please, please, oh please . . . help me. . . ."

SIXTY-SIX

NICO WAS DRIVING HIS RED PORSCHE UP THE Castello's long gravel drive when he saw Mifune hurrying from the thicket of pine trees. Nico was surprised. Mifune always moved calmly and slowly; he'd never seen him run before. Alarmed, Nico stopped the car and got out.

"Mifune," he called, catching up and grabbing his arm. "What's wrong?"

The old man rocked on his feet, sweat poured down his bony face, and he had trouble catching his breath.

"Take your time, time, your time . . . ," Nico said, but he already knew it was something bad.

"Aurora," Mifune gasped, and Nico's heart sank. "Your father told her about Isabella and Jon-Boy. . . . She went to find Lamour. She's taken her out on Lorenzo's boat. Something bad is going to happen, Nico. . . . I feel it. . . ."

Nico knew he was right. Aurora had never sailed the old fishing boat—she knew nothing about it—and a storm was about to hit. His instinct was to head immediately for the jetty and the Riva and go after them, but he knew he must tell his father first. . . . At least then somebody would know where he was and could call the coast guard.

He put Mifune in the Porsche and drove to the house. They found Lorenzo out on the terrace, watching the approaching storm.

"Oh, Nico, there you are," he said. "I'm glad you got home before the storm broke. Odd, isn't it, how I can never see a storm approach like this without thinking of Jon-Boy and Isabella, and Aurora of course."

"Aurora's out there," Nico said abruptly. He told him what Mifune had witnessed and immediately Lorenzo got on the phone and alerted the coast guard rescue service. Then he and Nico drove back to the road and took the elevator down to the cove.

The sea was already hurling itself at the jetty, rocking the Riva at its mooring. Lamour's little boat was smacking up against the pilings, but there was no time to worry about that now. Nico was already in the Riva, revving up the engine, while Lorenzo untied the lines. He leaped on board and they took off.

The rain hit as they emerged from the cove, sweeping over them like a curtain, soaking them in seconds.

Nico guided his boat by instinct and experience through the rocky channel and out to sea. "She'll head for the caves just past Pirata," he shouted to Lorenzo over the roar. "She thinks I don't know about them, but of course I do. It's where she'd take Lamour; I know it."

Lorenzo forced back his panic. Like Mifune, he knew instinctively his daughter had set out to kill herself at sea, in the place she had been born. And now she was going to take Lamour with her. He needed to control his emotions, to take charge, or both women would die.

The slender Riva crashed into the swells, hurtling over the top and flying into the dips like a carnival ride, even though Nico took it sideways-on. They were five minutes out when they spotted the fishing boat. It was headed toward shore, and even as they saw it, it caught the full onslaught of a wave and took on water, dipping and lurching.

"Dear God," Lorenzo cried, "there they are, Nico. . . ."

Nico gunned his engine in a futile effort for more speed.

"Bring her alongside," Lorenzo commanded, already fashioning the ropes into a makeshift harness that would secure him to the Riva. As Nico edged his speedboat alongside, the wind took it, scraping its length along the wooden fishing boat with a sound like an electric saw. Groaning, Nico looked up and saw Lamour's head pop out from the cockpit.

"Lamour's there," he yelled to his father.

Lorenzo saw Lamour and his heart did a double leap. She was shouting something to him, but he couldn't hear over the wind. He knew every inch of his old fishing boat, he knew where he could fix that line, and he knew how to do it, except the boat was a moving target. He motioned Lamour to catch the rope. She got it on the fifth attempt and staggered back, clutching it. Somehow she knew what to do, wrapping it around and around the wheel, anchoring it with the weight of her own body.

Nico held the Riva as stable as he could, as Lorenzo began to swing hand-over-hand across the line. He was almost there when a wave caught the boat, sending it slamming against his chest. Lorenzo yelled with pain, his fingers uncurled, and he lost his grip. He was falling. . . . He grabbed out, caught the line with one hand, felt the electric jolt of pain in his shoulder.

He swung himself up on deck. Lamour felt the line go slack; she hurtled out of the cockpit and into his arms. "Aurora's hurt," she cried. "We have to help her. . . ."

Lorenzo knelt over his unconscious daughter. He touched her bloody head, felt the sting of tears in his eyes. He loved her so. . . . He heard the clatter of the coast guard rescue helicopter overhead. "Thank God," he muttered, cradling Aurora's bloody head. But he knew it wasn't over yet.

Nico swung the Riva away from the boat and the swirl

created by the helicopter's rotors. He kept her as steady as he could, watching as the aircraft fluttered over the fishing boat, then sent down a crew member with the rescue basket. Nico saw them load his sister's inert body into the basket and winch it into the helicopter. Lamour was next.

When it was over, Lorenzo stood for a few seconds on the deck of his beloved old boat. Then, head bowed, he, too, was winched aboard.

Only then did Nico turn and, bouncing over the swells, make his way back to shore.

SIXTY-SEVEN

Lamour

I OPENED MY EYES AND STARED UP AT A VAULTED blue ceiling scattered with stars and looped with painted garlands. I was in bed, but not my own. I heard the rustle of a starched apron, soft footsteps; then someone was bending over me, her face close to mine.

"Ah, signora, at last you are awake," she said in Italian, confusing me, because I hadn't yet remembered I was in Italy.

"Where am I?" I asked.

"Why, at the Castello, of course, signora," she said cheerfully. "When you refused to stay in the hospital, the Signor Pirata brought you back here."

"Hospital?" I took a good look at her. Of course, she was a nurse. "But I'm not sick," I mumbled as she tucked a thermometer between my lips.

"Perhaps not, but you had a bad experience, out there in the storm. The doctor said we must keep you quiet, allow you to rest, make sure there are no ill effects."

Then I remembered. *I remembered it all.* Aurora planning to kill herself. Aurora joyful because of the storm that would drown me along with her. Aurora trapping my hands with ferocious strength so I couldn't turn the wheel and head the boat back to shore. Aurora lying unconscious, her bloody head. . . .

"Aurora?" I said urgently.

The nurse took out the thermometer, inspected it critically, then nodded her head. "Normal. And the Signorina Aurora is in the hospital still. She suffered a severe laceration to her scalp, but there was no fracture. She will be fine."

The nurse avoided my eyes and I guessed she wasn't going to talk about Aurora's other "sickness." I thought of Lorenzo, gazing, stricken, at his unconscious daughter, and the grief in his eyes. All her life he had sheltered her, protected her from dealing with the real world. He had found the best psychiatrists and psychologists, but he had never been able to remove the great weight of clinical depression that had brought Aurora to the point of attempted suicide. There were times, I realized, when love alone was not enough.

The door opened and I recognized Lorenzo's footsteps even before I saw him. I didn't want to cry, I didn't mean to, but when I looked into his concerned face I felt those stupid tears roll out of my eyes and slide onto my pillow.

"I'm sorry," I said, and heard him laugh.

The nurse arranged my pillows so I could sit up. I saw Lorenzo was carrying a tray with tea and toast and boiled eggs, chocolate chip cookies, and milk.

"Lunch," he said. "You've been sleeping for hours; you need nourishment."

He put the tray in front of me, then took my hand and kissed it. "How are you, *tesoro*?"

I nodded, still choked up. He had brought me to his home, put me to bed, gotten me a nurse, and now he'd served me breakfast. "I'm okay. Now you make me feel like a real *tesoro*."

"That's because you are." He buttered a piece of toast and handed it to me, watching as I bit into it. "I'm so sorry, Lamour. What can I say? What can I do . . . ?" He lifted his hands, defeated. "I never thought Aurora would go this far. She told me she had meant only to drown herself—like her 'father,' she said. She didn't mean to harm you, but then the storm came. She told me you were her friend, her sister. . . ."

I felt a sudden fierce loyalty to Aurora. She was a part of me. "And I am," I said.

"She asks your forgiveness."

I saw again her beautiful radiant face as she pinned my hands to the wheel. "Tell her there's nothing to forgive. She didn't know what she was doing."

"Is that the truth, Lamour? I must know, you see, whether it was a deliberate act? Whether Aurora really wanted to kill you?"

I shook my head. "No. No! She was crazy at that moment. She didn't know what she was doing, Lorenzo. I swear she did not."

I saw the relief in his eyes; then he bent over and kissed me. "Thank you," he said quietly.

"What will happen to Aurora now?"

"The doctor says she must be hospitalized for a few weeks. They have medication for these conditions, they'll stabilize her, then perhaps she'll be able to go back to the university, be back with people her own age. She'll try to get her life back on track, be 'normal.' We'll just always have to be aware that she's fighting this depression."

"You've always helped her," I said.

"And I always will."

We sat there, holding hands. "I couldn't bear to lose you," Lorenzo said after a long silence.

"Well, you didn't," I replied.

"Nico was superb; he came to your rescue. He managed that Riva in terrible seas like a born sailor, which of course he is. His only complaint is that he scraped her along the side of the fishing boat and ruined her paintwork."

I grinned. "It was for a good cause. He'll get over it."

I lifted Lorenzo's hand to my lips and kissed it. I liked his hands, hard workmanlike hands, scattered with dark hair. Hands that worked magic on me.

"Want to come to bed?" I asked cheekily.

I loved the sound of his laughter.

SIXTY-EIGHT

Lamour

FINALLY KNOWING THE TRUTH ABOUT HOW JON-BOY died left me bereft. After all these years I had thought what I would feel was relief that the mystery was solved and that I would finally be able to put my ghosts to rest. Yet the image of Jon-Boy falling, of his broken skull, of the poor crazed woman who had done this to him, and of Lorenzo holding my dead father in his arms haunted my days as well as my dreams.

Lorenzo was in Rome, and Mifune and I were working together in my garden, clearing ground for an old olive tree I'd bought and that was to be delivered the next day. I'd chosen its position carefully, placing it next to the steps leading from the terrace, where I would see its beautiful silvery leaves fluttering in the breeze as I drank my morning coffee. But Jon-Boy was on my mind and I needed to talk about him.

"I'm in trouble, Mifune," I said when we finally took a break. "You were right, when you told me that unlocking the door to the Amalfi house would unlock not only my past but also Jon-Boy's. You asked me if I was sure I wanted to do it, and I was so foolishly confident, I did. Now, I'm not so sure."

We were sitting side by side on the steps. He said, "It was not only because of Aurora that I did not tell you what happened that night; it was because I did not wish you to feel this pain. I had great respect for Jon-Boy. He was my friend. I went many nights after it happened to sit where I had last seen him, watching the sea, hoping for his body to be returned so we might honor him with burial, the way we should our ancestors. But it was not to be. Instead I put flowers on the shrine of Saint Andrew, the patron saint of men at sea, asking that he look after Jon-Boy's soul."

Our eyes met, and once again I felt embraced by this man. With his help my bruised spirit would be taken care of, and I believed that my shattered heart would eventually mend. "Life is granted to no man on a permanent basis," Mifune said. "It is a privilege, and we must use our time wisely. It is up to each of us to make of it what we can.

"Remember this, *piccolina*," he added, calling me by the affectionate diminutive he'd used when I was a little girl. "The soul is like a bird in flight. It escapes from us and flies free again without constraint. There are many more ways to remember Jon-Boy than his ending. Open your heart to those memories, *piccolina*, and let him fly free again."

For the first time in my life I took Mifune's hand. I held it in both mine. I was so grateful for his beautiful image of the soul as a bird flying free, I was moved to rest my cheek against his frail palm. "I never told you this, Mifune," I whispered, "but I've always loved you."

He patted my head and said, "Love transcends everything, *carina*, even death." When I looked up at him, he was smiling. And I was able to say my final good-bye to Jon-Boy.

SIXTY-NINE

L'amour

OF COURSE I CALLED JAMMY AND TOLD HER THE story. We cried together over the phone until she said finally, "Okay, so now you know, honey. It's time to get on with your life, remember?"

I did remember, but I wasn't sure there was anything I could do about Lorenzo and me. I wondered where our relationship could go from here. Was I content to remain the mistress, the way poor Isabella had? The woman left behind while her man got on with his real life?

In the end I sent Jammy a long e-mail in which I poured out my heart about my feelings for Lorenzo.

I don't think there is any future for us, I wrote, but I'm so in love, Jam, I'm living for the moment. I know he worries about the age difference, but hey, I'm gonna be thirty-nine next year. Do you think that helps? This is the first time since I was thirteen that I wished I were older, and it may be the last. It is odd, don't you think, that I fall for a man who remembers me when I was a child? But when I look at him I don't see an older man. I see Lorenzo, gentle, tender, handsome, and ohh, I see a wonderful lover who makes me feel the way a girl should when a guy makes love to her, hot with passion and sweaty with it, but at the same time sort of "treasured."

Of course I'm very much aware that he's an important man, a successful man. He knows everybody there is to know and he's invited everywhere . . . but he always comes back to the Castello, which is where he tells me he is happiest. Jam, as you know, I've never been one for the social whirl; I prefer my solitude and my gardens. Lorenzo's life is different from mine, and so many people from those business and social worlds make demands on him. Our lives are really poles apart, except on the neutral and anonymous ground of the Castello, and here at my house.

What I'm asking, Jammy, is can two such opposing lives ever mesh? Though why I'm asking I don't know, because Lorenzo has never mentioned any "future plans" and we both seem to be living for the moment, so I guess the point is a moot one.

Besides, there's the question of his children. Aurora is damaged; she's like a wary young horse shying away from anything new, especially anything that might take her father and her security away. As for Nico, the eternal happy playboy? Well, he's just an amusing flirt. It was interesting for a while to imagine myself a little in love with him; he made me feel good. But there again he might not enjoy the idea of his father being my husband.

Oh, Jammy! What with Jon-Boy's tragedy, and Aurora's illness, and my shaky love life, you can imagine how I'm feeling. Only Mifune remains steadfast, and I find myself leaning on his strength.

I think I'm going to pour myself a glass of wine and go sit in my belvedere and watch the sunset. At least that's no problem—it's just beautiful.

You know how much I love you and Matt—and the college kid—and how much I miss you. And thank you for letting me get all this off my chest.

SEVENTY

L'amour

A FEW DAYS LATER, I BUMPED INTO NICO AT THE Amalfitano, where I'd dropped in for lunch after a little shopping. He was alone, sitting over a cold beer. He glanced up. "I could use some company," he said.

"Then I'll buy you a pizza." I took a seat next to him.

Spotting me, Aldo came hurrying out from behind the bar. Nico and I ordered our pizzas; then I sat back in my seat and took a long look at him.

"So what's up?" I asked gently. He shrugged and looked away, unsmiling.

"Nico-o-o, come on; I can see something is wrong. Now tell me."

"It's love," he said.

"So . . . well . . . that's nothing to be upset about. There's nothing wrong with love."

"There is when the woman involved does not love me," he said, with that little sulky edge to his voice that let me know I was in trouble.

"When you say 'woman' are you by any chance referring to me?" I hid a smile because this was all too ridiculous.

He threw me a soulful glance, the kind I swear only Italian men know how to do, half dejected suitor, half hopeful lover. "Who else?" he asked sadly.

I laughed out loud. "Nico Pirata, you are not and never

have been in love with me. I loved *being* with you; you made me feel good. We had fun times together and you're a great companion, but . . . *love*? Oh, come on, Nico; we never even kissed."

"Not because I didn't want to," he said, bristling with injured masculinity. "And now you prefer my father."

"It's not a matter of preference. It's a completely different relationship."

"It's love with you and my father, then?" he asked gloomily. I agreed that yes, it was. He heaved an enormous sigh. "Then I guess we'd better drink to that."

"Thanks, Nico," I said, and we raised our beer glasses in a toast to "love." "You're really a good guy, you know that," I said. "And one day you'll make some gorgeous young woman a very good husband."

"Not if I can help it," he said with his usual happy grin, and I knew he'd been putting on the sulky-spurned-suitor act specially for me.

Still, I could tell something else was bothering him and I wasn't surprised when he said, "I'm sorry about Jon-boy, *cara*. I didn't want you to know the awful details because of Aurora and, besides, I didn't want to cause you pain."

I took his hand. "You're a very kind young man, you know that? And it must have been awful for you; after all, you were there that night, and you were just a boy." It was only the second time since I'd known Nico that I'd seen him completely serious.

"That night took away the innocence of childhood," he said. "One minute I was just a kid, worried I might be getting the measles or losing my boat; the next I was thrown into an adult world I never knew existed. I suddenly learned that grown-ups were not just there for us children; they had lives of their own and there was anger and violence. I never looked at the world in quite the same trusting way again."

"I'm sorry you were hurt." I patted his hand gently.

"Of course Papa did his best to help me. He was devastated I'd witnessed such a thing. He explained it all as best he could, and eventually I got over it. It seemed a kind of reward when we got the baby and I got a sister."

"Me, too," I said.

He looked at me and smiled. "She'll be okay," he said confidently. "She'll pull through; I know it."

"I do, too," I agreed, crossing my fingers. Aurora had the best help, and with the proper medication we all hoped her demons would be kept under control.

Our relationship resolved, Nico and I toasted each other with beer again. We enjoyed our lunch and being together, and afterward Nico carried my basket back to the marina, where my little boat was moored near his grand but still wounded Riva, where it had scraped along the fishing boat.

This time I kissed him on the cheek as I said good-bye. "Just a sisterly kiss," I said, laughing, before I jumped into my own little blue boat and sped off.

SEVENTY-ONE

Lamour

THE PHONE WAS RINGING WHEN I GOT BACK. IT WAS Jammy. "I'm on an Alitalia flight to Naples via Milan," she said briskly. "I'll be there at six P.M. Can you pick me up?"

"Are you for real!" I gasped, astounded and thrilled.

"You think I'm gonna leave you alone at a time like this? God, Lamour, I almost lost you—and you're my best friend. Besides, I need to keep you out of more man trouble."

I laughed. "Oh, Jam, I'm really not in man trouble—not like before, anyway. I just needed a shoulder to cry on."

"So now you'll have mine," she said. "See you in Naples, honey."

We took Lorenzo's helicopter to pick her up. He piloted it over my little house so that I might see it from the air. With its glittering tiled dome and fluted arches, it looked like a sultan's minipalace, tucked away in its folds of greenery.

"I can see how in love you are," Lorenzo said. I caught my breath, but then I realized he meant in love with my house.

"I'm the kind who falls in love for life," I said, then bit my lip because I knew that also had a double meaning. "I mean I loved the house as a child and I love it now and I'll love it when I'm old and gray."

"I hope I'm around to see that," he said.

I thought that could be interpreted in two ways. The first was that we might still be together when I was old and gray and he would like to see that. The second . . . well, I couldn't bear to think about that.

The blue and green coast drifted away under us; then the cone of Vesuvius shimmered in the distance and we were descending into a quiet sector of Naples Capodichino Airport.

The flight from Milan was late, so we hitched up at the bar to wait. Lorenzo drank espresso and I drank my usual cappuccino, managing as always to get foam on my nose and blaming it on the small cup. "I like to get the very last little drop," I explained as he took a napkin and wiped it away.

"I wish you'd licked it away," I whispered, and he grinned and said, "*Cara,* so do I." He kissed me anyway, just a light little kiss, but I felt such a glow come over me, I was afraid people might notice.

Jammy's flight was finally announced and we hurried to the gate just in time to see her shoot through the door like a minirocket.

"Jammy always does everything at high speed," I explained, running to her. We were wrapped in each other's arms, kissing, hugging some more, until finally she pushed me away and said, "Let me look at you."

I stood back for inspection while she took a long critical look.

"O-kay," she said, "I expected a frail little waif beaten down by the travails of life, and what do I have here? A hearty, well-fed girl who looks as though life is treating her pretty well."

"That's because Lorenzo's with me," I said, leading her to where he stood, discreetly waiting.

She inspected him quickly up and down. "It's the painter man," she said. "I'm glad to meet you again, Lorenzo."

"And I'm happy to meet you again, Jammy. Lamour's told

me so much about you, I feel I already know you," he said, hefting her bag and leading the way out.

Jammy was stunned when she saw the helicopter. We sat in it, holding hands like schoolkids, marveling at the passing scenery laid out below. When we landed at the Castello, Lorenzo asked us in for a drink—a Bellini made with Prosecco and peach juice, a drink Jammy had taken a liking to the last time she was here. She looked wonderingly around the beautiful rooms, then whispered in my ear, "Whoever it was that said 'the rich are different' was right."

Lorenzo was at his most charming. He asked us to stay for dinner, but Jammy was tired, so he sent a man down to the house with her bag, then personally escorted us through the gardens to the elevator.

"Sleep well, Jammy Mortimer Haigh," he said, taking her hand and kissing it. "I know Lamour will take good care of you."

"That'll make a change," Jammy said. "It's usually the other way around. I hope I'll see you tomorrow?" she added, and he nodded and said that if we agreed, he would meet us at the Amalfitano for lunch at one o'clock. Then he took my hand and kissed it, too. Our eyes linked as he smiled good night, and I felt that little pang of loneliness, even though I knew I was soon to see him again.

"I'm like a teenager in love," I told Jammy on the way down in the elevator.

"And so is he," she said.

"How can you tell?" I asked eagerly.

"It's all in the eyes, Lam honey," she said. "And I wonder if the guy who said that about the rich being different also said, 'The eyes are the windows to the soul.'"

Laughing, we went home. We sat on the terrace with the

breeze blowing our hair, and the wild scents of the garden, the rustle of the waves on the rocks, and the smooth fall of water down from the cliff. A tree frog croaked fit to bust and the crickets chirruped like gangbusters.

"I thought it was going to be quiet around here," Jammy complained, making me laugh because to me these were the sounds of silence.

I showed her my newly painted apricot room, which she was to share because I hadn't yet been able to bring myself to do anything about Jon-Boy's.

Jammy sipped a glass of wine. "I couldn't bear to think of you alone here, remembering the terrible way Jon-Boy died. And then the terrifying scene with Aurora. Oh, hon, I was so scared for you. And so sad for Jon-Boy."

I concentrated on the ham and cheese sandwiches I was fixing, telling myself I wasn't going to cry again. But then I remembered I'd hardly cried at all for Jon-Boy, so I just let myself go and had a good sob, huddled up with Jammy on the old blue sofa.

When the crying storm was over, we sat late into the night, eating our sandwiches and drinking wine, talking about the events of that stormy night until it was all out in the open and there were no more secrets.

"And Lorenzo?" she finally asked.

"What do you think?"

"Gut reaction? I think he's a great-looking guy. I think he's a nice person. I think he's rich and well connected, a man of the world. Actually, I think he's great. I also think he's too old for you."

"Jammy!"

She shrugged. "Well, you asked."

"Let me tell you this, Jammy Mortimer," I said heatedly. "*You* are one of the lucky ones. You met the right guy when you were both young. You fell in love, got married, bought a house in suburbia, had a child, got a life. *You* got it right, Jammy, but for some of us life turned out different. I married the wrong man and look what happened to me. Now I've met the right one and I admit the circumstances may not be all perfect, but . . ."

"*But?*" Her brow rose.

"But I love him."

"So—marry him," she said, yawning with fatigue.

"Oh, Jam, he hasn't asked me," I said, so mournfully I made her laugh.

"Then why don't *you* ask *him*," she said. And she went off to bed leaving me to mull over what she'd just said.

SEVENTY-TWO

Lamour

JAMMY STAYED FOR ONLY THREE DAYS, WHICH WAS long enough for her to fall in love. With my Amalfi house, that is. Of course she also managed to completely charm Lorenzo.

She told him she'd never met anybody as rich as him and that while she was impressed with his possessions and his business and his society friends, she wanted to know what he was really like. "When you're alone at night, and it's just you and your thoughts," she added.

I knew she was putting him through her personal security detector, but Lorenzo said, "Come with me, Jammy Mortimer Haigh, and I'll show you."

He opened the door to his tower. "This is who I am when I'm alone," he said, ushering her in.

I waited outside because I didn't want to hear Jammy's interrogation, but she told me later that as soon as she saw inside the tower she knew Lorenzo was okay. It was absolutely him, from the interesting personally chosen art to the well-thumbed books and the simple furnishings.

"Okay, you pass," she told him, and he shouted with laughter and threw his arms around her and kissed her.

Time flew by and too soon Jammy and I were back at the airport saying good-bye. "Lorenzo passed muster," she said.

"Now it's up to you to work out the rest of it. And don't forget what I said. Why not just ask him?"

I didn't forget. In fact, I kept it at the forefront of my mind. I'd never imagined I would be the kind of woman to ask a man to marry her, but if he wasn't asking me, what else could I do?

I laid my plans carefully. For once, I decided to behave like a real woman. Telling Lorenzo I had to be away for a few days, I drove to Rome. I had my hair cut at the same wonderful place I'd been with Jammy and I emerged looking brand-new, with a cloud of shiny dark hair that curled softly onto my shoulders.

I shopped on the via Condotti for a new outfit, explaining to the saleswoman at Alberta Ferreti that I wanted to look simple but sexy. Roman woman that she was, she knew exactly what I meant and soon had me in a slender silky dress with just the teeniest ruffle that swirled from the neckline to the split hem. The dress was a soft green color and so gorgeous I wondered how I had ever lived without it. Strappy silver sandals completed the look. When I viewed it in the mirror later, I realized that I looked the way the women Lorenzo knew looked: chic, elegant, cosmopolitan.

I dined alone that night at Da Fortunato, savoring the delicate sea bream and the ethereal pasta, enjoying the evening *passeggiata*: the Romans doing what they did every night, dressed to the nines, strolling their wonderful ancient city, enjoying one another. I lingered late, never feeling like "a woman alone," as I had so often before. Perhaps this time it was because I was a woman in love.

SEVENTY-THREE

L'amour

I HAD LEFT A NOTE FOR LORENZO INVITING HIM TO dinner at my house at eight o'clock. I'd brought back a basket of goodies from Rome, chosen carefully for their ease and speed of preparation. There was a mixture of wild mushrooms—my favorite—that I planned on sautéing and serving on slices of toasted brioche. There was the thin grass green asparagus I'd baste with olive oil, sprinkle with Parmesan cheese, then roast quickly in the oven. I bought veal escallops that I was told needed just a minute on each side in the frying pan, after which I should add a sprinkle of lemon juice and fresh herbs. I confess I cheated a little, buying Umberto's homemade gnocchi as well as his famous pesto sauce. I also bought ice cream, pistachio of course, plus mocha and vanilla—the like of which is never better than from Giolitti near the Pantheon. I had it packed in a container with ice, then drove too fast all the way back to Amalfi—a four-hour drive—praying it would not melt.

This time I put my simple meal together perfectly. I dressed in my new very female finery, then went out and surveyed my terrace table. The cobalt blue cloth picked up blue in the Vietri-tiled bench, and the napkins were sunshine yellow. The goblets were a deep shiny blue also, and I'd filled an old yellow enamel jug with daisies. No fancy silver and crystal for me. At heart I was a country girl.

Lorenzo arrived promptly, bounding down the *scalatinella,* managing to look distinguished in just a simple linen shirt and white pants. He stared at me, then at the table, and said, bemused, "I don't know which is more beautiful, you or your table."

He held me at arm's length, looking at me in my new incarnation, then said, "Oh God, oh God, how lovely you are," and I was in his arms and he was kissing me. I was kissing him back and passion flared between us like the red spark at the heart of a flame. It was ironic, I thought, as I led him up to my apricot bedroom, that after all my efforts I couldn't wait for him to pull off my lovely new dress so I could be naked in his arms.

Dinner was forgotten as we fell together onto my big new bed, devouring each other with our eyes and then our mouths, stroking, touching, kissing, tasting. Making love to Lorenzo was so much better than any meal I could ever cook, and I told him so. "Then let's have dessert," he said, and we started all over again.

Much later, with me in my old white cotton bathrobe and Lorenzo wrapped in a towel, our hair still wet from the shower and my new hairdo completely wrecked, we wandered down to the belvedere, clutching a bottle of champagne and two glasses. We sat holding hands, listening to the purr of the sea, watching a pale moon rising.

Contentment flowed like wine between our linked hands. I thought how wonderful life would be if I could spend the rest of it with Lorenzo. It hadn't turned out quite the way I had planned it, with the new hair, the new dress, the sophisticated new look. I was back to the package I'd arrived as— which was quite simply myself.

I took a deep breath. It was now or never. "Do you have any idea of how much I love you?" I said in a very quiet voice, because I was so nervous that's all I could manage.

His brilliant blue eyes met mine. "You know I love you, too, Lamour."

"Am I considered your mistress then? Like the pretty little Naples opera singer with your grandfather? The one whose house this was before it became mine?"

"I suppose we could call you that, if you wish."

I shook my head. "No," I said. "I do *not* wish, Lorenzo Pirata. I want you to marry me." I stopped. "Oh God, that's all wrong. What I meant to say was, Lorenzo Pirata, will you please marry me, because I love you the way no other woman will ever love you in your whole entire life, and I mean that sincerely and utterly, because I can't get you out of my mind and I don't want to and anyhow, if you say no I'll probably run away and never return here again and I'll end up in Chicago building gardens for other people and never having one of my own and never loving anybody and I'll be all alone." I looked him in the eye. "And I'll be afraid without you."

It all came out in a rush, all my love and fears. *"Tesoro,"* he said gently. "I am so much older. Did you never consider that when you are still young, I will be an old man? How many good years might we have left together? Five, ten? Twenty, if we are lucky?"

"Twenty years is a lifetime when you have love," I said fiercely.

"How can I ask you to marry me, my darling Lamour? God knows I need you in my life, but how can I be selfish and take your best years from you?"

"My best years would be the ones we spend together," I said. "I won't ask you again, Lorenzo. I've laid my cards on the table. Now it's up to you."

He swept me into his arms. "How could I ever give you up," he whispered into my cloud of hair. "You bring sanity into my life. You bring gaiety and youth and energy; you strip me of all my worldly conceits and make me human. Dear God, Lamour, you have no idea of the agony I've gone through, imagining life without you."

"Well then," I said, practical even in an emergency like this, "you don't have to, do you?"

And he laughed and said, "Lamour Harrington, will you please marry me?"

Of course I said yes.

We never did get around to that special dinner that night, and the Alberta Ferreti lay in a heap on the bedroom floor. Somehow, it didn't seem to matter.

EPILOGUE

L'amour

LORENZO HAS GIVEN ME DAISY AS A WEDDING PRESent. And there's more. With Mifune's connivance he secretly built a little barn for my cow in the meadow behind the Castello. Of course because of Mifune it looks more like a Japanese teahouse imported to Italy, set among an arrangement of geometric grassy squares.

The cow is beautiful, if you can call a cow beautiful. But yes, Daisy is quite definitely lovely. She's a creamy color, with soft brown eyes and long lashes that I told Lorenzo reminded me of my first love, Angelo.

When I go to visit Daisy, which I do each morning and evening, leading her from the meadow to the barn to be milked, she nuzzles my hand with her soft mouth. I know I shouldn't do this because it's too silly to kiss a cow, but I confess I drop a happy buss on that last velvet bit of fur just before her nose begins. She already answers to her name and I plan on taking milking lessons, even though Lorenzo has installed a milking machine, all steel and switches and suction. It does the job efficiently; nevertheless, I intend to learn how to milk Daisy by hand. That way I'll still keep up my rather tattered image of the self-sufficient woman. Don't even ask about the chickens. Let's just say I may never eat another egg.

Jammy and Matt will be here for the wedding. She told me she's having one of those old-fashioned three-legged milkmaid stools made for my wedding present. And I told her I expected something much more substantial, like at least a set of martini glasses. We'll see.

And what about my so-called new independent, self-sufficient woman status? Well, it seems I've independenced myself right into a happy relationship. And after all, isn't that what life is all about?

Nico took the news of our impending nuptials well. "The best man won," he said, smiling, "even if it is my father. But then my father always beat me at everything."

I thought there was an edge to his voice, but he was just being Nico, and we kissed gently—which was more than we'd ever done when he'd come romancing me.

"Pity it's too late," he said, giving me that familiar cheeky grin. "Just remember, never count me out, Lamour."

"I'm counting myself out and don't you forget it," I told him smartly.

As for Aurora, my new half sister, she has lost some of the insecurities that plagued her and has become less dependent on her father and more of her own woman. She takes her medication and is back at the university, trying to cope with life. I call her every day to remind her that I am her sister and her friend and she can always rely on me to be there for her. She told me she keeps Jon-Boy's picture at the side of her bed next to one of Lorenzo and Marella. "And also one of you," she added sweetly. *"Mia sorella."* She seemed to have forgotten the terrible night on the boat, and I believe she meant every word she said, including that she was happy I was marrying her father.

"Now you'll never leave me," she said, her insecurities surfacing once again, and I hastened to reassure her I never would.

"We're all family now," I said, and she laughed, a warm,

merry sound, and I knew she was glad. "Maybe there'll even be more children now," she said, giving me food for thought.

The idea of having Lorenzo's children is a delicious one: a part of him that I can keep forever. More little half sisters and brothers, or nieces, nephews . . . I still can't figure out exactly what the relationships would be, but it doesn't seem to matter. Aurora will be aunt to my children, and when she marries I will be aunt to hers.

And what of Lorenzo, the man of my dreams? Or, as I told him quite honestly, he would have been the man of my dreams if I'd known earlier that he existed and could have dreamed about him. There's a joy between us that's impossible to capture in mere words. It's in the glance across the crowded room, the telepathic way we seem to know each other's thoughts, the hand reaching out to take mine when I suddenly feel lonely. It's in the comforting weight of his arm around my shoulders as we take a stroll through Mifune's wondrous gardens in the evening. It's in his body, stretched along mine in bed at night, content after our lovemaking. It's in the tenderness I feel whenever I watch him, unobserved, reading the newspaper in his tower with his glasses on the end of his nose, in his tenderness to sweet, ugly Affare, and in his competitiveness when we swim together across the bay. It's in the passion I feel for him and he for me and the great comfort of a relationship where each puts the other first. Age no longer matters. We've agreed to take our happiness while we can and be very glad of it.

I have Jon-Boy to thank for teaching me what true love really is, though he himself never found it. Only, as he revealed in his diary, in me, his daughter. What a pity he never knew his other daughter; how different both their lives might have been. But there's no point in going there anymore. I feel that Jon-Boy has finally given me permission to go on without him.

And that brings me to Mifune. My childhood friend, the spiritual man who advised me to be true to myself, to my own emotions and feelings. The earthy man who taught me that beautiful gardens only came about by dint of hard, dirty work, but that the end results can surpass all your dreams and provide nourishment for the soul and be a lasting legacy. As the gardens here at the Castello and at my little house will be his.

He grows daily more frail and more inward looking. I believe he's searching his own soul before he has to go meet his ancestors. He has promised me he will be here for my wedding, and because of his strong spirit I believe he will honor that promise.

It's late now, and the half moon is up, pinned with sparkling Venus, as Lorenzo says. He told me he's buying a telescope so I can see it more clearly, see how it looks down on us lying in our big bed in the plain tower room that I love so much.

But here's the secret I will never tell him: I love my little golden house in Amalfi even more than the Castello. And then I tell myself what a fortunate woman I am to be filled with so much love. Whoever would have thought it just a year ago?

But as my best friend, Jammy, says, that's life, baby. You never know what it's going to throw at you.

Elizabeth Adler

Invitation to Provence

Nothing ever changes much in the village of Marten-de-Provence . . .

Until Rafaella Marten decides she has lived alone in the Château des Roses Sauvages for too long, and that the time has come at last to bring youth and energy, love and laughter back to the old house.

Franny Marten, hard-working California veterinary surgeon, accepts the invitation from a relative she has never heard of at a moment when her life is at rock bottom.

Jake Bronson can't resist – he is still a tiny bit in love with the charming woman who was once his father's glamorous lover.

And two more unexpected guests arrive: Rafaella's long lost son, and a terrified little girl from Shanghai with the Marten blue eyes.

Soon the sleepy French village is alive with more romance and danger than Rafaella ever dreamed of.

HODDER

Elizabeth Adler

The Hotel Riviera

Imagine a sunny sea-lapped cove, gift wrapped in blue and tied with a bow like a Tiffany box, and you'll get the feel of my little hotel. It's a place made for Romance with a capital R. Except for me, its creator.

Lola Laforêt doesn't have time for love. Her disreputable husband has disappeared, the police consider her a prime suspect and her beautiful home and business seems to belong to an ex-arms dealer.

Lola doesn't go looking for danger, it just seems to walk through the door. And when it walks through the door in the form of the delectable Jack Farrar she knows she's in real trouble.

HODDER

Elizabeth Adler

Summer in Tuscany

An American woman in Tuscany to claim an inheritance encounters the frustrating yet delightful workings of a small town, and finds the love that has eluded her all her life.

Gemma Jericho is an overworked New York doctor with a handful of a teenaged daughter and a mother who worries that Gemma has no life. So when her mother Nonna receives a mysterious letter telling her about an even more mysterious inheritance in Tuscany, the three of them throw caution and convention to the wind: they leave for Italy.

What they encounter is a crumbling old village and a town divided: half believe Nonna's villa belongs to Ben Raphael, an unnervingly handsome American. As cultures clash, gossip soars and intrigue unfolds, Gemma is caught up in the most disturbing – and delicious – trouble she's ever had.

And her summer in Tuscany will change her outlook and her life forever.

HODDER

Elizabeth Adler

The Last Time I Saw Paris

Lara Lewis's marriage is fizzling. Her surgeon husband is far too busy for her – too busy even to go on their long-planned second honeymoon to France and Lara suspects that he's backed out of it because he's found another woman to replace her.

The she meets Dan Holland, earthy, unsophisticated, California-handsome and a good guy, and takes him on the second honeymoon that was meant to have saved her marriage. Except that Dan doesn't know this.

What follows is a madcap, romantic adventure that begins with missed connections and lost luggage, then fights and making up, losing each other – and finding love. Starting in Paris, they retrace the exact same path Lara had taken years ago with her husband, revisiting the same towns and villages, the same *auberges*, the same restaurants and cafés, a pair of inexperienced tourists stumbling through France.

Trouble comes when the lover finds out he is the stand-in for her husband on the second honeymoon – and then her husband shows up in Paris and wants her back.

HODDER